RUBY LARK

JACK MASSA

 Triskelion Books

Published by
Triskelion Books
www.triskelionbooks.com

Ruby Lark

ISBN: 979-8-218-76340-4

Print Edition published September 2025.

Cover Design and interior art by Masa Radanic, bgsauthors.com

Part One
The Fall of Duneidan

It is certainly a curious age. Hand-in-hand with the rediscovery of ancient science, mechanics, and technologies, has come the revival of long-abandoned magical practices. Some of these reappeared among the Norrling wizards, others in the Warmlands. Most notable in terms of historical effect of course is the set of psithic-alchemical techniques known as the cold fire, which enabled the creation of the so-called "deathless warriors," the zolgars.

—*The Terrestrial Histories of Fystus the Emu,*
Volume 38, Chapter 5.
Norrling year 6270.

Chapter 1

The ballroom floor shone silvery-blue, the sheen brightest near the Duke's throne. Mirafra noticed this because her eyes were downcast, her habit whenever she felt nervous.

"Eyes up, songbird," Sharam her mentor admonished through the corner of her mouth. "We must always look Warmlanders straight in the eye so they'll respect us—especially the nobles."

Easy enough for Sharam. She was a maestra, her *psithe* a Crested Crane. She had spent many years as an ambassador wizard in the Warmlands. As an apprentice, Mirafra the Tree Pipit wondered if she would ever attain such composure.

Lifting her gaze, she discovered a woman staring at her—Jovadia the Bittern, Court Wizard to King Alaric, whose visit to the Duke's palace was the occasion of tonight's reception. Jovadia loomed behind the King's throne, a tall woman in gold and yellow robes, her narrow face compressed in a sparkling wimple. Her eyes burned in Mirafra's vision.

Mirafra glanced at her feet.

No. Her mentor was right. Though a mere apprentice, she was a member of the Duke's court and had every right to be here. She must pretend the self-confidence she lacked. Gripping her nerve, she lifted her eyes again to confront the King's wizard.

Jovadia caught the glance and returned it calmly, measuring Mirafra in a way that caused a pang of fear to squeeze the young woman's stomach.

Off in the corner, the stringed orchestra played a stately march. Mirafra and Sharam moved forward in the line—the Duke's

3

courtiers, officials, and soldiers here to be presented to the King. Duke Keltonn himself occupied a throne next to the visiting monarch. On his right sat the Duchess and beside her stood their children, a daughter and three sons dressed in maroon velvet and silver brocade.

Mirafra's eyes roamed to the last in the line, Arwyn, the youngest son at age 17. His face evinced boredom and restlessness as he tugged on his tight collar. Catching her eye, he showed a sardonic half-smile that appeared and quickly vanished. Arwyn was an oddity among highborn Warmlanders. While most young noblemen concerned themselves with hunting, arms training, and courting girls, Arwyn's interests ran to philosophy, science, and other obscure studies. In the two months Mirafra had been at court, Arwyn had become her only friend.

Reaching the front of the line at last, Sharam and Mirafra climbed the four steps of the dais. Duke Keltonn nodded kindly and gestured with a hand.

"Your majesty, I present the esteemed Sharam, wizard of Ombernorr and my close advisor, and her apprentice, the honored Mirafra."

They bowed to the King, who showed a vague smile and lifted a hand toward his own wizard. "Honored. Perhaps you have already met my own royal wizard, Jovadia of Ombernorr."

"We have not, but it is certainly a pleasure." Jovadia spoke in a silky voice. She crooked a finger, signing for Sharam and Mirafra to join her for a conversation.

While the King and Duke continued with the receiving line, Jovadia led her fellow wizards to a red velvet curtain at the side of the dais. She exchanged pleasantries with Sharam, asking the last time she had been to Montodoro, the High Sanctuary of the female wizards, mentioning a few names of high-ranking sisters. Mirafra was a bit surprised when the Bittern addressed her directly.

"And you, Mirafra, are you an operio or an adept?"

4

Her eyes sank to the floor. "Neither, Honored Maestra, merely a tyro."

"Oh, indeed? But you are young. Unusual for one of your age and rank to be assigned to a mission to the Warmlands, is it not?"

"I especially asked for Mirafra on my last visit to Montodoro," Sharam answered. "She hails from my native village, and I liked both her spirit and her curiosity. I thought a sojourn in the Warmlands would bring her benefits. Her psithe is the Tree Pipit."

"Ah, a songbird of the tyro grade. A good mimic, I believe. Is illusion one of your better talents, Mirafra? I expect you are skilled with the disk, and perhaps the cup ...?"

The psithe, the living essence of a bird, could be changed into four shapes. The disk gave power over the mind and could cause illusions; the cup was an instrument of healing. Mirafra sensed that the Bittern was implying she must be weak in the other two attributes, the wand of levitation and the sword or dagger used for creating fire—and for combat.

Sharam answered for her: "She is quite talented for one so young, but of course needs development. I would not be surprised if, the next time she enters the Birdhouse, she does not draw the psithe of an operio, or even an adept."

Jovadia's eyes brightened. "Indeed, that would be quite an advancement."

She excused herself to return to her duties attending the King.

As they ambled off into the crowd, Sharam murmured, "Tell me your impressions, Mirafra."

"Do you mean of the King or of the Bittern?"

"Ha-ha. The King is a king. His ambition and gluttony for power are plain enough. Of course, I meant our sister wizard."

"To be honest, she frightens me. There is something in her eyes ..."

"Hmm. Do you think this is a valid psychic perception, or just the unease of an apprentice confronted by a powerful majja?"

Mirafra lifted her shoulders. "How can one tell?"

They took seats at an empty table at the edge of the ballroom. The reception line was nearing its end. Presently, there would be introductory speeches, then mingling at the banquet tables, and dancing. Courtesy required that the wizards stay at least through the speeches.

"What were *your* impressions of Jovadia, maestra?" Mirafra asked.

Elbow resting on the table, Sharam stroked her chin. "A powerful presence, for certain. No doubt she delves in spurious practices. But then, for a majja who has been away from the High Sanctuary for so long, and concerning herself with politics and power, the temptations must be great."

Like everyone at court, Mirafra had heard strange stories. In the past several years, King Alaric's power and influence had grown in the region, to the point that he was on the verge of establishing an empire. Towns and estates that could not be convinced to become his clients had been invaded. His army was supreme in the region. And Jovadia the Bittern was said to be a power behind the throne. Some claimed she weakened the resolve of Alaric's adversaries through mental enchantments. Others that she delved in strange, potent magic rediscovered from ancient times.

Sharam seemed to read Mirafra's thoughts. "I think we can discount the more outlandish tales: that she practices evil sorcery, that Alaric has become her puppet."

"But can we be certain?"

"Yes, Mirafra. Never listen to the gossip of Warmlanders about our wizardry. Naturally, they exaggerate what they cannot begin to understand."

Mirafra gazed off to the throne dais, where the Bittern conversed with two of the Duke's knights. An inner sense warned her that the rumors of Jovadia's influence should not be so easily dismissed.

But, no doubt, Sharam was right. The maestra had so much more experience with the world. Mirafra knew herself to be impressionable—and easily intimidated.

When the speeches of welcome were completed, the courtiers rose from their seats to mingle. Amid the convivial babble of conversations, music began, the orchestra playing a stately dance. The Duke and the Duchess stepped to the center of the dance floor. After the first chorus, they were joined by others, courtiers in fine doublets, ladies in samite gowns. King Alaric watched from his seat on the dais, the Bittern at his shoulder.

At a signal from Sharam, Mirafra rose and gladly made ready to leave. Formal occasions always tired her—the fear of social missteps combined with her sensitivity in large groups. But as they wended their way through the tables, a voice hailed her.

"Mirafra! You're not leaving already."

Arwyn, the Duke's son, hastened toward them through the crowd.

Mirafra glanced at the floor, then at Sharam. "Well, yes. The maestra and I are withdrawing. Dancing is not one of our offices."

"Of course not." Arwyn nodded politely to the Crested Crane. "Nor is it one of my pleasures, as you well know. I thought we could sit and talk a while, have some sweets and punch. I'm going to be forced to attend meetings with the King the next few days, so I won't be available at all."

With a polite smile, he glanced at Sharam, then back to Mirafra. He was long of limb and body, like his father and brothers, but lacked their muscular builds. Slim and lanky, he moved with an awkward gait. Still, Mirafra thought him good-looking.

She glanced uncertainly at the maestra. "May I stay?"

Sharam offered a smile. "Of course, if the young lord wishes your company. Not too late, mind. We rise at dawn for our psithe practice."

"I won't forget." Mirafra laughed as Arwyn grabbed her arm and hustled her toward the buffet.

She selected two candies and a small square of cake, while Arwyn piled his plate with samples of all the sweets. They carried their dishes and cups of punch to an unoccupied table off in the corner. While they sampled the delicacies, Mirafra asked him about the King's visit.

"Well, naturally, Alaric will be pressuring my father to swear fealty to him," Arwyn said. "My father expects it; why else would the King have arranged the visit?"

He spoke casually, but Mirafra could sense nagging fear beneath the bluff manner. The Duke's domain was near the edge of Alaric's territories and so far had escaped the King's expanding ambitions.

"Alaric fancies himself a warlord," Arwyn muttered softly. "Everyone expects he plans to invade Occitan and the lands to the west. He wants to conquer an empire, like the Moldorns used to have."

Mirafra knew the history. The Moldorns were a people from the mountains of Ibor, the continent to the south. Decades ago, they had developed new weapons of war—rigid and navigable airships and firebombs that could destroy whole towns. They had conquered most of Ibor and begun incursions into Tann when a rebellion in their own capital toppled their Emperor—a rebellion instigated by a wandering Norrling wizard called Teron the Mooncrow. The Emperor's daughter came to the throne and reversed the military policies. In the years since, Moldorn technology had gradually spread to other nations—airships, steam engines, new metals, even the formula for the so-called Moldorn fire. Monarchs throughout Tann were in a kind of race to arm themselves with the advanced weapons, either for protection or conquest.

"What will your father do?" she asked.

"Who knows?" Arwyn answered with his mouth full. "I suppose it will depend on how forcefully the King leans on him. My father wants no part of Alaric's ambitions. But he will probably have to make concessions. The negotiations will be hard, perhaps nasty."

He set down his fork. "I've been listening to this gloomy talk for days. I suggest we take a respite."

"What do you mean?"

"I've heard there's a new show in town—at the music hall."

"Oh, I couldn't."

"Traveling performers: acrobats, a bard from Llorrland, and a conjurer they say is truly amazing. He might be one of your people, a Norrling."

"If so, he's a renegade." For a generation or more, certain majja who came to the Warmlands had decided to stay, seduced by the balmy weather, the rich and pleasant lands. In the High Sanctuaries of icy Ombernorr, most considered these strays to be rebels, fallen creatures. To many among the older and stricter majja, Jovadia the Bittern would certainly be considered one of them.

Of course, among the first and most famous of those wandering wizards was that same Teron the Mooncrow, who had overthrown the Moldorns and changed history.

"Wouldn't you like to find out?" Arwyn was saying. "Isn't your curiosity piqued?"

She found his good humor hard to resist. "It does sound tempting. Oh, but I couldn't."

"Yes, you can." He clasped her wrist. "In these grim times, we both deserve a little fun!"

Chapter 2

Mirafra and Arwyn left the castle through the main gate. Recognizing the Duke's son, the sentries on duty simply snapped to attention and let them pass over the drawbridge. Descending the hill in the twilight, Mirafra felt a mixture of excitement and unease. She had changed out of her formal attire, wearing now a plain cloak, tunic, and trousers—nothing to indicate her identity as a majja. Still, she doubted her mentor would approve of this late excursion into town. But, on the other hand, Arwyn had all but insisted, and Sharam did encourage her to maintain good relations with the Duke's family.

Below the hill they crossed the market commons, a rolling meadow occupied by tents and wooden booths. Beyond spread the town of Duneidan, where lamps winked along the curling streets and alleys. But Arwyn and Mirafra's eyes were drawn to the airships that floated near the ground on opposite sides of the meadow.

The three larger ones were war galleons, with gold-painted bows and rails below their massive silver balloons. These had arrived today, bringing the King and his entourage. The smaller ship, on the other side, was a trading vessel of a type that carried passengers and cargo. These had become a common sight in Tann over the past decades.

"I heard the new performers arrived on that one," Arwyn said. "I wonder if they'd be open to letting us go onboard. Wouldn't that be grand? Have you ever ridden on an airship, Mirafra?"

"No. Never." Though she had journeyed from northwestern Ombernorr, in the opposite corner of the continent, all of her travels had been by sea or overland. Riding in an airship did sound exciting.

The music hall stood in a neighborhood of shops and taverns near the edge of town. Loud music and boisterous laughter spilled into the street, where parties of townspeople passed by or lingered. Arwyn and Mirafra strolled through the brightly lit doorway. In the foyer, the Duke's son paid their admission price and ordered a tankard of ale for himself. Mirafra politely declined any drink.

Entering the main room, they weaved through the crowd and found a table on the side. On stage, behind a row of glimmering lamps, a blond, bearded minstrel performed. He sang and skillfully plucked at a mandolin, accompanied by a drummer, lute player, and piper. The song was a comic ballad, and the crowd sang along with each chorus, filling the hall with raucous cheers and laughter.

"He must be the traveling bard," Arwyn said. "The other three players are regulars."

When the song ended, the minstrel bowed and left the stage. The crowd was still applauding when the remaining musicians started a new tune. Three acrobats ran out onto the stage, dressed in multicolored tunics and leggings. They leapt and danced, cartwheeled and flipped, all in time to the music. Next, they produced hoops that they juggled in the air and tossed to one another.

In the midst of these actions, a slim figure in a hooded cape appeared on the side of the stage. From within his shirt he produced a silver wand. The drum's tempo increased; the acrobats flung the hoops higher; and the newcomer thrust out the wand.

He pointed at each hoop as it rose to its summit, and the hoop instantly vanished in the air. The crowd gasped and applauded. When the last hoop was gone, the acrobats bowed and scampered off to the wings.

"People of Duneidan," a loud voice announced. "Please welcome Zeneon the Enchanter!"

The cheers rose in volume as the conjurer walked to the middle of the stage. After bowing, he waved the silver wand. One by one, the three missing hoops rolled out on the stage and settled near his feet. Circling the wand and shouting an incantation, he caused the hoops to float into the air. They twirled around, danced for a while in time to the merry music, and then finally fluttered off to the wings. Zeneon bowed to the wild ovation.

Arwyn turned to Mirafra with a puzzled shrug. "What do you think? Norrling wizardry?"

"I doubt it," Mirafra replied. "Warmlander stage magicians know many kinds of tricks to fool a crowd."

Now the bard appeared, with the mandolin slung on his back. He carried a black brazier, which he set down before the conjurer. Then he backed away to join the other musicians. Together, they summoned a slow, eerie tune.

Zeneon lifted his wand again, then tapped it sharply on the brazier's rim.

"Inferno!" he shouted.

Fire exploded from the black iron bowl. The onlookers gasped. The flames raged bright orange, yet produced no smoke. Zeneon lifted the edge of his black cape and waved it through the fire.

"Scomparire!" The flames disappeared.

But the conjurer was not done. Now he lifted the other hem of the cape and swept it over the brazier.

"Uccelli!"

Instead of flames, a flock of tiny black birds appeared and flew off toward the ceiling. Zeneon bowed to the applause.

The music changed again, rising in volume and tempo. The conjurer seemed to rise on his toes. He twirled around three times, then pointed the wand at the brazier.

"Inferno me stessa!"

This time, when the fire appeared, it was not in the brazier but bursting over Zeneon's body. The auditorium erupted in cries and groans. On fire, the conjurer twirled again and lifted into the air, higher and higher as he burned.

"Scomparire!" he shouted.

Next instant, the flames were gone, the music stopped, and Zeneon stood unharmed and smiling at center stage.

"What do you say now?" Arwyn asked amid the explosion of cheering.

Gazing wide-eyed, Mirafra murmured. "Now, I'm not sure."

Rising from a bow, his cape spread like wings, Zeneon smiled down from the stage. Suddenly, he seemed to notice Mirafra staring at him. For just a moment, she sensed his mind examining her.

Next morning, Mirafra and her mentor Sharam climbed the winding steps of a tower and emerged on the highest battlement of Castle Duneidan. It was just after dawn, the air cool and clear. From this vantage, one could see for miles across the highlands, a country of rugged hills and forests, meadows, and shining lakes.

"You are distracted this morning, songbird," Sharam remarked as they walked along the parapet.

"Sorry, maestra."

"Out too late celebrating with the young lord?"

"No, I ..."

In fact, she had been thinking about Zeneon the Enchanter. Trying to fathom the truth of his nature had kept her restless all night. It was certainly possible all of his tricks were clever illusions. But when he peered at her from the stage, she had sensed more—that he might indeed be a Norrling—or at least that his act was a masquerade, that he was hiding his true identity and powers. And if so, did this masquerade have anything to do with King Alaric's arrival in Duneidan?

"... You what?" Sharam prompted.

Mirafra shook her head. "Sorry, maestra."

"All right then," Sharam said. "Let's get on with our practice."

They stopped at a broad area of the battlement, away from the nearest sentry. Sharam pulled the psithe from inside her feathered robe. The life essence of a crested crane, it now appeared in its formless state, a hand-sized sphere of shimmering light. With a gesture and a word, Sharam flicked it into the disk form.

Mirafra took out her Tree Pipit psithe and also made it a disk. This was the fourth attribute of the psithe, called *qorm*, the eye of the bird. Its power was of the mind, to influence the thoughts of others, to create and cast illusions.

"Begin," Sharam said.

As a tyro, Mirafra could make the disk display different shapes and shades of light. She had only begun to master the art of forming more elaborate illusions. Now, focusing her thoughts, she circled the disk over her head and chanted. Soon, it appeared that trails of color fell from the psithe, drifting down over her body. Next, she tried to shape the colors into a veil, with the intent of hiding herself within. Some days she managed to create a translucent curtain, but this morning the colors just hung in threads and tatters.

"Your focus is poor today," Sharam remarked. "Let's try the wand."

Her hand circled, and her psithe transformed into a silver wand as long as a quarterstaff. This attribute was called *honer*, the wing of the bird.

Mirafra matched the gesture and spoke a command. Her disk became a thin wand of amber metal the length of her forearm.

Sharam gripped her wand in both hands and raised it over her head. The wand's power of levitation lifted her until she floated a yard in the air.

Levitating herself or other objects was above Mirafra's grade, but she did manage to make the wand itself float, though it wavered at moments, and she had to steady it.

Next, they practiced with *treel*, the bird's claw. Sharam made her psithe into a sword that pulsed with fiery light. Mirafra's psithe changed to a dagger. Together the two majja practiced producing heat and light from their blades and also ritual thrusts and cuts as used in Norrling combat.

Lastly, Sharam invoked the attribute called *duod*, associated with the bird's tongue. In shape, this attribute was a cup, its power to distill water from the air. To this water, the majja learned to add powders and tinctures to produce medicines and potions. This morning, Mirafra succeeded in manifesting her psithe in its copper goblet shape and then filling it with water.

"Well done," Sharam said. "Now I must go and attend the Duke. Keep practicing as usual. Our meeting with the King and his party commences at the fourth hour in the great hall. I want you to attend and see what impressions you gather."

"Yes, maestra, I shall."

Like everyone in the Duke's household, Sharam was worried about what King Alaric would demand and what pressures he would bring to bear. Given Alaric's recent conquests and military strength, Mirafra wondered if resistance was even possible. She found herself staring over the parapet at the three warships anchored in the meadow below. Alaric reportedly had ten airships in his fleet, with more under construction. Like the Moldorns before him, the King had used the vessels to firebomb villages that tried to resist his rule. Would such horrible war come to Duneidan?

Mirafra strained to push those worries from her mind. Standing back from the wall, she willed the psithe into its dagger shape. For the next quarter hour she practiced, summoning heat and light into the blade, then expelling it with bursts of fire.

Suddenly, she felt someone watching. She whirled and saw Jovadia the Bittern regarding her with an amused expression.

"Very nice," Jovadia said. "I sense strong passions, which you are mostly successful in channeling."

"Majja." Mirafra bowed, then forced herself not to cast her eyes down. Odd that the Bittern should be strolling early in the morning on this high battlement, and alone.

Jovadia took a deep breath as she gazed out over the land. "A lovely view, is it not?"

When the Bittern met her eyes again, Mirafra felt an intuition. Jovadia was not here to admire the scenery but to examine the castle's defenses.

Jovadia might have read her mind. For an instant the Bittern looked startled, then she smiled. "Yes, a very lovely view. But tell me about yourself, Tree Pipit. How long have you been in the Warmlands?"

"Less than a year. I left Montodoro at the start of summer and arrived here just over two months ago."

"Quite an opportunity for one so young. But then the Crested Crane plainly thinks highly of you."

Mirafra looked down without replying.

"And what have you learned in your apprenticeship?"

She glanced at her dagger. "Well, I continue to train to master my psithe ..."

"I mean about the Warmlanders."

"Oh." She hesitated. "Their ways are strange to me, of course. Particularly, their science and crafts—mysterious and powerful."

"And their politics?"

"I know little ..."

Why was she asking all this? Probing Mirafra's mind as she had the castle's defenses?

That thought brought another sharp look from the Bittern. Then a nod. "Yes, I do think you are quite talented, Mirafra. And I will say this to you: There are many paths to magical attainment possible for majja with potential. Some involve arts taught long ago in Montodoro but then abandoned. Others have risen in far-flung

16

corners of the world. You might have quite a future—if you are flexible and brave."

Mirafra felt an incipient fear. "I don't understand you."

The Bittern smiled. "Think about what I've said. Perhaps we will talk again."

With that, she folded her hands in her sleeves, turned, and continued on her walk.

The great hall of Castle Duneidan was walled with rough stones and hung with ornamentation—coats of arms, crossed pikes, family banners of the Duke and his vassals. Along the sides of the chamber were hunting trophies, the heads of great elks and boars.

At a long ebony table, the Duke's courtiers sat facing King Alaric's entourage. The majority of the assembled nobles were men, but there were also women—the Duke's wife, his Court Wizard Sharam the Crane, and, across the table, Jovadia the Bittern. All present were dressed in colorful dyed wools, rich brocades, and velvets. Some wore sparkling jewelry, including gold chains and amulets of office. Others of the lords were clad in chainmail, as were the guardsmen who stood with pikes and swords at either end of the hall.

Seated on a bench behind the Duke's party, Mirafra struggled to keep her emotions calm. Sharam had charged her to attend the meeting and gather mental impressions. But as she scanned the hall, Mirafra's thoughts kept returning to her encounter that morning with the King's wizard.

Jovadia sat a few chairs down from Alaric, staring across the table with a thin-lipped, fierce expression of ... *What? Concentration? Malevolence?* Was the Bittern probing for impressions like Mirafra herself? Or was she casting power, seeking to mentally influence the members of the Duke's court?

Mirafra suppressed a shiver.

Duke Keltonn stood and rapped his hand on the table for quiet. "My Lords and Ladies, once again, our court is honored to receive King Alaric and his entourage. They have traveled far from their capital at Tonnsburg in their wonderful airships and have already made visits to principalities to our north. We understand that the King's mission is to propose an alliance, and we are pleased in all honor and humility to hear him."

The Duke resumed his seat, and all faces turned to the King. Alaric slowly stood. Slim and bearded, adorned in a fur-trimmed robe and jeweled crown, he smiled.

"Lords and Ladies. Once again we thank Duke Keltonn for his reception and hospitality. But now I must speak bluntly, for my visit is critical. As you probably know, there is growing tension in the north between my kingdom and that of Occitan. True, there have long been disputed borders in some places. But, in the past months, these have erupted into fighting. King Carswell has increased his sea fleet and is building more airships and manufacturing bombs. His intentions are plain: he will not rest until all of Eastern Tann falls under his rule. Historically, the lands of Arabhedden have mostly been spared from continental wars because of your remoteness. But that will not avail you this time—not with Carswell's ambitions and Occitan's mobile forces. That is why I have come, to make an alliance with you and all the rulers of this peninsula, for our mutual protection."

Gesturing with an open hand, the King indicated men seated to his right. "With me at table are your neighbors, Duke Brool of Sardia and Lord Pegaro of Jurrland, who have already agreed to this alliance. They will explain to you the benefits."

Mirafra scanned the faces of the two nobles, their mouths clenched, their eyes unreadable. The King turned to his left.

"I will also introduce in turn select ministers of my court and commanders from my army and air fleet. They will discuss military and logistical details."

Stretching to view the faces of these men, Mirafra felt a wave of dizziness. Her eyes shifted again to Jovadia, who sat with hands folded before her chin and wore a placid, distant expression. But behind that mask, Mirafra sensed rage and power that seemed to flood across the great hall.

Chapter 3

"Tell me your impressions, Mirafra." Sharam stared into her teacup, her tone weary and her manner grim.

With the meeting in recess for the midday meal, the two majja had retreated to Sharam's apartment. They sat huddled before the fireplace. A tray of tea, breads, and cheeses had been served to them, though neither showed much appetite.

Mirafra tried to collect her scattered thoughts. "I sensed so much anger and fear among the Duke's people. The King does not mean them well, but ..."

"But what, Mirafra?"

"My mind was overwhelmed by Jovadia. I know you told me not to believe the extravagant rumors the Warmlanders tell of her, but ... I cannot deny the impression that she is doing something with mental power. I know not what or how."

"Yes. She is doing something. That is certain." Firelight wavered over the maestra's face. "I too am finding it difficult to fathom. The Bittern psithe is present but does not seem to be the source of the power she is tapping. Or, if it is, she is concealing it in some profound way."

"I met her this morning on the castle roof," Mirafra said. "She mentioned unorthodox arts, some that were practiced in the past and others from outside our tradition."

"What more did she tell you?"

"That was all ... except to hint that such practices offered powers well beyond what we can learn at Montodoro."

Sharam frowned. "So the rumors about the Bittern are true. I suspected as much." She turned to Mirafra. "I have not concealed from you the fact that some Norrlings who have chosen to stay in the Warmlands have abandoned the proper rules of our order. This is true in varying degrees. But I must warn you again, Mirafra, that such deviations are dangerous. The Norrling way has been refined over centuries both to control our magic and to keep our minds and spirits safe."

These principles Mirafra had heard recited many times. Her tutor's repeating them now with such intensity surprised her.

"Well," Sharam said. "As to the Bittern, we do not need to understand her methods. Her intent is plain enough: to sway Duke Keltonn and his court, to bring them into line with the King's plans. And our duty demands we do all we can to counter her."

Rising from her seat, she went and opened a tall cabinet next to the hearth.

"What will you do, Maestra?"

"First I will warn the Duke. The knowledge alone will help him to shield his mind." Sharam had opened a jewel box and was shuffling through the contents. She lifted out a small bronze amulet and held it up by its chain. "And I shall urge him to wear this, concealed in his garment."

She brought the amulet closer. "Can you tell me what it is?"

Mirafra examined it with her mind. "A qorm token, attuned for protection."

"Exactly. No matter what arts the Bittern is using, this should scatter their energies."

Sharam met with the Duke in his private quarters prior to the resumption of the meeting in the great hall. She wanted to warn him about the Bittern's mental attacks, and to strongly suggest he wear the protective amulet.

Mirafra waited outside in the corridor, bowing to the Duchess and the Duke's sons as they emerged on their way back to the hall. When Arwyn appeared, he smiled, plainly glad to see her. He tugged her sleeve and led her a few steps to a round-arched door. They stepped onto a balcony. Far below lay the meadow and the town of Duneidan.

"We've got a little time before they start again." Arwyn drew a deep breath of the chilly air. "I will be glad when this is over."

"What do you think is going to happen?" Mirafra asked.

His expression fell. "I don't think anyone knows, yet. My father discussed it with us over lunch—my mother and brothers, Count Baglan, a few of the knights. The King will pressure him, that's for certain. But Father seems determined to resist." He shook his head. "Alaric is such a liar. King Carswell did not start any fighting, Alaric did. We have a cousin, a lady-in-waiting in Carswell's court. She writes to my mother. She claims Alaric's vassals have been raiding Occitan without provocation, and Carswell has tried hard to make peace."

Mirafra nodded, her heart full of sympathy.

"I suppose my father may be forced to make an alliance of some sort. Count Baglan is urging it ... I don't know, Mirafra. What do you and Sharam think?"

"We think your father is good and noble to resist the King. But there is something else." She explained to Arwyn their suspicions about the Bittern, and how Sharam would urge the Duke to wear the protective amulet. As she finished speaking, another thought occurred.

"I have something." Reaching behind her neck, she lifted a chain over her head. "You can wear this, if you like. I mean, I'd like you to."

She showed him a small bird cast in silver. She had bought it in the marketplace and, as part of her ongoing practices, imbued it with energy from the Tree Pipit psithe. "It's probably not worth much, but it may give you some protection."

Arwyn looked startled, then showed a wide grin. He took the chain and placed it over his head. "I shall wear it with honor."

Then, to Mirafra's amazement, he leaned over and kissed her cheek.

"They'll be starting again," he said. "We'd best get inside."

The day was growing colder, and so a fire had been lit in the hearth of the great hall. Its warmth did nothing to allay the chilly atmosphere of the council.

As promised, two nobles from the north, who had accompanied the King, explained details of their alliance and extolled the benefits of Alaric's protection. Next, the King's high-ranking officers discussed the military treaties, the mobilization of the allies' troops, command structures, and plans for deployment. His ministers explained the legal ramifications of the treaties and finances.

Through it all, the Duke and his family listened in stoic silence. A few of his vassals commented or asked questions. Count Baglan in particular seemed to favor the King's proposals. Tall and broad-shouldered, wearing a steel breastplate, he smiled gently as he spoke. Mirafra wondered if the Count might have made some secret arrangement with the King—or if, perhaps, he was especially susceptible to the Bittern's subtle influences. As for Jovadia, she sat still and erect and never spoke. All afternoon she simply stared straight ahead, like a figure of stone.

When the presentations by the King's allies were concluded, a silence settled in the hall. All eyes turned to the Duke. He scanned the faces on his side of the table then slowly, as if reluctant, stood. In formal words, he thanked the King and his party for their visit. Next he reviewed at some length the details of the alliance that had been proposed, demonstrating his understanding to a degree that Mirafra found admirable.

The Duke's eyes settled on the King. "Having listened to all of this, I say again we are honored by the offer of an alliance. However, for the good of my dukedom and my people, I must decline. We have no interest and see no advantage in fighting a war far from our borders, a war that does not concern us."

"It does concern you!" Alaric slapped the table as he bolted to his feet. "We have explained at great length how the King of Occitan will not stop until he rules all of eastern Tann!"

Duke Keltonn fixed him with a cold stare. "While your proposed alliance makes us a vassal to your kingdom. I honestly see small difference."

Before the King could answer, Keltonn raised a calming hand. "But if your majesty will permit, I offer this compromise. Duneidan will swear to a treaty of non-aggression with your kingdom and its allies. What's more, we shall allow any of our vassal knights who wish it to volunteer to join your forces, under whatever terms you and they might choose."

Still standing, King Alaric shook his head. "Not good enough. You would use my armies to shield your lands from the coming war without committing to your fair share of the fighting." His voice rose as he pointed angrily across the table. "I call this what it is, cowardice!"

Amid gasps and hisses, two of the Duke's knights leapt to their feet. Keltonn gestured with both hands to calm them, his gaze fixed on the King.

"Insults will not avail you here. We must decide according to what is best for our people."

"Then there is nothing more to be said." King Alaric answered in an icy tone.

Thrusting aside his chair, he turned and marched toward the doors, his courtiers and allies hastening to follow.

Hands clasped behind his back, feet spread wide, King Alaric stared through an open window of his command ship, the *Purple Dragon*. Below him spread the roofs and curling streets of Duneidan, lamps and torches flickering in the gray twilight.

"The man is a coward, I tell you. Desiring to keep all his rich lands but unwilling to defend them." The King turned to face the luxurious cabin, his tone changing from angry to unsure. "And yet, how can he be a coward and have defied me so boldly?"

Jovadia the Bittern relaxed on a satin couch, her slippered feet propped on an ottoman, a cup of wine in her hand.

The King stepped toward her with a dissatisfied grunt. "And your powers seemed completely useless in swaying the Duke to our cause."

"My powers were blocked by the Crested Crane." Jovadia stared somberly into the red wine. "In this, her psithe proved more effective than I expected. Or, perhaps she gave the Duke some token to wear."

"Whatever the details," the King flung up a hand. "It is our next move that concerns me. I can hardly leave Duneidan with Keltonn's defiance unanswered. That would undermine all of our efforts in the peninsula. I see no alternative but to attack."

The Bittern regarded him calmly. "Your majesty's thinking is wise, as always."

"Yes, but that too has its risks. Firebombing the castle will not be precise. His soldiers and allies, even the Duke himself, might escape. And when word reaches the rest of the peninsula, the clans may band together against us. We could incite a whole second war on our southern flank." He ended by shaking his head dolefully.

"There is another way, your Majesty. A more *precise* form of attack."

Alaric gazed in puzzlement for a moment, then his head tilted up. "The zolgars, you mean?"

The Bittern had risen to her feet. "Yes, my King. A surprise attack in the night, quick and efficient. Eliminate the Duke and his family, preserve our allies in the castle, and any other men who will likely then join us. Preserve the castle itself."

Alaric paused, fingers touching his sealed lips. She called them zolgars, "deathless ones"—normal men converted to unnatural warriors by her magic. The King had seen them demonstrated in the dungeons below his castle, where Jovadia kept her workshops. Tall, brawny, tremendously strong. But that was only the start of it. Fearless, invulnerable to pain, they kept fighting no matter how badly wounded.

The King had never used them in combat. The idea both fascinated and appalled him.

"How many did you bring? Will they be enough?"

"Thirty, asleep in the hold of this ship. More than sufficient, I assure you."

"And you're certain you can control them, make them do your bidding."

A thin smile appeared. "Only I."

Alaric paced to the window, concealing an inner chill. Imagining such an attack felt horrible, yet fascinating. Back turned to the wizard, he stared into the dusk.

"I don't know, Jovadia. Yes, I've used airships and firebombs against my enemies. But taking advantage of scientific weapons is one thing, a sneak attack in the night with unnatural creatures? It feels ... dishonorable."

The Bittern had crossed the carpet silently to stand at his shoulder. Her voice came as a whisper. "Your notions of honor do you credit, my King. But my arts are only another form of ancient science. Wars may be won in many ways. What matter the methods so long as they bring the ends you seek: your noble plans for your people and your kingship?"

Her voice was soft and soothing, her arguments, as usual, so persuasive. What a marvelous ally she had proven to be, Alaric thought. Her counsel and powers had brought him conquests and riches—and now to the brink of empire.

"And you can be ready to attack tonight?" he asked.

"Yes. In the night."

Chapter 4

Mirafra experienced a horrible dream. In a courtyard in far-off Montodoro, she stood with a class of tyros, lined up in ranks and files, practicing measured exercises with their gleaming psithes. Suddenly, alarm horns sounded in the distance. As the young women glanced at each other, mystified, darkness appeared. It swept over the courtyard, over all of the ancient Sanctuary. Within the darkness flew glittering swords. They swooped out of nowhere, stabbing the majja, leaving them writhing in pools of blood.

She sat up with a gasp.

An alarm horn blared. Faint in the distance, she heard roars, shouting, the clash of steel. In a panic, she surged out of bed, pulled on shoes and her feathered robe. Halfway across the narrow room she stopped, ran back to retrieve her psithe from the bedside table where it lay, locked in the disk form on a bronze neck chain.

Her bedroom adjoined Sharam's apartment. Entering the antechamber, she saw in the lamplight that the door to the hallway was open. The noise of battle was louder. Thinking Sharam must have gone to investigate, Mirafra ran for the corridor.

Then she stopped, seized by horror. Sharam lay face down on the carpet, limbs contorted—like one of the fallen majja in her nightmare.

"Maestra!"

Mirafra knelt, gently lifted a shoulder and rolled Sharam over. The Crane came awake, grimacing. The feathers on her robe shimmered in silvery light cast by her psithe, which lay beside her. Mirafra spotted no blood.

Sharam clutched her skull with both hands. "I am wounded, dying."

"No!"

"Listen to me, Mirafra. The castle is under attack. I was running to help when I was struck down, a bolt of force to my brain. Jovadia, it must be ... Where is my psithe?"

Mirafra picked up the white energy ball and placed it in the Crane's open hand.

Somewhere above, amid the clash of weapons, a woman screamed.

"Open your mind, Mirafra. I must attune my psithe to you."

"No, Maestra!"

"Yes! Do as I say!"

Mirafra shut her eyes and sought to calm herself. Waves of gentle power moved into her brain and down her spine.

"Use the magic to hide yourself," Sharam whispered. "Get away from the castle. Return my psithe to Montodoro, if you can. Above all, do not let the Bittern get it. She will seek to possess it, I am sure."

As Mirafra opened her eyes, Sharam pressed the gleaming sphere into her hand.

"Draw on this power only as you must, lest it overwhelm your mind. Now go!"

Mirafra shuddered. "Maestra, I cannot leave you!"

"You must!" Sharam stared wild-eyed for a moment. Then she exhaled and touched the young woman's wrist. "You are a good majja, Mirafra. We all must do our duty. Promise me you will!"

Fighting back tears, she answered. "I promise."

The maestra closed her eyes and let her head sink back. A look of peace came over her, and she ceased to breathe.

Mirafra stared in shock at the dead woman, then down at the Crane psithe, which sizzled in her hand. Gathering her will, she commanded the psithe to assume the disk shape. After quivering for a moment, it did.

Stunned, overwhelmed by grief and dread, Mirafra moved cautiously to the doorway. The clamor of battle sounded farther away now and mostly from above—the level of the Duke's quarters. The stairs and corridors leading to the ground floor might be empty. Mirafra might escape the castle unseen, even without invoking the Crane psithe.

Yet she hesitated, thinking of Arwyn.

She had promised to conceal herself and get away if she could. But she had not promised to go alone.

The feathered robe rustled as she ran up the corridor. Reaching a central staircase, she did not pause but chose the upward flight, in the direction of the fighting. The Tree Pipit psithe hung on a chain over her heart. The Crested Crane psithe, with its much greater energy, lay concealed in an inner pocket.

Near the top of the stairs, she jerked to a halt and ducked. Two huge warriors were marching up the hallway. Clad all in black armor, they carried longswords in each gauntleted hand. Helmets with visors concealed their faces.

For a terrifying instant, Mirafra thought they might spot her. But they walked on, silently and with an uncanny smoothness—flowing like creatures formed of black water.

Mirafra reached into her robe and touched the Crane psithe. Breathing slowly, chanting in her mind, she invoked a spell of concealment. Energy fluttered like misty curtains over her body. Though she felt the power, she could not tell if it truly made her invisible.

She would simply have to trust.

Quietly, she climbed the remaining steps and hastened along the corridor. Within the magical mist, she was hardly aware of her footsteps, as if she floated.

Ahead she saw the two armored warriors. They trudged over the bodies of four men-at-arms, all of them lying still, one decapitated. Mirafra followed the hulking creatures into the Duke's reception hall.

Inside was chaos: dead bodies strewn across the floor, clumps of men still fighting with swords and pikes. But the black-armored creatures seemed impervious to steel. They continued to hack and stab, though their own arms and chests bled. One fought on despite a sword driven deep into his belly.

Unseen, Mirafra moved over and around the carnage. On the dais, she found the body of the Duke, lying with an arm chopped off. Behind him lay the Duchess, gown drenched in blood, dead eyes staring at the ceiling.

In an antechamber behind the dais, she found Arwyn, still alive, wielding sword and shield, fighting in company with his eldest brother and three of the Duke's soldiers. Six of the deadly warriors attacked them. As she crossed the chamber, Mirafra saw the elder son struck down. With a cry of rage, Arwyn used the opening to dart in and stab the warrior in the groin. The creature merely straightened and lifted its two swords.

Arwyn whirled and fled. The warrior started after, then turned to counter another attacker. Mirafra followed Arwyn through an archway, down a short corridor. He darted into another chamber, a vault used to store weapons. When Mirafra reached him, he had lifted a pike from the wall and was starting back to the fray.

"Wait!"

To Arwyn, the voice seemed to issue from the air.

Mirafra parted the mist and showed herself. Arwyn swayed back in shock.

"Mirafra!" Leveling the pike, he waved her aside. "Get out of here. Save yourself if you can."

"You can't fight them. Come with me."

He looked startled. "No. I can't. They've killed my whole family. I must fight!"

The mist had vanished. She stood in the doorway, blocking him. "You'll have a better chance to win justice for your family if you escape now."

He considered that for just a moment. "No. It's not possible."

Mirafra showed him the glimmering disk. "It might be, with this."

Footsteps and the faint clink of armor sounded from the corridor.

"Please come with me," Mirafra urged.

Arwyn's shoulders sank. "Well, there seems no hope any other way."

Mirafra stepped closer and enveloped them both in the mist.

Head swimming, Jovadia the Bittern leaned over a cauldron of black iron that bubbled and hissed with cold fire. For nearly two hours, she had stared into the cauldron, watching the swirls of light and darkness, and within those veils, visions of the attack on the castle. And, from another level of her mind, she had controlled the attack. Marching the zolgars past the gates, through the chambers and corridors that she had studied so carefully, directing the creatures to find and destroy the Duke and his family and close advisors, while sparing Count Baglan and the other, weaker men who would now fall in line for the King.

Nor was that all. In the midst of the battle, the Bittern had launched a separate attack, a psithic arrow to slay the Crested Crane, catching her at just the right moment when her mind was distracted by the chaos sweeping over the castle. That had gone well enough—except for the cursed apprentice. Jovadia had glimpsed in the cauldron that the Tree Pipit had taken the Crane psithe. Remarkably, a mere tyro, she'd succeeded in tapping the maestra-level power to conceal herself.

The strain on the young woman's mind must have been severe. How far could she have gotten?

Her own skull flashing with pain, Jovadia stubbornly cast her will into the cauldron. After a few moments, the energy conformed, revealing jagged images: the Tree Pipit moving invisibly through the Duke's reception hall, then standing beside one of his sons in a doorway. Then worse: using the maestra's psithe to conceal them both, the young majja and the boy fleeing downstairs.

They will seek to escape the castle, Jovadia realized. Given the remarkable strength shown by the tyro, they might succeed.

A minor failure, but one Jovadia refused to tolerate. The Duke's entire family must perish. Besides, she wanted that Crane psithe for herself.

Gritting her teeth, the Bittern cast more mind-force into the cauldron.

Black pain stabbed the back of her head. She swayed and had to grip the iron rim to steady herself.

Too exhausted.

She swept both hands over the cauldron, calming the energy. And a massive torrent of energy it was, cast not only from the Bittern's psithe but from the psithes of her three apprentices, who at this moment sat in trance in Tonnsburg Castle far to the north. Those and three other psithes, which had been thrown into the cauldron itself—psithes the Bittern had appropriated from majja who had failed to satisfy her as apprentices.

Too much energy to settle just now; she would complete that process later. She placed a black lid over the cauldron. She must speak to the King.

Though it was still a few hours before dawn, she found Alaric awake in his cabin, awaiting her report. Dressed in a robe of velvet trimmed with white fur, he sat at the dining table, attended by a butler and chamberlain, a pitcher of wine at his hand. He looked up expectantly as Jovadia lurched into the room.

"What news, my lady?"

"The attack went well." Still dizzy, she slumped into a chair beside him. "Our enemies are dead, all except—"

"Except who?"

"The Duke's youngest son and the apprentice majja—they might have escaped the castle."

"How is that possible?"

"She used her maestra's psithe for concealment. You must send troops at once to hunt them down. Search the castle first, then if need be, the town and outlying farmsteads."

"You're certain all the others are all dead?" Alaric reached for his cup. "Well, if it's only the boy and a girl wizard ..."

Jovadia leaned fiercely toward him. "This is urgent! We don't want any of the Duke's family left alive! The boy must be killed, and the girl killed or brought to me. And I must have that psithe!"

The King leaned back, flinching. "Of course, you are right, Jovadia." He stood and called for the captain of the guard.

Moving quietly, Mirafra and Arwyn slipped through the main castle gate, past the bodies of the Duke's sentries. Only when they had crossed the drawbridge did Mirafra finally release the psithic energy. The strain of wielding so much power had grown tighter and tighter as they descended through the castle, stopping at times to hide in an alcove or behind a closed door while monstrous warriors marched past.

Now, setting her feet on the grass of the meadow, Mirafra allowed her will to relax. Immediately, darkness rushed up through her body. She collapsed to her knees.

Arwyn clasped her shoulder. "Are you sick? We'd best keep moving."

"Yes." She leaned on his arm as he lifted her. "Into the town."

"Just what I was thinking."

Bent low, they hurried across the meadow. Mirafra struggled to keep her feet, fighting back the dizziness. *So much power.* So much more than her body had ever absorbed or cast. Another time, the achievement would have thrilled her.

But not now, not this night.

The town lay ahead, only a few streetlamps burning at this late hour. But the sky was clear with a bright, waning moon overhead. Moonlight shone on the long balloons of the King's three airships. Mirafra and Arwyn gave those wide berth, circling toward the other side of the meadow, where the lone trading ship hung near a cluster of tents and market stalls.

Mirafra felt a surge of relief when her feet touched the first cobblestones. Here they could hide in the maze of streets and alleys, at least until morning.

But then what?

"You there! Halt!"

The loud command brought back her panic. Spearmen circled the corner ahead, two holding lamps, all of them clad in the King's livery.

"It's them!" one man shouted. The soldiers rushed forward.

Mirafra reached for the Crane psithe, then froze. No time to invoke a concealment, even if she could summon the power.

Arwyn tugged her sleeve. "Run!"

They turned and fled back into the meadow.

But now they were crossing open ground and clearly visible in the silvery light. Desperately, Mirafra looked for cover. Arwyn pointed toward the rows of tents and market stalls.

They ran that way.

Behind them, the soldiers were gaining.

The fugitives dashed down a curling lane, turned a corner, and ran down another. With no other place to hide, they ducked into the shadow of a merchant's tent. Behind them, the trading ship hovered against the starlit sky, stout lines anchoring it to the ground.

Mirafra reached into her cape and clutched the maestra's psithe. She tried to feed it power, to cast another concealment.

No use. Too exhausted. Too frightened.

The soldiers were closing on their position.

From behind them sounded a creaking noise. Mirafra whirled to see that a gangway ladder had dropped from the hull of the airship. A light appeared, a silvery glow that descended the steps. Peering at the light, Mirafra saw a man in a black cape. She recognized him—the conjurer from the music hall.

Reaching the ground, the conjurer walked calmly down the lane past their hiding place. He reached the corner just before the onrushing soldiers. He lifted the gleaming disk high, and the men halted, staring at its light.

"Gentlemen," the magician said. "I saw the ones you are chasing. They ran that way, back to the town."

Baffled, the men looked in the direction he pointed.

"If you hurry, you can catch them."

The soldiers looked at one another. Suddenly, they turned and ran back down the lane.

The conjurer waited till the guards were out of earshot, then lowered the disk. "You can come out now," he murmured over his shoulder.

As Mirafra and Arwyn crept away from the tent, the magician faced them.

"I'd recommend you come with me."

"You are Zeneon the conjurer," Arwyn muttered.

"And you are a Norrling," Mirafra added. "Because *that* is a psithe."

"Yes," he hefted the disk in his hand. "Time for that later. You, I believe, are the Crane's apprentice, and you the Duke's son. I felt the storms of energy that thundered over the castle. I entered trance and glimpsed some of the details. Such horrible evil. I am sorry for your family, young lord, sorry that I could not help. But at least I can help you now to escape. If you'll trust me and come aboard my airship, we'll cast off at once and get away while we can."

"*Your* airship?" Arwyn asked.

"Yes. It belongs to me." He offered a bow. "Allow me to tell you my true name. I am Teron the Mooncrow."

Mirafra's jaw dropped. *Mooncrow.* The first and most famous of all the Norrling wanderers. *Could this be true?* Too much to fathom. A new wave of dizziness surged through her head, and she fainted.

Part Two

The City of Highest Beauty

The Moldorns were the first to rediscover the methods of colossal architecture. Their towered citadel of PonnTherion was the tallest structure to have been built in the world for many centuries.

But these technologies were soon adopted by neighboring nations. In Occitan, most notably, there arose a city renowned across the West for not only the height but also the artistry of its giant buildings.

— Ivan Demmering, *The Ancient Technicians*.
1368 New Calendar.

Chapter 5

Mirafra wandered long, dim corridors, crawling, scraping her hands and knees. Often, she cast her eyes down to avoid the scenes around her: scenes of chaos and terror, stabbing blades and murder. Piles of men with twisted limbs lay dead. Arwyn's mother, eyes fixed wide, stared at nothing.

Other times, Mirafra floated, as if swimming in cool, bubbling water. But then the water turned to fiery energy the color of blood, blinding her sight, scalding her chest and belly.

"Mirafra. Can you hear me?"

In her dream she stood in a crypt in Montodoro. Sharam the Crested Crane floated above an open sarcophagus, pointing her finger. "You must do your duty, songbird."

"Mirafra?"

She woke, staring into Arwyn's worried face. Blinking, she gazed past him into a small chamber with wooden walls and low, arcing beams. The sensation of floating was with her still.

"Where are we?"

"Hah! You are with us again. I am so glad!"

She tried to rise, sank back, dizzy. "With you, but where?"

With a somber smile, Arwyn spread his hands. "On the airship. Flying. Teron gave the order, and we took off before dawn. The ship really does belong to him. And he really *is* Teron the Mooncrow, I am convinced of it."

Mirafra sat up, slowly this time.

"Easy," Arwyn cautioned. "Teron said you will recover, but it might take a few days. He gave you a potion that he mixed in his psithe-cup. He explained your condition with some Norrling words.

The translation he gave was that you were 'overextended,' the strain of too much power."

"I think he's right about that." Suddenly she looked around. "My psithe—?"

"Here," Arwyn opened a drawer in the bedside table. "Both of them."

Relieved, Mirafra picked up the chain with the Tree Pipit disk and placed it over her head. She was still wearing her nightdress. The feathered cape lay at the foot of the narrow bunk. She reached for it and slipped the Crane psithe-disk into an inner pocket.

"I'll have to find a safe place for that." She sank back on the pillow. "Where are we going?"

Arwyn's face turned grim. "That's still to be decided. Occitan, I hope. Anyway, I must travel there, one way or another, to join King Carswell's service. That seems the best chance to avenge my family."

Mirafra stared at him, thinking of what they had both lost, wondering what she would do, what she could do ...

"Teron said we would talk about it over dinner. You're invited, if you feel well enough."

Teron. Mirafra wondered if the man really could be the famous Mooncrow. It seemed so unlikely. And the fellow *was* a stage magician, a trickster ...

Teron sat in trance, feet tucked at his hips, the Mooncrow psithe in its wand shape hovering over his knees. The wand also lifted his body so that it floated a yard above the cabin floor. Before him, wide windows gave a spectacular view of the blue sky and the green hills of Arabhedden. But Teron's eyes were closed, his mind searching behind and around the airship, penetrating even the distant clouds to the west.

He searched for some time before relaxing, satisfied that no ships pursued them. They had indeed escaped.

Teron withdrew the energy from the psithe and let his body sink onto the cushion below. Staring through the wide window, he spied blue water in the distance. He sensed a presence, smiled, and called over his shoulder.

"Come in, Topiedeon."

The cabin door opened, and the blond minstrel strode through. "Forgive the interruption, Teron, old lad. But I am wondering as to our destination. That is, I and everyone else on board are wondering."

Topiedeon had crossed the cabin and stretched out on a couch. He lifted his bearded chin toward the window. "As you can see, the day is growing late, and the ocean is now in view. You ordered Dona Delores to sail east with the wind, to flee Duneidan as fast as possible. I get that. But unless you're planning to sail on to Afrique—which I think would put quite a strain on our fuel supply—a new course would seem to be in order."

The Mooncrow had stood and was stretching. "Yes, I know. I had thought to sail south to the coastal towns, then the islands. Warmer weather this time of year and all that. But I spoke with the boy this afternoon. He's hoping to travel to King Carswell's city in Occitan."

Topiedeon frowned. "Occitan, is it? A long way around, and not much chance of commerce between. I don't think Dona Delores will be happy."

"No! Dona Delores will not be happy!" The captain herself marched through the open door. A stout, broad-shouldered woman, she wore a dark blue coat and airman's hat. She stopped in front of Teron, fists at her hips. She spoke Tuvarian, the common trading tongue, but with an Iboran accent. "You are the owner, Senor Teron, but you must think of your ship and your crew. We did not take on any cargo in Duneidan, and as you know, we flew *to* Duneidan without cargo because you had a whim to go there. I do not know why."

Topiedeon smirked. "She's right about that, lad. And, as we left so precipitously, the troupe did not get paid for our five nights of performance."

"I still have some coin," Teron answered, thinking uncomfortably that his coffer was rather low. "The troupe will be paid. And so will your crew, Captain."

Dona Delores frowned.

Topiedeon gave a shrug. "I trust you on that, Teron, of course. Yet I have to wonder why you would consider conveying the young nobleman all the way to Occitan. For that matter, I'm still not sure why we flew to Duneidan in the first place, when more business was to be had along the coast."

Teron shrugged. As Dona Delores said, the decision came on a whim. Meditation led him to it. He had sensed enormous psithic power would be unleashed when King Alaric visited Duneidan. For some reason, that intuition brought back recurring memories—the terrible night, years ago, when he had witnessed the firebombing of Telyrra by the Moldorns. But why that made him decide he had to fly to Duneidan remained a mystery. Some Norrling doctrines taught that each magician had a rightful course in life, which they might choose to accept or not. Sometimes, the rightful course was only revealed by contemplation.

"I'm not sure myself," the Mooncrow admitted. He turned to Dona Delores. "How long would it take us to reach Carswell's capital at Baivonne?"

The captain threw up her hands. "Two days, four days, depending on the winds."

"And we have sufficient fuel?"

"Yes, I suppose. Barely."

"So it's Occitan then?" Topiedeon asked.

Teron considered. "Turn south for now, Captain. I will speak more with our guests and decide over dinner."

Dona Delores turned with a grunt and marched from the cabin. Topiedeon stretched his arms but did not rise. Teron settled into a chair.

"Teron, old friend," the minstrel said, "I do hope you're not going to get us involved in another war. Remember, you said that on leaving the Moldorn court you had sworn off politics for good."

Teron weighed the psithe-disk in his hand, then tossed it in the air as if flipping a coin. "But did I say 'positively'?"

"Acch!" Topiedeon's mock screech of alarm made the Mooncrow laugh.

Mirafra had been given a plain tunic and trousers, borrowed from one of the crew. Dressed in these, along with her shoes and feathered cape, she followed Arwyn down a narrow passage. The woozy sensation of floating still lingered, and at moments the floor sank or shifted under her feet, forcing her to lean on the wall for balance.

"The nature of airship travel, I suppose," Arwyn remarked with a nervous laugh.

Up two flights of steps, they reached the upper deck and entered a luxurious cabin set in the prow. Wide windows gave a spectacular view of the sky and the ground far below, now growing dim in the twilight.

A long table was set for dinner, already occupied by nine persons. From the head of the table, the conjurer Teron (or Zeneon?) welcomed Mirafra and Arwyn and gestured them to seats beside his own. He introduced the other diners: Topiedeon, the blond bard who had played in the music hall; the Bonatores, two men and a woman who were the acrobats of the troupe. Opposite Teron sat a strongly built woman named Dona Delores who—Mirafra was surprised to learn—was the ship's captain. With her were two airmen who the captain introduced as her cousins, Ricardo and Emilio.

Two junior crewmen stood in attendance, and now they poured wine and fresh water. The magician raised a cup to welcome and salute the young guests.

After the toast, one of the Bonatore men addressed Teron in the Tuvarian tongue. When the magician reminded him to speak in Galintaan, he tried again, gesturing with his hands.

"Excuse, Senor Teron. But is it true we are ... sailing to the north again, rather than the islands?"

"I have not yet decided that, Felix," Teron answered. "But I do understand your concern. We had to leave without collecting our pay. But you will all be recompensed, I promise."

"You have been a good partner to us, Senor Teron," Lisa, the woman acrobat, put in. "But we wake up, and the ship is taking off. Later we hear we are sailing to Occitan. We are confused."

"They are not the only ones," Topiedeon muttered with a smirk.

Food was being served: steaming venison, dried fruit, and brown bread. Mirafra had felt too dizzy to eat earlier in the day but now discovered she was hungry. She picked cautiously at a piece of bread, drank some water. Soon, she was eating eagerly.

The mood around the table lightened as the food was enjoyed and the wine flowed. The captain and performers laughed and reminisced about places they had visited, taverns and carnivals where they had played. Teron, though he smiled at times, said little. Mirafra sensed in him a deep mind, full of many thoughts, which he was adept at concealing.

Only when everyone had eaten their fill did Teron turn the conversation back to serious matters. He began by addressing Arwyn.

"My lord, in our conversation earlier you said you hoped to reach King Carswell's castle at Baivonne."

"Yes, sir. I feel I must travel there, however I may. It would be wonderful if your ship could take us, but I understand you have other concerns, and I cannot pay for our passage."

"That is not expected," Teron answered. "But I would like the company to understand your reasons. We know already that your castle was attacked last night by King Alaric, and all of your family killed. But why seek Carswell's protection?"

Arwyn cleared his throat. "For several reasons. Carswell's and Alaric's kingdoms are already in conflict. With the coming of summer, this will likely become a war. I have a cousin who is a lady in Carswell's court. Based on her correspondences, I believe the King to be a man of honor. I am confident that when he hears my story he will give sanctuary to Mirafra and me. Also, I want to make sure he knows what is happening in Arabhedden. In particular, I would warn him about the strange warriors who attacked our castle. I believe they were not normal men, but creatures spawned by magic."

Prompted by Teron, he went on to describe how the black-armored warriors had fought and seemed unbothered by wounds. Scanning the faces of the listeners, Mirafra sensed fear, confusion, but also skepticism.

Teron turned to her. "And you, young majja, you have been trained in the Norrling arts. What is your opinion of these warriors?"

She stared into his eyes and answered frankly. "Everything Arwyn said matches what I saw. Weapons did these creatures no harm. When wounded, though they bled like men, they went on fighting. I concluded that they were mortal men but remade by magic—certainly not Norrling magic—but perhaps, I think, some evil perversion of our arts."

Teron nodded, lips taut. "Your description is apt, and it accords with what I sensed in psithic visions." His glance traveled around the table. "Some unknown power is at work in this—unlike anything I've ever encountered."

"Jovadia the Bittern," Mirafra murmured. "She spoke to me about raising ancient secrets."

Teron stared at her, deep in thought. Finally, he stood. "My friends, I agree with the young lord that King Carswell and his court must be informed of this, and the sooner the better. Captain, please set our course for Baivonne."

With a wry smile, Dona Delores rose from the table and went to inform the rest of the crew. After muttering among themselves in Tuvarian, the three acrobats finished their wine, thanked Teron for the meal, and took their leave. As they were departing, the crank of cables sounded, and the airship turned into the wind.

"Sure, and the Bonatores are not happy with you, Teron," Topiedeon leaned back in his chair, stretching. "They're wondering if we will find work up in Occitan, and if we don't find work, how we will eat."

Teron had walked to the windows and was staring out into the night. "We will find work. Baivonne is one of the busiest ports in Tann. I'm sure there is no shortage of music halls and taverns."

"But also plenty of competition," the minstrel answered. "Especially in the winter months."

Teron waved the objection aside. "We'll find work, I'm sure. Also, Carswell is a wealthy king, and I would not be surprised if he rewards us handsomely for bringing him these two young allies and the information they carry."

He indicated Mirafra and Arwyn, who had not left the table.

The magician stepped back to his seat and reached to pour himself more wine. "Besides, Topiedeon, given what these two young people have been through, we can't just drop them in some island town with no resources. My conscience won't allow it."

"Oh, I agree with you there," Topiedeon smiled and topped up his own cup. "Just remember, you don't want to get involved in any politics."

A corner of Teron's mouth turned up as he brooded over his goblet.

Mirafra glanced at Arwyn, then decided to speak up.

"If I may ask ... Teron. That is, I *must* ask. Are you really Teron the Mooncrow? And if so, how did you come to be a traveling conjurer and the owner of an airship?"

"Ah, my child." Topiedeon reached for the mandolin, which hung from the back of his chair. "That is indeed a strange story. How does the Mooncrow, the daring wizard and breaker of empires, end up a stage magician in a ragged troupe of traveling players?" He strummed a chord, frowned, reached to adjust a peg.

"Topiedeon has written ballads about it, and no doubt will write more." Teron said. "But in the interest of accuracy, I will give you my own version. Tell me first what you've heard of my story, so I know where to begin."

Mirafra exchanged glances with Arwyn, who answered. "The popular tale, of course, says you were a Norrling wizard from the Sanctuary of Ptolloden, that you witnessed the Moldorns' attack on the island of Telyrra, and that you later arrived in disguise in the court of the Moldorn Emperor in PonnTherion. There, you fought the Moldorn nobles, the Pallantines, first as an assassin who haunted the city by night, later as the leader of a rebellion that toppled the Emperor. When his daughter was installed on the throne as the Empress Rania, you became her advisor and Court Wizard."

"All true," Teron muttered. "More or less."

"All completely true!" Topiedeon struck a loud chord. "As I can attest, having witnessed the events both in Telyrra and PonnTherion."

"In tales I heard in Montodoro," Mirafra added, "it was also said that you were the consort of the Empress Rania. A few years ago, she died in childbirth, and her young son ascended to the throne."

Teron's thin face had grown sad. "True again. But do not assume Rania's children were mine. Rania was a remarkable woman, and we loved each other dearly. But to keep the throne, she was forced to choose a husband from among the Moldorn nobles. That ended our love affair, though I continued to serve her as Court Wizard."

"Nothing more was told of you after the death of the Empress," Mirafra said.

"Not surprising." Teron frowned. "Politics, you see? With Rania gone, the new Emperor, a child of seven, quickly became the tool of the Pallantines. They had lost much of their power and were intent on regaining it. It soon became obvious that I had little influence on the boy. Rania had provided for me richly in her will. I settled for this airship and a chest of gold and left PonnTherion. At first, I thought I might return to Ombernorr and resume my studies. But from talking with traveling wizards I met, it became obvious that the regime in Ptolloden had grown even more strict and aloof from the world than when I first left. The course of austere detachment has never satisfied me, you see? So, for a while, I simply traveled, letting Dona Delores and her crew ply the trade routes. Then one night in a tavern in Istria, I discovered this rogue of a minstrel, performing with the Bonatores. It didn't take much for them to convince me to join the act."

His mouth quirked into a smile. "That is my tale, such as it is. I left Ombernorr at age 20 to become a wandering performer. Now, age 40, I am a wandering performer again."

Chapter 6

The next morning, Arwyn convinced Mirafra to leave her tiny cabin and explore the airship. She had slept soundly during the night—after prolonged meditations with the Tree Pipit psithe—and was feeling almost fully recovered.

They walked up the same narrow passageway as they had the evening before but this time kept on past the stairs. At the prow of the ship, they came to a large compartment where crewmembers worked an array of wheels and levers. The captain, Dona Delores, spotted them in the doorway. To Mirafra's relief, she greeted them with a smile and invited them to enter.

This chamber, she explained, was called the wheelroom. From here the pilot controlled the fins and rudders that steered the ship. Mirafra stared out the broad glass windows to the hills far below. For the first time, she appreciated the wonder of flying.

"What about the boilers that make the steam?" Arwyn asked, ever curious.

"The boiler room is amidships," Dona Delores explained. "From here we must relay orders if we want more or less steam to control altitude. Would you like me to show you?"

The captain was obviously proud of her airship and more than happy to conduct a tour. She ordered the crewman to hold a steady course, then led the two visitors back the way they had come. Along the way she explained the layout of the ship.

The hull had three decks, with cargo holds in the center. The passageways along the sides gave access to smaller compartments and cabins. Overhead, three "balloonets" floated within the oblong envelope, which Dona Delores called "the bubble."

A chamber between the two cargo holds housed the boilers. Four of them burned constantly, three to vent hot air to the balloonets and a larger one to power the tail propellers.

"What fuel do you burn?" Arwyn asked.

"Lifting gas, when we can get it," the captain answered. "But we burn coal or wood when we must." The gas, she explained, was manufactured from coal and stored as liquid in metal canisters. When released, it turned to a gas that burned more efficiently than the other fuels.

"If the question is not impolite," Arwyn said, "how did you come to be captain? Is this an unusual position for a woman?"

"Ah, it is," she replied. "Airships at first were built only for the military. But this changed when the Empress came to power. Then, more and more, they became vessels of trade."

Her father, she explained, had been a sea captain and among the first traders to acquire an airship. From childhood, she had traveled with him, following the trade routes of the Capdian Sea and Eastern Ibor. When her father died, his ship had been taken by creditors. Now a skilled pilot, Dona Delores had found work on one of the imperial trading ships, and had soon risen to captain. That ship, the *Pomegranate*, was the one given to Teron when he left the Moldorn court.

"I think of the ship as my own," she said. "But Teron is a good owner, and he does not interfere with me running things—at least not too much."

Arwyn and Mirafra glanced at one another.

"We are grateful to you," Mirafra said. "For changing your plans and conveying us to Occitan."

The captain shrugged. "In this business, sometimes you must blow with the wind. No?"

Weeping, soft and inconsolable. So painful, it seemed to express all the sorrows of the world.

Waking in her narrow bunk, Mirafra realized the crying came from the room next door—Arwyn's cabin. For a time she lay listening, staring into the darkness. It was the middle of the night, Arwyn deserved his privacy, and surely he had ample reason for weeping.

But finally, not able to help herself, she got out of bed, donned her robe, and placed the Tree Pipit disk around her neck. She stopped at his door, hesitant. Then she pushed the door open and went to stand beside his bunk.

In the faint glimmer of the psithe-disk, Arwyn saw her. He sat up, wiping an arm across his eyes.

"Mirafra. I didn't hear you."

Holding back tears of her own, she sat down beside him. "It's all right," she whispered.

He gazed into her eyes, then suddenly threw himself into her arms, sobbing.

"Oh, Mirafra, I've lost everything. How can I go on? ... And yet, I must go on, for my family's honor."

When his weeping subsided, he leaned back, wiped his eyes. "I am so ashamed for you to see me like this."

She squeezed his wrist. "It is all right."

"I did not think I was so loud."

Her glance drifted down. "Perhaps I felt it rather than heard it."

He gazed into her eyes, understanding. "We are close, aren't we?"

Embarrassed, she nodded. "Very close."

He embraced her and spoke close to her ear. "I have not lost everyone. I still have you. ... You saved my life, at the risk of your own. I still don't understand why you did that."

She held him in her arms. "I had to. I could not leave you to die if I could help it. I never ... never had a friend before. Teachers, fellow students, but no one I cared for so much."

After holding her a moment longer, Arwyn tilted back, gripping her shoulders in his hands. "We will both go on. And do our duty. Because we must."

Next day, while wandering the ship, Mirafra and Arwyn heard voices and music coming from the forward cargo hold. With a laugh, Arwyn pushed open a door. Mirafra followed him into a broad, airy space that rose the height of all three decks. Daylight filtered through rows of windows high above, just beneath the metal-coated curve of the envelope.

Topiedeon the bard was playing a tune, while the three acrobats leaped and tumbled over a spread of carpets. From the shadows of the wall stepped Teron the Mooncrow, startling Mirafra.

"Greetings, my young friends."

Arwyn gave a courtly bow, and Mirafra mimicked him.

"The acrobats must practice every day or lose their edge," Teron said. "Stay and watch us, if you like."

When the performers finished their routine, the Mooncrow went to join them. The players exchanged a few words and took up new positions. Now the minstrel strummed a slower tune. Mirafra watched as Teron took the Mooncrow psithe from inside his robe and formed it into a wand.

The Bonatores circled him with slow, rhythmic steps. As the music grew louder, Teron raised the psithe-wand and shouted a

Norrling word. The acrobats increased their pace as they floated into the air. Soon they were moving around the magician at shoulder height, twisting and tumbling as the mandolin played. Finally, as the music slowed, Teron brought the acrobats gently back to the floor.

They bowed to Arwyn and Mirafra, who applauded.

Telling the troupe to practice another routine, Teron walked back to rejoin the two young people.

"That was wonderful!" Arwyn exclaimed. "I cannot imagine there are many acts in all of Tann so accomplished."

Smiling, Teron bowed his head. "Simply a blend of illusion and levitation." With a sudden thought, he eyed Mirafra. "Would you like to try?"

She tilted away. "Oh, I couldn't."

"I think perhaps you could, or I wouldn't suggest it."

"But my psithe is merely of the tyro grade."

"But you have another psithe, that of a maestra, if I am not mistaken." He was staring at the pocket of her cape, which contained Sharam's psithe.

Mirafra's lips parted. Hesitantly, she brought out the heavy disk.

"You wielded it quite competently the other night," Teron observed. "The maestra must have attuned it to you."

"Yes. Sharam the Crested Crane. She charged me to use it to escape, to keep it from falling into the hands of the Bittern. And to return it to Montodoro, if I could."

"And so you should," the Mooncrow said. "But for now, it is yours, and you should use it. We wizards are like acrobats, you know: if we do not practice, we too can lose our edge."

He gestured toward the carpet. "Come. I realize that carrying so much power overwhelmed you. But a short dose should do no harm, and that too will improve with practice."

Mirafra's fingers tightened on the disk. She did not want this challenge.

"I will teach you how to work the trick," Teron said. "Of course, you don't have to, if you are afraid."

Perhaps the Mooncrow had calculated that *that* suggestion would make her angry. Since childhood, Mirafra had been beset with many fears. But, as a majja, she was taught to overcome them. If she was to fulfill her duty, to return the Crane's psithe to the Sanctuary, and perhaps also to help Arwyn, she could not let fear stand in her way.

Clenching her lips, she nodded and marched off in the direction Teron indicated. First, he took her aside, some distance from where Topiedeon and the acrobats practiced. Standing far below the curving airship bubble, Mirafra transformed the Crane psithe to its wand shape. The surge of energy washing through her brain was powerful, but she kept her balance.

For a time she practiced levitating the gleaming white wand, raising it above her head and lowering it to her knees. Next, Teron coached her to use the power to lift her body off the floor. Keeping balance was harder with this, but the Mooncrow used his own psithe to nudge and guide her efforts. Soon, Mirafra was raising and settling herself with ease.

Teron then invited Lisa, the young woman acrobat, to join them. He explained that he was teaching Mirafra a few of his stage tricks. While Lisa stood relaxed, Mirafra fed power to the wand, attempting to lift the acrobat. This proved much harder. As Mirafra strained with the effort, a shimmering dizziness washed through her head.

"Perhaps that is enough today," Teron suggested.

"No. I can do it!" the Tree Pipit said.

Slowly, white wand shaking in her hands, Mirafra succeeded. Floating at shoulder height, Lisa grinned, waved her arms, and gracefully pirouetted.

Grimacing, Mirafra gently lowered the young woman to the floor. When she relaxed, her head drooped, and she came close to fainting. Teron grabbed her elbow to hold her up.

"That is definitely enough for today."

"Well done!" Arwyn stood nearby, clapping loudly. "Mirafra, you are amazing!"

Jovadia the Bittern stared into the swirling depths of her psithe-disk. In the form she had fashioned, the disk was larger than typical for a psithe. Resembling a platter with a razor edge, it flashed with sparks as bright as the firebombs dropped from the King's warships.

But for all her power, and though she had tried several times, Jovadia could discover no trace of the apprentice Tree Pipit or the Crested Crane psithe she believed the girl had taken. And the Duke of Duneidan's young son was also not yet accounted for. They must both have gotten far away—perhaps on that airship that disappeared from the town on the night of the attack.

With a sigh, Jovadia waved a hand, converting the psithe into the smaller disk, which she wore like an amulet on a gold chain. The loss of the Crane psithe was a minor annoyance, one she would have to accept. For now.

After draping the chain over her neck, she stood and surveyed the luxurious bedroom she occupied in the fallen Duke's castle. For the most part, her plans were going well. The thirty zolgars had captured the castle with ease, killing all who resisted. With wounds patched, the supernatural warriors now rested in a castle crypt, lifeless until Jovadia chose to rouse them again. Within a day, Jovadia had recovered from the psithic strain of raising and directing the creatures.

Now it was time to plot her next moves.

Jovadia dressed, put on boots, and wrapped herself in the Bittern cape. Without touching the breakfast tray that a servant had brought, she went to find the King.

Alaric was in the throne room, consulting with his officers and newly installed vassals. Just three nights ago, this chamber had been a scene of carnage. Now, the blood had been scoured away, and the King's banner hung beside that of Baglan, the new Duke.

Silent as a shadow, Jovadia approached the throne. After bowing to the King, she observed the reactions of the other men. The King's soldiers bowed to her, and the local nobles followed suit, observing the Bittern with uneasy glances.

"Do not let me interrupt," she told Alaric.

"Not at all, Lady. I am glad you are here. We were just reviewing the status of things here in Duneidan."

Jovadia ascended the three steps of the dais and positioned herself next to the King. Hands folded in sleeves, she listened. The new Duke Baglan reported that the town had been subdued with almost no fighting. Riders had been dispatched to nearby estates and villages to proclaim the new regime and their alliance with the King.

"Oaths of fealty must be obtained from all noblemen," Alaric said. "Then, after things settle down in a month or two, you can start calling up troops."

For now, the King planned to remain in Duneidan to support Baglan in consolidating his rule. Once word of the conquest had spread, Alaric intended visits to the two other dukedoms on the southern peninsula. From all indications, he did not expect that force would be needed to add those to his domain.

"By the coming of spring," he said with a satisfied air, "all of Arabhedden must be under our control. Then, my lords, we shall look west, to Occitan."

Jovadia waited until the Council had finished before requesting a private word with the King. Without rising from the throne, he directed Baglan and the others to leave. When the sentries had moved to the far end of the hall, he turned to the wizard.

"I am happy to see you looking well this morning, my lady. Your recovery seems complete."

"Indeed."

"Your work with the deathless warriors is appreciated. It made taking this castle much easier."

"As we intended, my King. Going forward, you may count on the zolgars as a strong force in your service, in fact, a main component of your army. That is, if you provide me the necessary support."

Alaric tilted his head back. "What further support do you need?"

"This is an ancient and potent magic, my liege. It requires me to draw on many psithes. The more of the bird-spirits I can acquire, the better."

"What do you propose?"

"Any wandering Norrlings found in your territories must be arrested, their psithes confiscated. Also, the court wizards in service to your vassals must either become my subordinates, or their psithes too must be surrendered."

Alaric frowned. "That second part will be difficult. There is sure to be resistance. Is there no other way? No ancient magic you can use to fashion new psithes?"

Scowling, the Bittern leaned closer, displeased at his questioning. "For hundreds of years, psithes have been created only in the High Sanctuaries of Ombernorr, using power embedded in the very stones by generations of wizards. Over time, no doubt, I could discover a way to duplicate the process. But that would be difficult at best and require much research and time. I don't think your plans should have to wait for five or ten years, do you?"

"No, of course not."

"Then mine is the better way. And think of the rewards. With just seven psithes I was able to command 30 zolgars. With 70, the number would be much higher—maybe a thousand, maybe more. Imagine an invincible army marching against your foes. By next summer, you might conquer not only Occitan, but all of Tann."

The King's eyes grew round and bright.

"And after Tann," Jovadia whispered, "there are other continents."

Chapter 7

The Bay of Omez sparkled far below, waters gray and silver in the morning light. The *Pomegranate* sailed with the wind abeam above the curving coastline. Ahead in the distance, the land turned to marshes and wide channels—the delta of the great Machtiges River. On the eastern edge of the delta stood Baivonne.

Approaching the city, the airship turned off-wind, maneuvering toward the harbor where scores of boats and ships floated out in the wide channel and along the docks. Mirafra nervously gripped a steel rail as she gazed through the windows. She stood in the observation room in the bow of the middle deck, along with Arwyn, Topiedeon, and the Bonatores. Teron had not chosen to join them. "Busy plotting his own maneuvers," Topiedeon had explained.

From the wheelroom on the deck below, Mirafra could hear Dona Delores calling out orders. Cables groaned and rudders twisted. The air hissed as steam was vented. Soon they were floating over the vast city, which rose on low ridges from the marshland—a vista of concrete, glass, stone, and tile. Walls, plunging roofs, and towers shone in a dazzling array of colors brighter than rainbows.

"I've always dreamed of visiting here," Arwyn murmured. "But I never imagined ... Surely this is the greatest city in the world."

"Well, I've not seen all of them yet, lad," Topiedeon answered. "But t'is a pretty town, to be sure." He glanced down at Mirafra. "What about you, young majja? Have you not passed this way on your travels?"

The Tree Pipit shook her head. From Montodoro, she and Sharam had journeyed across the tundra and the Forests of Bhakthorn, then taken a ship down the coast. "Except for Arabhedden, I've seen almost nothing of the Warmlands."

On a hill near the center of the city stood a fortified castle with tremendously high walls and spires. Close by lay an airfield, where a half-dozen vessels were moored—two warships, Arwyn noted, and the others outfitted as traders.

From the deck below came more shouted orders and the whir of cranks and cables as the ship began its slow descent. Given the brisk wind, navigating onto the airfield proved tricky. Several turns and slow reversals proved necessary, and Mirafra was not the only one gripping the rail for balance.

As the *Pomegranate* finally settled to the ground, Teron appeared. He was dressed in a way Mirafra had not seen before, all in black with a feathered cape and a Mooncrow mask worn atop his head, the psithe carried as a wand in his hand.

"Well, don't we look fine this morning?" Topiedeon laughed.

"Representing the wizards of Ptolloden," Teron answered dryly. "Must dress the part."

While Dona Delores and her crew stayed on board to secure the ship, Teron led the rest of the party down the steps of the forward gangway. There, they were met by a group of guards and airfield officials. Teron confirmed that they were a trading ship and showed papers of ownership. After paying what he called an exorbitant fee for rental of the berth, he was given a permit.

The field was bordered by cargo warehouses and a fuel depot. A steam-powered machine was in use, hoisting cargo into one of the trading ships. Mirafra and the others crossed the complex on foot. Arriving at an outer gate, they hired two horse-drawn carriages. One was to take the Bonatores into town to scout out taverns and entertainment venues. Teron, along with Arwyn and Mirafra, was bound for the palace. Topiedeon decided to accompany them.

"Sure, I wouldn't want to miss this," he laughed.

As the carriage jostled over cobblestones, Mirafra glanced around, thinking what an odd-looking group they were: she and Arwyn still dressed in ill-fitting crewmen's trousers and shirts, Topiedeon in multi-colored minstrel garb, and the Mooncrow bedecked as a Norrling wizard.

"I wonder what kind of reception we'll meet with," she muttered. "Getting an audience with the king may be difficult."

With a grim smile, the Mooncrow tilted his wand. "We'll manage."

But Mirafra's words proved prophetic. After arriving at a main entrance, the party walked across a broad, open drawbridge. The massive iron gates too stood open, but six sentries with halberds ordered them to stop.

"We are here to see King Carswell," Teron told them. "We have urgent news from Arabhedden that he will wish to hear."

The sentries looked at each other. Then one left to summon a sergeant. When the sergeant came out from the guardhouse, Teron repeated that they had important news for the King.

"This young man is Arwyn, son of the Duke of Duneidan. The Duke's castle was attacked four nights ago by the forces of King Alaric. There is war brewing in Arabhedden. King Carswell will want to hear our story."

The sergeant appeared perplexed. "Story indeed. You look more like a troupe of carnival tricksters to me."

"Our business is urgent." Teron kept his voice level, though Mirafra could feel his anger.

The sergeant raised his hands. "No matter. It's not for me to decide. All who wish an audience with the King must see the Advocate of Petitions." He ordered a corporal to conduct the visitors inside.

Teron and Topiedeon marched on the heels of the corporal, with Mirafra and Arwyn following in the rear. Traversing a long, arched corridor, they emerged in a broad courtyard bordered by stables set below forty-foot-high walls. Across the court stood an even taller building, with sheer walls that shone like rose quartz and soared hundreds of feet into the sky. Mirafra had glimpsed the King's palace from the airship, but up close it was even more impressive. Even the Sanctuary at Montodoro could not compare with this in grandeur.

"Fantastic," Arwyn whispered.

Passing through bronze doors, they walked up a high-ceilinged hallway and were greeted by an even more splendid view. They stood in a vast chamber of the same spectacular height but with walls of different-colored translucent stones, set with windows and balconies rising up twenty or thirty stories.

The floor of this chamber featured steps and platforms at different levels, some carpeted, some of polished stone. Near the place they entered, groups of people milled about, some resting on couches or benches. Beyond them, on a raised platform sat an official in red velvet robes and a wide gold hat, flanked by uniformed attendants and scribes.

The corporal conducted Teron's party to the front of the official's imposing desk. "More petitioners for you, my lord. Just arrived at the main gate."

With that, the corporal pivoted and walked off, leaving the Advocate of Petitions to examine the newcomers with a sour curiosity.

"Who are you then, and what is your business?"

The Mooncrow took a step closer. "I am Teron the Mooncrow, a Norrling adept. This young man is Arwyn, son of the Duke of Duneidan, who was recently killed in an attack on his castle by the forces of King Alaric. We come to warn King Carswell that war has broken out in Arabhedden and will, we believe, soon threaten his own kingdom."

The Advocate looked surprised. "That is quite a statement."

"Obviously," Teron answered. "We have further details to disclose to the King and his Court Wizard. These matters are urgent."

"All the petitions we hear are urgent," the man replied. He directed a scribe to read back what Teron had said.

When the scribe was done, Teron nodded. "How long before the King receives this?"

The Advocate waved a hand. "All petitions are taken at once to the proper officials. What happens from there is up to them."

Teron turned away, frowning.

"It sounds like there will be at least some delay in getting the King's attention," Mirafra confided to him. "Perhaps I could also petition the Court Wizard?"

Teron looked at her with surprise. "Yes. Good idea." He addressed the Advocate. "This young woman is also a Norrling."

"If I may," Mirafra told the official, "I would like to address a petition to the King's wizard; I believe she is called Clorinda the Ibis."

"Yes, yes," the Advocate answered. "She is known."

"Please inform her of what is stated in the Mooncrow's petition. And add that the Duke's wizard, Sharam the Crane, was also killed in the attack, and that I have the Crane's psithe in my keeping."

When this petition had been recorded and read back, Arwyn decided to add his own.

"My cousin, Lady Lorraine, is a member of the court. Please see that she is also informed of the attack on Castle Duneidan. Inform her further that her cousin Arwyn is here. I am all that is left of our family, and I have come to seek King Carswell's protection, and to serve him in any way I might."

The Advocate scrutinized him with twisted lips, perhaps sympathetic to the young lord's plight or perhaps skeptical that this ill-dressed fellow could be what he claimed.

When all three petitions had been completed and verified, the Advocate handed them off to a courier.

"Wait there in the lobby for your answers." He gestured toward the benches and seats where a few dozen people were gathered. "If you hear nothing today, come back tomorrow by the third hour of morning. All petitioners must be present when their names are called."

Mirafra and the others stepped back from the high desk. But Teron lingered at the edge of the dais, staring past the Advocate and officials. Mirafra realized he was watching the courier who had been dispatched with their petitions. She watched also as the man reached the far wall and stepped onto an elevation platform. This device, framed in glass and with brass rails, rose smoothly up the wall.

"Must be steam powered," Arwyn observed.

"Aye. Far too many stairs to climb to the top of this heavenly building," Topiedeon chuckled.

Teron watched until the elevator stopped some three stories below the blue glass roof. Then he placed a finger on his chin, turned, and ambled down into the lobby.

"Judging by this crowd and by our reception from that officious official," Topiedeon grumbled. "It may be days before the King is informed, if not weeks!"

"Yes." Teron answered. "That won't do at all." After surveying the area, he added, "You three wait here. I'll come back for you."

"Where are you going?" Mirafra demanded.

Teron didn't answer, just strode determinedly back toward the doorway where they had entered. Along that wall was a colonnade of shiny white pillars. Mirafra and the others watched as Teron slipped furtively behind one of the pillars.

Moments later, Mirafra detected an odd flicker of light. Then a large black bird flew out from behind the column.

Beating his wings rapidly, the Mooncrow soared above the many-leveled floors of the indoor court. It had been months since he last invoked the *quinteer*, the fifth and quintessential attribute of the psithe. Control of the bird body was imperfect at first, and Teron had to focus hard. Possessed by the exhilaration of flight, part of him wanted to swoop down and caw loudly at the humans below.

But he needed to attract as little attention as possible. As self-possession returned, he flew higher, aiming for the place below the roof where he had seen the courier disembark from the elevator car. It made sense that King Carswell would reside at the uppermost levels of the palace, and Teron was determined to visit the King as soon as he could.

Flying along the wall at that high level, he found a balcony with open glass doors. He perched on the railing and peered inside: a grand bedroom, but the inner doors were shut.

Of course he could transform back to human shape and easily open the doors. But then he would be seen as an intruder, possibly an assassin who had somehow gotten past the guards. He'd never get to the King that way. He needed a more wizardly entrance.

He flew off to another balcony. This opened on a corridor, high and wide enough that the crow could easily make his way.

Flying near the ceiling, as quietly as he could, he navigated a series of hallways and palatial chambers. Before long, he was spotted. Servants and guards on the floors below pointed and shouted. But, as Teron hoped, the stray bird was seen as a curiosity rather than a threat. Several people even laughed.

At last he discovered a wide, curved dining room where one bank of windows gave a sweeping view of the city and the river beyond. At the head of a long table sat a red-headed man in colorful robes trimmed with white fur. By the crown on his head and the deferential postures of those around him, Teron knew he had finally found King Carswell.

The King was finishing up his breakfast, sipping from a delicate teacup. Three richly dressed courtiers had joined him at the meal, and nearby a girl strummed a golden harp. Except for attendants and sentries posted at the three doors, the wide chamber was empty.

"Look!" One of the courtiers pointed as the crow swooped in near the table.

All but the King bolted to their feet. The harp music stopped, and Teron could hear the footsteps of sentries rushing toward him. He settled to the floor and mentally spoke the spell to break the quinteer bond.

Light flashed, and the next instant the crow was gone and Teron stood before the table. With everyone gaping, Teron spread his cape and gave a deep bow.

"My lords, forgive the unorthodox entrance. I am Teron the Mooncrow, and I bear crucial news for King Carswell, who, I am guessing, would be this majestic person." He bowed again.

A babble of confused and outraged voices sounded. Sentries hurried forward with the clatter of arms and armor. But King Carswell had stood and was laughing.

"Relax, good guardsmen." The King raised a hand. "Let the wizard be. I see no harm in him—as of yet." He pointed at Teron. "You know, sir, I have often heard of this Norrling trick of transformation into a bird. But never before have I witnessed it."

"A powerful conjuration, Your Majesty. Reserved only for the most important matters."

"I see. And did I hear your name correctly? Do you claim to be the famous Teron the Mooncrow, late of the Moldorn Court?"

"That is in the past," Teron replied. "My business now is of the present and most urgent. I come from Arabhedden, where King Alaric is making war. He seeks to subjugate all of the peninsula. And when that is done, I have no doubt he will turn his eyes on your domains."

Several men spoke at once. The loudest was a thin, bearded man who stood near the King.

"What evidence do you have to support these wild claims?"

The King gestured toward the speaker. "This is my cousin, Count Halsark, who recently served as our ambassador to Alaric and has, in fact, negotiated a treaty of peace between our two realms."

Noting Halsark's vehement stare, Teron answered calmly. "I would not be easy in trusting any promises made by King Alaric. For example, he recently paid a visit to Duke Keltonn of Duneidan. His stated intent was to discuss terms for an alliance. But without warning, Alaric's warriors sacked the castle in the night and murdered the Duke and his family. This was doubtless a warning to the other unallied lords of the land. Alaric is intent on conquest, and there is no reason to believe he will stop once his armies are reinforced by those of Arabhedden."

"Bah!" Count Halsark answered. "I have lived in Alaric's court and know him personally. I believe him to be an honorable ruler, else I'd never have recommended the treaty. Whereas I know nothing of this conjurer, even if he is who he claims. Who knows what other tricks he may be planning?"

Raising his eyebrows, Carswell looked back at Teron.

The Mooncrow ignored Halsark. "I came to the palace this morning with Arwyn Keltonn, the only surviving son of the Duke's family. With us also is Mirafra, a young Norrling whose mentor, the Duke's wizard, was slain in the treacherous attack. They both have filed petitions for an audience with the King. I ask only that you grant the audience and hear the truth from their lips."

The King gave a solemn nod. "The Duke of Duneidan was always on friendly terms with us. I shall read these petitions at once and hear what these young people have to say."

Chapter 8

Mirafra gazed down at the sparkling floor of the King's council chamber, black stones with flecks of silver. Like all of this palace, it seemed, the chamber was huge, with a rounded colonnade on one side, curved exterior windows on the other. Attendants, soldiers, and courtiers gathered in small groups along the edges. The Tree Pipit, along with her friends, stood before a dais with a high table occupied by the King and twelve of his officials.

As the Mooncrow promised, he had returned in less than an hour to lead them up the many stories of the castle and into the presence of the King. How he had done it, she could not begin to imagine.

From the highest place on the dais, King Carswell spoke: "We have reviewed the three petitions and spoken already with the honorable Mooncrow. I assume the young man to be the Duke of Duneidan's son and the young woman the apprentice majja. But who is this fourth person, in the garb of an entertainer?"

"My friend, Topie—" Teron started to say.

"Topiedeon the bard, great King. Here as a friend to Teron and one who attempts, in my poor way, to chronicle his adventures. I also play the mandolin and am known for love songs and ballads."

Carswell smiled. "You are welcome, Master Bard. Perhaps we shall have the pleasure of hearing you play some time in the future. But now to business. First, let us hear from Arwyn. I have read your petition, young man, addressed to your cousin. Lady Lorraine, would you please come forward?"

From the edge of the colonnade stepped a tall young woman in a rose-colored gown and headdress. The chamber was hushed as she walked up to Arwyn and peered closely at him. After a moment, she gave a sad smile.

"Hello, cousin."

"Can you confirm," the King asked, "that he is in fact the Duke of Duneidan's son?"

She faced the throne. "My liege, I have not seen him in several years. But I know him for certain as my cousin, Arwyn." Turning back to the boy, she squeezed his hand. "I am so sorry for your family. We shall speak more later, I know."

As she returned to her place, the King spoke. "Arwyn, son of Duke Keltonn. Please tell us everything you recall about King Alaric's activities in your father's realm."

In a strained but steady voice, Arwyn recounted all he had seen and heard, from the first news of Alaric's impending visit, to the negotiations with the Duke and neighboring nobles, to the night of the attack.

"The storming of our castle was unprovoked and came without warning," Arwyn declared. "The attackers killed not only warriors but defenseless men and women. But even that is not the worst of it. Because, they were not mortal men who committed this crime, but armored creatures who carried two swords and moved with unnatural agility. And, though they bled when wounded, their wounds slowed them not at all. These were not mortal soldiers I say, but creatures forged by sorcery."

"Bah! Supernatural warriors now." This was spoken by a thin-faced man seated beside the king. "Remember, we are dealing with performers, my liege. I lived four months in Alaric's court and heard no talk of magical soldiers."

"Whatever Count Halsark may have heard or not heard," Teron answered coldly, "I myself and these two young people know what we witnessed."

"Since the question touches on magic," Carswell said, "let us hear from our own wizard. Lady Clorinda, what is your view?"

Everyone turned to the woman who sat at the far edge of the table. She was slim and pale, with a long nose and keen, blue eyes. From her headpiece and ceremonial feathered cape, Mirafra had already figured her to be Clorinda the Ibis.

Clorinda was smoking a long pipe, which she pulled contemplatively from her mouth. "As we have two other Norrlings present. I would like to hear their opinions. Master Mooncrow?"

Teron cleared his throat. "I was not present in the castle, and I saw the creature only in visions. But I can confirm a tremendous wave of psithic energy circled over the castle during the attack. For the rest, I defer to Arwyn and Mirafra, who both witnessed the creatures first hand."

"Young apprentice. Mirafra is your name?" The Ibis scrutinized her.

Straightening her shoulders, she replied. "Yes, maestra. I can confirm all that Arwyn said. I saw the black-armored warriors stabbed and bleeding, but they fought on with little or no harm. I believe they were conjured, or transformed, by some twisted use of psithic magic. Jovadia the Bittern is Alaric's wizard. She has been rumored to practice forbidden forms of magic. She as much as admitted this to me in a private conversation on the battlement the morning before the attack."

"And if she can create indestructible warriors by these arts," Teron added, "who can measure the threat she may pose to all of King Alaric's neighboring lands?"

That question brought a worried quiet to the figures on the dais. Even Count Halsark raised no dispute.

"I too have heard rumors about the unorthodox practices of the Bittern," Clorinda said. "I shall undertake investigations, my King, and report back what I learn."

Carswell nodded soberly. "I believe investigations are certainly in order. I shall dispatch riders and one of my airships to Arabhedden to survey the situation there. As we have a standing treaty with King

Alaric, it would not be proper or courteous to query him directly. Instead, we shall learn all we can by other means and then consider if further actions may be warranted."

He stood, and all at the table did likewise. Addressing the Mooncrow's party, he said, "Meanwhile, you four will remain at our palace as honored guests." Before turning away, he added. "And perhaps Master Topiedeon will give us the pleasure of a performance one evening."

Mirafra and Arwyn stood side by side, staring through the glass wall at the grand inner courtyard.

"Such a building," Arwyn murmured. "I do believe we are four times higher than the highest tower of Duneidan Castle."

Their apartment was spacious, with three sleeping chambers arranged around a central sitting room—all high-ceilinged, carpeted, and hung with tapestries and paintings. By far the most luxurious quarters Mirafra had ever seen.

There was even a steward, who approached now and cleared his throat to attract their attention.

"The Lady Lorraine requests to see you, Lord Arwyn."

Shown into the sitting room, Lorraine gave Mirafra a courteous bow and then threw her arms around Arwyn.

"Dear cousin, I am so saddened by your terrible news. Our dear Duke and Duchess, and our brothers ..."

She called them *her* brothers, Mirafra knew, because Lorraine had been raised partly in Castle Duneidan, her own parents having died of a pestilence when she was ten. She had known Arwyn since he was a baby. Her placement as a lady-in-waiting here in Baivonne had come about through the Duke's cordial, if distant, relations with King Carswell.

They sat down together on a couch, and Mirafra took a chair close by. Lorraine asked what Arwyn might know of the fates of other folk from the castle and the neighboring clans.

"Nothing, I fear," Arwyn answered. "Those who were not killed in the attack must now be under the rule of Alaric. I'm afraid all of Arabhedden will soon be bound to his so-called alliance."

Lorraine seemed ready to weep.

"I myself only escaped because of Mirafra." Tallwyn gazed at her fondly. "She saved my life at the risk of her own."

Lorraine reached over and squeezed Mirafra's wrist. "For that I will be forever grateful, honored majja. My condolences also on the loss of your mentor."

"Thank you," Mirafra responded. "Truth is, we were very fortunate. First, because my maestra passed me her psithe, and then because of the sudden appearance of the Mooncrow."

"Oh, yes. A remarkable man," Lorraine whispered, glancing around. "Is he here now? Is he in truth the famous Mooncrow?"

"He is for certain," the Tree Pipit said, for she no longer harbored any doubts.

"He and the minstrel have returned to the airfield," Arwyn explained, "to see about securing and supplying his ship. King Carswell has been most generous to us in that regard."

Lorraine nodded. "Indeed, he is a noble and gracious ruler."

In answer to Arwyn's questions, she went on to describe something of the character of the King, and the overall atmosphere of his court.

"There are different factions, of course, but little intrigue that I am aware of. Most nobles of Occitan support the King, whose main desire is always the welfare and prosperity of his people. He is an able and intelligent ruler, with a keen interest in science and new inventions."

"I love those things also," Arwyn said.

She smiled. "I know that the King wishes peaceful relations with all, but he is not afraid of war and will defend his realm if he must."

"And I will serve him as best I can," Arwyn vowed. "In whatever may come."

"What about his Queen and children?" Mirafra asked.

Lorraine's expression grew sad. "Esmeralda is a wonderful, kind woman. But she is not in the best of health. She succumbed to the *tertian fever* two winters ago and has mostly been bedridden since. She seldom appears in public now, though the King still loves her dearly and spends part of every day at her side. I think it fair to say she is his most trusted advisor and guide."

"There are also children," Arwyn remarked.

"Indeed, Prince Darien is now 18 and is training as a squire in a castle to the north. If war comes, I fear he too will be called to serve. His sister, Elena, is 10, a wise and intelligent child, much like her father."

"I am sorry to hear of the Queen's ill health," Mirafra said.

"We do all we can for her." Clorinda the Ibis spoke up as she strode across the room, one step ahead of the steward.

"Clorinda, the Court Wizard," the man announced, unnecessarily.

The three young people rose hastily and bowed.

"Forgive my abrupt entrance," the Ibis said. "I wish to speak to Mirafra. No need to depart, Lady Lorraine. Simply some wizard business to discuss. Mirafra, perhaps we might withdraw to another room?"

"Of course, maestra."

With a nod to Arwyn and Lorraine, Mirafra led the wizard into one of the bed chambers. As soon as she had shut the door, she asked, "You said you do all you can for the Queen. You treat her with the cup then?"

"Oh yes, frequently. This helps her some, as do the potions and remedies favored by her Warmlander physicians. But Esmeralda is a delicate lady, and complete recovery has so far eluded her."

Mirafra nodded her understanding. She had studied the Norrling healing arts, of course, but had almost no practical experience.

She offered Clorinda a chair, but the maestra instead told her to sit while she walked back and forth.

"I need to know more about you," Clorinda said. "What is your grade in the hierarchy?"

"I am a tyro, maestra."

"Indeed? You seem more than that. Is my reading correct, that you presently possess not one, but *two* psithes?"

Mirafra explained how Sharam, about to die, had entrusted her with the Crane psithe. "She attuned it to my mind, hoping I could use it to escape the castle."

"Ah, that would explain the levels of power I've sensed in you—far above a typical tyro. Have you used the Crane psithe since your escape?"

"Not at first. But ... to be honest, the past few days Teron has encouraged me to practice with it."

"Has he indeed? Well, I'm not your mentor, so it's not for me to allow or forbid, but I would advise you to be careful. Too much power attuned to a mind that has not had sufficient training—this can lead to imbalance and damage."

"Yes, I know. I've had dizziness and fainting, but it's getting better. In any case, Sharam instructed me to return her psithe to Montodoro if possible, and that is what I hope to do as soon as I can."

The Ibis nodded, satisfied. "I am glad you said that. I agree the proper course is to return it to the Birdhouse at the Sanctuary. When you take it there, I expect you will be given the opportunity to draw a new psithe, one to match your new levels of power."

Mirafra had not considered that. "I hope I shall be ready. My maestra only gave me the psithe in desperation. She feared it would fall into the hands of the Bittern."

"Yes, the Bittern again." Clorinda frowned as if from a sour taste. "I've heard rumors of her activities, of course. When I was last in Montodoro, Jovadia was viewed as one of many talented majja who have gone astray in the Warmlands. But if all that you and the Mooncrow say is true, she has certainly become a menace. The Supreme Gathering should be informed."

Having paced throughout their conversation, Clorinda suddenly sat down. "For now, my course shall be this: I shall do some concentrated mental probing of the Bittern and her activities. And I will wait to see what news the King's messengers return with from Arabhedden. Assuming they confirm your story, as I expect they will, I shall ask that the King provide me airship transport to Ombernorr. Perhaps we shall both be traveling to Montodoro sooner rather than later."

In the cold, crisp air, the *Pomegranate* floated low to the ground. One of the hatches was open, and a lift machine was conveying steel canisters of fuel up into the hull. Nearby, another cart stood packed with barrels of water, crates of food, and other supplies. Standing beside Topiedeon and Dona Delores, Teron watched as crewmembers worked with stevedores from the airfield to load the materials on board.

"I trust all this will keep us for ten days or so, Captain?"

"Oh, easily," Dona Delores answered. "But after that, Senor Teron, do you know where we'll be bound?"

"Not yet." The Mooncrow lifted a shoulder. "I want to see what the King learns from Arabhedden, and what he decides to do. It's possible hostilities may start soon after. You wouldn't want to go cruising into a war, would you?"

"Certainly not! And I hope you'll not be steering us into one!"

"Don't worry, Dona Delores," Topiedeon chuckled. "Teron has promised not to get involved in any more wars—at least, not *too* involved."

The captain frowned, and Teron raised his hands.

"By the way," the minstrel said, "are the Bonatores onboard? Did they find work?"

"Yes and no," the captain answered. "They returned late last night, and not happy. Felix said there is a big festival coming, and every performance venue they tried is already booked."

"Well, I can fix that," the bard said. "I've been invited to perform before the King. I'll invite them along. They can even stay at the palace with us. That grand apartment has plenty of room, don't you agree, Teron?"

"Of course."

"So everyone gets to sleep at the luxurious palace except for the captain and her crew!" Dona Delores's complaint was half-joking, half-serious.

With a laugh, Teron reached into a pocket and pulled out a purse. "This will make you feel better about things. The King is most generous. Use it to buy anything you might need, including entertainment for the crew."

He dropped the purse in her outstretched hand. Feeling its weight, the captain grinned.

"Just make sure one shift is always on board," Teron added. "And that a watch is posted day and night."

The captain's smile became a confused frown. "You are expecting trouble?"

"Probably not. But I did notice that not everyone in Carswell's court is friendly to us."

78

On his return to the palace, Teron was met with a summons to attend the King. He followed a young woman page up an elevator to a level he had not set foot on before, near the very roof of the castle.

He found Carswell at a desk in a modest-sized room crowded with bookshelves. Behind the King, a broad window set in the outer wall of the palace gave a distant view of the land below and the river to the north. Entering the room, Teron noticed Clorinda the Court Wizard, who was walking up and down with her odd, strutting gait. Teron bowed, and the Ibis gave him a curt nod.

"Welcome, Sir Mooncrow." The King waved him to a chair. "I hope the arrangements made for your party and your airship are adequate."

"Much more than we are used to, good King, I assure you."

"Excellent. I also wanted to inform you that both horsemen and an airship have been dispatched this morning, as planned. The ship will survey the south and east coasts of Arabhedden. The riders will visit principalities near our borders, with the cover of carrying letters to certain lords, inviting them to the Festival of Harvest in Baivonne next autumn. I expect the first reports back in a fortnight or so, with more filtering in after that."

Teron nodded. "With your permission, I would like to remain at court for that time, in case I may be of further service, either to Your Majesty or to Lord Arwyn or Mirafra."

"Yes," said the Ibis. "I understand you have become something of a mentor to the young majja."

"Hardly that," Teron replied. "But I am concerned with her welfare and that of the young Duke, given the ordeal they both have suffered."

"Indeed," the King said. "Your concern for the young people does you credit. Permission is granted, of course. You and your party are welcome for as long as you wish to stay."

Teron glanced up at Clorinda, who had paused near his chair. For the first time, she let slip a smile.

"There is one other matter I wish to discuss," the King went on. "It may in fact be another service you can do me—one most important to myself personally and to my kingdom. As you may have heard, my Queen Esmeralda has suffered from ill health for some time. She is being treated by the best physicians we can find, as well as by our good friend Clorinda. Yet her illness persists. In the stories we have heard, the Mooncrow was skilled as a healer."

"I fear those stories are exaggerated," Teron said. "Also, my practice of the healing arts has been neglected these past years. But, of course, I will do anything I can to help."

He questioned Clorinda about the Queen's condition and the remedies that had been tried. The answers showed that her methods and those of the other physicians went well beyond his own knowledge of medicines. That left only one technique. Known as *pure invigoration*, it was an art in which psithic energy, not from the cup but from the disk, was poured directly into the organs and nerve centers of the body. Clorinda affirmed she was using this method on a daily basis.

"Then there is one assistance I may supply," Teron said. "Among the wizards of Ptolloden, in stubborn illnesses, *pure invigoration* has sometimes been shown to be effective if more than one psithe is used."

"Exactly what I hoped you might suggest," Clorinda's blue eyes sparkled. "I have heard of this combined technique but was never taught to use it. I would not know how best to orchestrate the energies."

"Well, as I said, my practice has been neglected. But I am sure that together we can at least make a good effort."

The King was smiling hopefully.

Another thought occurred to Teron. "As two psithes are better than one, so three are even stronger. I suggest we ask Mirafra to join us."

Chapter 9

Nervous and excited, Mirafra followed the Mooncrow and the Ibis across the threshold of the Queen's apartment. Her first thought on hearing the idea was that using the pure invigoration technique was beyond her skills. In her schooling, she had been taught the basic theory but had no training in the application. Still, when both Teron and Clorinda insisted she might be able to help, she of course agreed to try.

In an antechamber, the wizards paused to consult with the Queen's chief physician, a white-haired Occitanan named Doctor Yahn. He reviewed the patient's symptoms and the ongoing courses of treatment. He also showed a surprising understanding of the invigoration technique and was quite pleased that they were going to try it.

Stepping into the next chamber, they found the Queen in bed, surrounded by servants and attendants. Esmeralda rested on a pillow, stroking the hair of a girl child who lay beside her. The Queen gave a faint smile of greeting when the wizards were announced. She looked pale and sickly for certain, but Mirafra sensed a strong, gentle spirit.

As the attendants filed out, Lady Loraine stopped, squeezed Mirafra's wrist, and whispered her thanks. Behind her walked the girl child, Elena, the Queen's daughter. She paused and stared up, wide-eyed, at the mages.

"You are going to heal my mother, I hope."

"We hope so too, dear child," Clorinda answered.

The three wizards stepped to the bedside. The room was cleared except for two attendants who stood near the door and Doctor Yahn who observed from the foot of the bed. Weak though she was, Esmeralda watched the majja with bright and curious eyes.

"You must be the famous Mooncrow, and you the apprentice. My King has told me of your visit. I am thankful to you for offering me your help."

"How are you feeling today, my lady?" Clorinda had taken out her psithe in its cup shape.

"Not so well, I fear." She smiled sadly at Mirafra. "One must be frank with physicians."

Closing her eyes, Clorinda distilled a clear potion into the cup. "Well, I am hoping we three will help you to feel better."

"Thank you," the Queen murmured. Suddenly her gaze sharpened, and she turned to Teron. "Do you think there will be a war?"

"Not for you to worry about now, my lady." The Ibis swirled the cup in her hand. "You must focus on getting well."

Esmeralda sighed. "You are right, I know."

"Please drink this," Clorinda pressed the cup to the lady's lips. "It will relax you so that we may do our work."

When the Queen had swallowed the potion, the Ibis transformed her psithe into a disk. Teron took out his disk, and Mirafra lifted the chain over her head, clasping the Crane psithe in her fingers.

Staring at their psithes, the three majja entered light trance. As if from far away, Mirafra heard the Mooncrow's soft voice as he intoned ritual instructions.

"See the power within the psithe. See it stirring. White light that moves like water. Now the light flows out into the air. In a gentle current, it streams into the body, moving first into the center of the head."

Earlier, they had reviewed a book from Montodoro with instructions and drawings of human anatomy and had discussed the nerve centers and organs where they would send the light. But now, as her energy stream joined that of the other two psithes, Mirafra swayed backward, overcome by the charge of power.

"Steady," Teron urged her.

Sucking in a breath, Mirafra regained her focus. She visualized the light moving through the Queen's brain in gentle, healing waves.

After a few moments, they shifted the energy to the throat, then down to the heart and lungs. Finally, the light was streamed down to the base of the spine.

At last, the wizards drew the energy back into their psithes.

The Queen blinked. She took a breath, looking both relaxed and puzzled. "That felt very nice."

The three wizards repeated the healing each morning. Everyone agreed the treatments were having salubrious effects. Soon, the Queen felt strong enough to leave her bed, move around on her own, and take tea with the King, who showed deep gratitude.

On the fourth day, when they left the Queen's quarters, Clorinda requested a private word with Teron. Mirafra offered to withdraw, but the Ibis shook her head.

"No, no, my dear. You may hear what I have to say."

She led them to the end of a pink stone corridor, where they emerged on a balcony high above the grand inner court.

Clorinda leaned over the balustrade, touching her fingertips before her lips. "I wanted to inform you both that I have been mentally probing the atmosphere of Llorrland. And I have indeed seen chaotic power emanating from the vicinity of Alaric's capital. What exactly it means, I do not know, but it certainly supports your warning that Jovadia the Bittern may be tampering with dangerous power."

"I have no doubt of it," Teron answered.

"In any case, it is proper that Montodoro be informed. I shall attempt to do so by invoking a qorm dream and communicating with the Supreme Gathering."

Teron nodded. Communicating in the dream state was a fairly common practice among advanced wizards. "Will that be enough," he asked, "to convince them of the seriousness of the matter?" Dreams, even qorm dreams, were subjective and apt to be influenced by emotion. Important decisions were almost never based on qorm communication alone.

"Enough to alert them, at least," Clorinda said. "Once the King has gathered definite intelligence, and I have a clearer idea of matters, I may travel to Montodoro in person to give a full report." She turned her head to scrutinize him. "I would think you might also want to inform the High Masters of Ptolloden."

Teron snorted. "Small use in that, I fear. I am sure they will have sensed the disturbance just as you have. If they choose to do nothing about it—as I expect they will—then an exile such as myself will not likely change their minds."

"This puzzles me," the Ibis said. "From the stories we've all heard, you were once a wandering tyro—in the days before wandering in the Warmlands became common as it is today—and yet you convinced the High Council of Ptolloden to let you intervene against the Moldorns."

Teron sighed. "I was younger and more energetic back then. In any case, from what I've heard lately from fellow wanderers, the rulers of Ptolloden are even more adamant and isolationist than they were in the past."

"Is that why you have not returned there?" the Ibis asked him.

Teron gazed down at the grand courtyard. The height of this palace reminded him of the great towers of the Moldorn capital. But while PonnTherion was built to show indomitable power, the design here was all of harmony and beauty.

"Forgive my asking," the Ibis said. "But you have carried the Mooncrow psithe for many years. Given your obvious talent, I would think you would want to resume your studies. You might advance to master or even high master."

Teron took out the psithe disk and weighed it in his hand. "After leaving Moldorn, I did think about returning to Ptolloden, but could never bring myself to make that decision. The teaching there is all aimed at detachment from the world. That course has never suited me." He tossed the disk into the air, deftly caught it, and gave a rueful smile. "And so I remain a wanderer, a Mooncrow, but never a master."

Near the palace roof stood a vaulted hall many yards across. Tall windows set in galleries above filled the space with daylight. The hall served as a gymnasium, typically used for exercise and arms practice.

At the moment, the space resounded with the music of Topiedeon's mandolin. The Bonatores leapt and spun and circled in the air, lifted by Teron's wand, while Mirafra and Arwyn watched from nearby.

The group had come here to practice each day since the Bonatores moved to the palace. The troupe had already performed once for the King over dinner. Now they were preparing for several shows during the annual Festival of Good Fortune, which started tomorrow.

When the song ended, Teron walked over and pointed his wand at Mirafra.

"Your turn," he said.

With a grin, Mirafra produced her wand and went to practice with the acrobats. Teron remained beside Arwyn to watch. One by one, the Bonatores threw their hoops into the air. Mirafra used her psithe-wand to slow the rings' ascent. Soon, three hoops hovered motionless high above her head. Next, she let the hoops drop, and the performers did a tumbling routine. As they leaped, Mirafra pushed them higher. Finally, she lowered them to the floor.

"She's getting quite proficient," Teron remarked. "I believe the healing work is improving Mirafra's control of the Crane psithe."

"She says the Queen is improving too," Arwyn noted.

"Yes, the Lady's condition is of long standing, but she does seem to be gaining strength." Teron twisted the wand in his hand and changed it to a sword. "Now, young lord, would you also like some exercise?"

With a smile, Arwyn drew his own sword. "Very much so!"

They walked to an empty place on the floor and faced off, saluting each other with their blades.

Arwyn had been practicing each day with Teron and also with one or another of the King's fencing masters. Like Mirafra, the boy was improving. At first awkward and hesitant with the blade, he was showing increased strength and stamina. While they parried and thrust, the Mooncrow sprinkled in some coaching of his own, teaching the boy a few tricks he had learned in Ptolloden, and also from the swordsmen of Moldorn.

When not working on arms training, Arwyn had kept himself busy. Upon learning of their shared interest in science, the King had introduced the young lord to his engineers and alchemists. Occitan was a leader in the study of the sciences that the Moldorns had first promulgated years ago. And Arwyn was more than eager to learn. He questioned the scholars and diligently read the books and papers they offered. He was particularly interested in alchemy, the science of converting materials into different forms, which Teron knew was a kind of magic all its own.

When the morning's practices concluded, the party returned to their quarters. Topiedeon fell into step with Teron as they strolled along a walkway high above the vast inner court.

"You are enjoying the company of both our young friends," the bard remarked. "And is that a smile I keep seeing on your face?"

Teron chuckled. "I admit they inspire me. Intelligence and bravery, combined with the resilience of youth. Don't you find them heartening?"

"You know, as a poet, I must maintain a certain artistic detachment."

"Hah! But admit it, aren't you glad I decided to help them? You and the Bonatores have plenty of work, Dona Delores and crew have been well paid, and even the Queen of Occitan has benefited. Haven't things turned out well for everyone?"

"Oh, I am not unhappy that you helped them. I simply observe that you seem more satisfied than you have since we first met up again." As they approached their door, the bard added, "As to how things will turn out, that remains to be seen, doesn't it?"

"As always," Teron said. "But I'm not expecting to stay much longer. As soon as the King sorts out his plans, and our two young friends are settled, I mean to sail. I still like being a traveler much better than a courtier."

Count Halsark stared solemnly into his own eyes in the mirror. In the dim bedroom, lit by a single oil lamp, his sharp face was drawn and dark. Yet the eyes possessed an eerie gleam.

"Is everything all right, my lord?"

Halsark had forgotten the servant. "Yes. Leave me."

After the door closed, the sheen on the mirror seemed to waver and brighten. A figure took shape, standing at Halsark's shoulder. A beak-nosed woman in a feathered cape—Jovadia the Bittern.

Straining his thoughts, Halsark seemed to recall that he had experienced this once or twice before since leaving King Alaric's capital. But he always forgot it afterward.

His lips whispered, "You have summoned me."

"Yes, my friend. I sensed disturbances in your mind. What is happening in Carswell's court that worries you?"

How well he remembered Jovadia's probing interviews when he served as ambassador in Tonnsburg, her serpent-like influence over both himself and King Alaric. She had convinced the Count to negotiate a treaty favorable to Alaric, and had promised that after Occitan was conquered, it would be he, not Carswell, who would sit on the throne as Alaric's vassal.

Now, more in thoughts than words, he revealed the events of the past days, the arrival at court of the Mooncrow and the Duke of Duneidan's young son, their reports of the conquests in Arabhedden, and their growing influence over the King.

"The Norrling is even treating the Queen, and her condition is improving."

"So, Carswell will likely marshal his armies for war. This is obviously not favorable to our plans. And these two interlopers will remain an annoyance. The young Duke could serve as a rallying point for the nobles of Arabhedden. And who knows what further troubles the Mooncrow may stir up? I suggest you get rid of them both. And sooner rather than later."

Halsark stared in bewilderment. "Me? But how?"

"I leave that to you. A man able to win a throne can certainly manage something so simple."

The Festival of Good Fortune was celebrated each year following the winter solstice. For nine days and nights, the streets of Baivonne were decorated with wreaths and banners and thronged with parades and rowdy celebrations.

On the fourth night of the carnival, Mirafra and her friends went down into the city. The Bonatores were scheduled to perform in one of the main music halls. Along with Arwyn, Teron, and Topiedeon, Mirafra wended her way through the boisterous crowds. Brass bands marched along the lighted streets. Citizens in elaborate costumes rode dray wagons decorated with flowers, and threw wreaths and beads and even coins to the crowds. Somewhat nervous with all the excitement, Mirafra could not help but also feel exhilarated.

Inside the music hall, Topiedeon went on stage and performed a set with the acrobats. Teron stayed in the audience with his young friends. He and Mirafra were reserving their magical attentions for other matters.

Later, Topiedeon walked with them back toward the castle, while the Bonatores stayed to enjoy the celebrations. As the party marched away from the center of town, the crowds grew thin, and a faint worry crept into Mirafra's mind. She started glancing over her shoulder.

Finally, as they moved down a deserted street, she glanced up at Teron. "I have a feeling we're being followed."

"I know." The Mooncrow spoke without turning his head. "Be ready to make your sword. Topiedeon, do you have your knife?"

"Well, yes," the minstrel sounded abashed.

Moments later, Mirafra heard footsteps hurrying behind them.

"No one turn around." Teron reached into his pocket. "Follow me."

Suddenly, he wheeled and ran into an alley. A few steps in, he stopped and gestured for everyone to back against the wall. The psithe-disk flickered in his hand as he murmured an incantation.

Four men turned into the alley. They drew swords from beneath their cloaks and rushed forward. They moved past Mirafra and her friends without seeing them—thanks, she realized, to Teron's trickery.

Halfway down the alley, the men stopped, looking around in bafflement.

"Looking for us?" Teron stepped from the shadows. His psithe was now a sword.

"Kill them!" The men charged.

Mirafra crouched, psithe-sword in hand, terrified. She had never been in a real battle. Arwyn leapt in front to shield her. Deftly, he parried the first attacker.

Teron feinted and in a blur ran the first man through. While he leapt aside to face the next assassin, Topiedeon stooped to pick up the fallen man's sword.

Two psithe-swords swooped and flashed, illuminating the dark alley. Mirafra's training with the third attribute had mostly been with a dagger, not a sword. But she drew on what she remembered: first, to discard all fear. She brightened her blade to distract the opponents' eyes and focused on parrying to protect both herself and Arwyn. For a few moments, they held off two of the assailants. Then Topiedeon darted in to aid them.

Across the alley, Teron jumped like a dancer. His point circled and stabbed his opponent through the shoulder. The man dropped his sword and stumbled back against the brick wall.

The two remaining assassins, now outnumbered, glanced at each other for an instant, then turned and fled.

Her sword hand shaking, Mirafra looked around in amazement. Arwyn strode over to Teron, who crouched beside the wounded man.

"We should kill him," Arwyn said.

"No." Teron answered through gritted teeth. "More useful to us alive." The Mooncrow held his disk before the man's eyes. "Who sent you?"

The man's mouth lolled open. "I—I don't know ..."

"Speak," Teron commanded. "This was no random waylaying. Someone hired you to kill Lord Arwyn, or the Mooncrow, or both. Who was it?"

The man stared, sinking into trance.

"The name!" Teron shouted. "The name!"

Head drooping, the man whispered something Mirafra could not hear.

"Ah, I thought so." Teron lifted the man by an arm. "Come, my friend. We'll take you to the palace and get you patched up."

Topiedeon picked up the man's weapon. He weighed the two swords in his hand. "Well, I suppose I can sell these for some coin. But really, Teron, leading them into a dark alley? That was rather risky, no?"

Holding up the wounded assassin, the Mooncrow shrugged. "There were only four of them."

At that, Arwyn laughed. Near to collapsing, Mirafra braced herself on his shoulder.

Chapter 10

Summoning a burst of power from her wand, Jovadia the Bittern unlocked the iron-barbed door. As she pulled it open with hinges shrieking, she glanced over her shoulder at the six figures lining the torch-lit corridor—all dressed in capes and feathers.

She led them into a broad, low-arched chamber, a dungeon underground in Tonnsburg Castle. The air was wet and cold, but in this room there was no need of torches. A five-foot-wide cauldron of black iron shimmered with pale, liquid light—the *cold fire* that had become Jovadia's magical obsession.

The Bittern stopped at the edge of the cauldron. She twirled a finger, instructing her followers to group themselves beside her. They moved with a rustle of garments: six Norrlings—Jovadia's three apprentices and three others. Those were new recruits brought to the castle under orders from the Bittern, part of her campaign to collect as many psithes as possible. One of the neophytes was female, the other two male—wizards strayed from Ptolloden. One or more of these three might not be leaving the chamber alive.

"The cold fire." Jovadia's sharp face was lit from below. "It burns with the power of 10 psithes, surrendered by majja like yourselves. This power, when combined with our own psithes through the arts I teach, grows vast—its limits no one can tell. And this is only the beginning. A much larger cauldron is being constructed at a secret location. It will contain as many psithes as we can acquire."

She scanned the faces of the three neophytes. Were they shocked, afraid, or eager? Of the seven wandering majja Alaric's men had acquired, these she had judged powerful enough to be of use. The others she had simply killed and tossed their psithes into the cauldron.

Now, at her command, the wizards produced their psithes and held them up as disks. While they stared into the glowing disks, Jovadia uttered an incantation to settle their minds.

"Stare into the cauldron," she commanded. "Feel the power. Attune your psithes to the cold fire!"

The minds of the majja slipped into trance. The light in the cauldron circled, growing brighter, white gold with swirls of scarlet. The power of the cold fire expanded, rising as a globe.

As the globe spun slowly under the ceiling, Jovadia turned her thoughts on the newcomers, testing and probing. First, the woman, Zaria the Snowhawk. She was talented, an adept in rank, formerly a court wizard to a duke of the north. She would do well.

Jovadia turned next to the first of the males. He was young, his psithe a Golden Sparrow, an operio, or "journeyman," as that rank was called among the wizards of Ptolloden. But he was dedicated, eager for power. He too might prove suitable. Jovadia would reserve her judgment for now.

Lastly, she stared at the third newcomer, a male adept, the Blue Gull. He was strong-willed, and all along Jovadia had sensed he kept his thoughts hidden. Now, his brain completely absorbed in the cold fire, she was able to pierce his defenses.

Reading his mind, she saw her suspicions were justified. The man was a spy, sent by the High Masters of Ptolloden. She had known that her activities, involving so much magical power, must eventually attract the attention of the Norrling Sanctuaries. Still, she was surprised that it was Ptolloden, not Montodoro, that moved to investigate.

Well, the disappearance of the Blue Gull would disappoint them.

With a slow movement of her hand, the Bittern changed her psithe into a wand. A sudden pull was enough to yank the Blue Gull off balance. His body jerked and fell forward, then rose suspended over the cauldron. He gave a brief cry as the cold fire flashed. Next instant, the man was transformed into a twisted statue of ice. The ice lasted only a second before splintering, the shattered pieces falling away.

As the Blue Gull psithe merged with the cold fire, Jovadia surveyed the faces of the other majja. "Do not be afraid. The Blue Gull was a spy, an informer sent to probe our activities. Now his psithe will serve us, though he will not. But remember this lesson, my followers. Deception will never fool me. Your decision to join our mighty cause is irrevocable. Doubts or hesitations will not be tolerated."

On the next-to-last day of the Festival of Good Fortune, King Carswell held a council session in his great hall. The King's advisors and courtiers attended, along with the highest-ranking nobles of Occitan, who were visiting Baivonne for the Festival. Mirafra was pleased to see that Queen Esmeralda felt strong enough to also be present, seated at the high table beside the King.

She and Arwyn sat at one of several crowded tables arranged across the floor. Along the walls, in front of statues and marble columns, stood lines of armored men—more guards than Mirafra had seen assembled since her arrival. Harbingers, she supposed, of what was to come. Mirafra was confused as to why Teron the Mooncrow had not joined them. She knew he had been invited.

"My lords and ladies," the King began. "We are here to discuss a grave matter. Intelligence has reached us, confirmed by multiple sources, that King Alaric has made conquest of most of the principalities of Arabhedden. Moreover, he is requiring the lords of these newly acquired territories to muster their armies. We have therefore concluded that Alaric is preparing, in the months ahead, to invade Occitan."

Muttered conversations sounded across the hall. Mirafra knew that most of the nobles already suspected that something like this was afoot.

Carswell raised his hands for silence. "I am therefore calling upon all of you to be prepared to march and defend our realm from attack. Now, we shall hear discussion."

As the King sat down, a renewed clamor arose. Mirafra discerned that several parties of nobles had already discussed what might happen at the council and had prepared responses. The first one who rose to speak was Count Halsark.

"My lords and ladies, with all respect, I must ask if we are not jumping to conclusions. Whatever steps Alaric may have taken in Arabhedden need not concern Occitan. We have a treaty with Llorrland, a treaty I myself negotiated. I have had more contact with Alaric's court than anyone here, and I believe there is no cause for alarm, no reason to conclude that he intends to move against us."

Shouts of agreement rose from some quarters, amid the rumbling of many voices.

"Count Halsark makes a good point," a lord called out. "I see no reason yet that we ought to break our treaty."

"I do not propose breaking the treaty," Carswell answered. "Only that we be prepared if Alaric breaks it. And since Count Halsark has spoken, I will inform you now of a related concern—one that may prove most dire. It is reported that Alaric's Court Wizard, known as Jovadia the Bittern, has developed a formidable new weapon. By her arts, she has transformed normal men into creatures of sorcery, warriors who are nearly impossible to kill."

Amid the uproar, Halsark shouted, "This is nonsense!"

"I do not think it nonsense," the King raised his voice to be heard. "The report was first conveyed to us by the son of the slain Duke of Duneidan and by Mirafra, an apprentice wizard, both of whom witnessed these deadly creatures in action. My own Court Wizard Clorinda gives credence to their account."

Seated by his side, the Ibis gave a curt nod.

A lord seated near the King rose and affirmed that his own Norrling advisor had also expressed suspicions regarding the activities of Jovadia the Bittern. Two other nobles shouted that they had heard rumors as well. Mirafra glanced at Count Halsark, who was still standing and appeared increasingly unnerved.

"Now we must fear not only war, but war with wizards," he cried. "What next preposterous alarm shall we hear?"

King Carswell stared with cool anger. "Since the Count asks the question, I shall raise one further alarm, not in the least preposterous. It has been proven to my satisfaction that sorcery in the service of King Alaric has penetrated this very court, seducing one of my close advisors, causing him to turn traitor. Bring in the prisoner!"

In answer to his command, a door opened at the far end of the hall. Two guardsmen came forward, marching a bedraggled man between them. Mirafra recognized the assassin the Mooncrow had wounded in the alley. The man stared warily around the hall as he was dragged before the King.

"The traitor of whom I speak," Carswell said, "hired this man and others to assassinate two guests of this court who have become my advisors, the young Duke of Duneidan and his friend, the wizard Mooncrow."

The hall was hushed as the King pointed down at the prisoner. "Now, fellow, speak. If the one who hired you is present, point him out to this assembly."

After glancing about, the assassin slowly raised his arm, finger pointing. "That is the man, Count Halsark."

In the chaos that ensued, the men at Halsark's table jumped to their feet, backing away as if from fear of contagion. But, to Mirafra's surprise, the Count himself made no protest. He stood frozen, wild-eyed, a picture of confusion and fright.

"The Count is in a trance," Clorinda the Ibis spoke for the first time. "I thought this might happen."

"Guards, arrest the Count and place him under confinement," Carswell ordered. "As we said, we believe his will has been subverted by sorcery. Therefore, his treachery will not be punished at this time. Instead, a cure will be sought."

Halsark did not struggle, merely stared in bewilderment as guardsmen came to the table and led him away. As they marched from the hall, the King spoke.

"My lords and ladies, I see this as further evidence of the dangerous magic that may be loosed against us. I ask those of you who employ court wizards to consult them and have them confer with Clorinda the Ibis. I am entrusting her with gathering further intelligence and seeking means to counter the Bittern."

Clorinda stood, resting her fists on the table. "All we know at present, aside from Jovadia's dastardly intents, is that she has found a way to collect and harness the power of multiple psithes. We believe that is why King Alaric is arresting all unattached Norrlings discovered in his territories. But I can promise the people of Occitan that I, and my sister majja of Montodoro, will do whatever is necessary to counteract this dangerous misuse of magic."

She resumed her seat, and the King nodded grimly. "Now, lords and ladies, let us discuss specific plans for the defense of our kingdom."

Concentrating hard, Teron wheeled the glimmering wand slowly above his head, levitating the three acrobats, moving their bodies in a circle. The Bonatores lay face down in the air, arms and legs outstretched, fingers touching. Nearby, Topiedeon leaned against the gymnasium wall, strumming a slow and stately tune.

Suddenly a strident chord broke up the music. Teron glanced down to see the King and others striding into the chamber.

"Hey!" Lisa Bonatore cried.

Startled, Teron looked up and sent power to keep the acrobats from falling. Dipping the wand, he settled them to the floor.

"Please forgive our intrusion."

Carswell strode up before the Mooncrow, followed by Clorinda, with Mirafra and Arwyn trailing behind. They must have come directly from the council meeting, which Teron had decided to skip.

"Of course, your majesty." Teron said.

The Bonatores climbed to their feet and gave hasty bows. Topiedeon came over to listen.

"I wanted to inform you about the council and the decisions made," the King said.

"And also to get your help," Clorinda inserted, to Teron's surprise.

"Yes, well." The King lifted his hands. "First, you should know that, as we planned and expected, Count Halsark's treachery was exposed in front of the assembly. He is placed in confinement and should cause no further trouble. The dramatic revelation of his betrayal did help convince the council of the seriousness of the threats we face. Plans are now in place to mobilize forces throughout Occitan to stand ready to protect our borders."

"This brings us to what we need from you," the Ibis added.

Teron glanced behind her to see Mirafra and Arwyn, watching him expectantly. He wondered where this was leading.

"Yes." The King cleared his throat. "You have already been of great service to us, Teron, and you are under no obligation to do more. But we are mobilizing for war. Clorinda is being sent to the High Sanctuary at Montodoro to seek aid from the Norrlings. Since the Bittern is their own renegade, we hope they will take responsibility and ally with us to counteract her powers. Of course, the fastest way to travel is by air. I have eight airships in my fleet. But as a key element of our defenses, all will be assigned to patrol our southern shores and borders with Llorrland."

Teron now saw where it was going. Clorinda spelled it out.

"That is why we are hoping to borrow—or hire—your airship, Master Mooncrow."

Teron's mouth tightened. He glanced from the Ibis to the King, then noticed a sardonic smile on Topiedeon, and the eager, hopeful faces of Arwyn and Mirafra.

"I'd really rather not," he answered. "I've already kept my company here longer than expected. We are planning to sail to the Islands and Ibor to resume trading and performing."

"How long would a trip to Montodoro take?" Topiedeon piped up.

"I don't know." Teron could only guess from maps he'd seen. "Five to seven days maybe—each way. And as for how long we'd be delayed once we reach the Sanctuary, who can tell?"

Topiedeon turned to Felix. "Well, we did have that other offer." The bard explained to the King: "From a promoter at the Festival. The man wanted to hire our company to perform on a steamboat that travels up and down the river. That might be enjoyable and profitable both."

Felix Bonatore smiled and shrugged.

Teron turned on the minstrel with astonishment. "Why are you trying to talk me into this?"

"Because I know you want to do it," Topiedeon laughed.

"No, I do not!" Teron replied stubbornly, forcing down an urge to consider the idea.

True, part of him was tempted. These past days had reminded him of the wild adventures of his youth. But those memories were also painful, because of all that he had lost: first his relationship with the Empress Rania, then his place of power and influence at the court.

He addressed the King. "Please understand, Majesty. When I left Moldorn, I promised myself I was done with intrigue and war. I made an exception to rescue Arwyn and Mirafra because of their great need. But we've already lingered here longer than I planned."

"Oh!" The Ibis scoffed. "Is this the daring, venturesome Mooncrow we've heard so much about?"

Teron only glared at her.

"I understand your reluctance," Carswell said. "But you might also reflect on this: One cannot always avoid conflict. Alaric and the Bittern might sooner or later extend their threat to the Islands, even Ibor."

Teron's mouth twisted. There was no avoiding the truth of the King's words. His eyes wandered to Mirafra.

"Please," she whispered, fixing him with her dark, intense gaze. "We need you."

Her plea touched his heart—a heart, he thought, that had grown cold over the years, but might now be warming. The Mooncrow laughed at himself, tossed his wand into the air and made it hover.

"Well, I always did have a curiosity about seeing Montodoro."

Mirafra's clothes lay scattered on the bed: tunics, trousers, undergarments, and stockings, both for indoors and cold weather; an extra pair of boots; even slippers, a gown, and a shawl for formal appearances. The King's staff had been most generous, even more so once Mirafra started to assist in treating the Queen. These were far more clothes than she had ever owned. Certainly more than she would need for the voyage to Ombernorr.

As she considered what to pack into the two small satchels, Arwyn leaned against the doorframe, watching her. She had smiled at him when he came in, but they had not exchanged any words. His somber stare was painful to her.

Finally, he made a decision and walked over to the bed. "Mirafra, I have something to say to you. I know I should not ask this, but I must: Would you consider *not* going to Montodoro, staying here with me in Baivonne?"

That she had known this was coming made it no easier. Avoiding his eyes, she said, "Arwyn, I cannot. I must return Sharam's psithe."

"Clorinda can do that for you."

"No! I must go. Duty requires it. I'm the one majja who has seen the indestructible warriors in action. For that reason alone, I may be of help."

"I know. I shouldn't have asked it of you." He stared at the floor, eyes moist. "It's just that, we were friends from the start, because we are both different. Now, you are all I have left."

Mirafra harbored similar emotions. In many ways, she had been closer to Arwyn than any other person in her life. "I am sorry, dear friend. My hope is to return with a more powerful psithe of my own and knowledge that will help us defeat the Bittern and King Alaric. I owe that to Sharam and to you."

Arwyn turned away. "My fear is that you may decide not to return at all."

Mirafra winced. She could not deny that she had wrestled with that notion. To quit the Warmlands altogether, to stay at Montodoro where all was safe and peaceful. But no, she could not believe that was her proper course.

"I promise you. I will return if I possibly can."

With a grim smile, the young Duke started for the door. After two steps, he turned.

"Here's another thought: would you mind my coming along? I don't think the King or Teron would object. After all, I fought the creatures and might be able to add information."

Now Mirafra felt ready to cry. "I would love to have you sail with us."

Grinning, Arwyn put his hand on hers. "Good. This way, we can keep watching out for each other."

"We are going *where*, Senor Teron?" Captain Dona Delores gaped at the Mooncrow.

Face shadowed by the curve of the airship envelope, she stood with Teron, Topiedeon, and her cousins Ricardo and Emilio under the hull of the *Pomegranate*. Nearby, a steam engine rumbled as it lifted extra fuel and supplies through a hatchway.

"Surely you've heard of Montodoro," Topiedeon explained. "T'is the great Norrling Sanctuary in northwest Ombernorr. Don't worry, Captain. It's only 2,000 miles into the wilderness, built, so I understand, before a glacier."

"Airships don't fly to Ombernorr. At least, I've never heard of such a route!"

"Moldorn ships did once," Teron replied. "But it's true; we may be the first to visit the western coast. You might become famous, Captain. For certain, your logs of the voyage will be prized by the Airship Guild."

"I'd much prefer to keep my ship and crew safe in the Warmlands," the lady answered. "How shall we even find this wizards' Sanctuary?"

"We have maps of the terrain, supplied by the King's geographers," Teron said. "Even some drawings that estimate the prevailing winds."

"But only barbarians and snow tribes live in Ombernorr! What will we trade for? And how will you and your troupe find work?"

"King Carswell is financing the expedition," Teron said. "And the troupe will not be traveling with us. They've accepted a contract to perform here in Occitan, on the river. Topiedeon is here to pack up his things, and the Bonatores will be along later to do the same."

The minstrel raised a finger. "Actually, that's not entirely true. I know I did *say* I would stay with the acrobats. But after thinking it over, I'd decided to stick with you."

"What?" Teron could not hide his surprise.

"It must be so." Topiedeon chuckled. "If I'm going to continue to chronicle the adventures of the fantastical Mooncrow, how can I miss this part of the story?"

JACK MASSA

Part 3

The Birds of Montodoro

As in the Sanctuary of Ptolloden, the order consists of 640 levels arranged into eight octodens. Here the levels carry slightly different names: 1 Fledgling, 2 Apprentice, 3 Tyro, 4 Operio, 5 Adept, 6 Maestra, 7 High Maestra, and 8 Supreme Maestra. And, while many of the wizard species are the same as in the eastern Sanctuary, there are also differences, most notably a profusion of songbirds and strutting birds.

—*The Terrestrial Histories of Fystus the Emu*,
Volume 39, Chapter 2.
Norrling year 6270.

Chapter 11

Chill twilight hovered over Castle Tonnsburg.

Thirty warriors stood in the courtyard, three rigid lines of tall figures in black armor, each holding two broadswords. The soldiers were strong and tough, seasoned men-at-arms. They had already been trained in the combat techniques of wielding two swords. Over the past month, their brains had also been conditioned with a drug to make them dull and pliant.

On the parapet above, Jovadia perched in a feathered cloak and beaked mask. Her five apprentices, lined up beside her, stared into their disks.

"Within your psithes you now see the cold fire," the Bittern instructed, "that same fire that burns in the cauldron in the lair below us. It burns in the depths of your psithes and also in your brains and bodies. See its unfathomable light! Feel its power!"

Jovadia felt the first stirrings, a tingling of the nerves, a tightening behind the eyes. She glanced up from her own psithe to gauge how the apprentices were adjusting. They showed varying degrees of power, of course, but their concentration seemed good. Zaria the Snowhawk, one of the new recruits, seemed to be adapting especially well.

Gazing back into her disk, Jovadia resumed the spell. "The cold fire builds within you. So dazzling to wield such power, it causes discomfort, even pain. But you are strong, and you love this feeling of power, and so you adapt."

As the energy built, some of the apprentices began shaking. The Golden Sparrow, the young journeyman, fell to his knees with a groan. To his credit, he fought his way back to his feet, forced himself to concentrate on the task.

The cold fire became a visible cloud, circling the six wizards. At last, Jovadia judged it ready.

"Now cast the power down into the brains and bodies of the men below."

The apprentices followed as Jovadia lifted her disk. As instructed, they began with the front row, the first man on the left. Frosty light beamed from the psithes, collected in a ball, then swooped down to strike the head of that first warrior. The majja chanted the words composed by the Bittern.

You are no longer mortal man
You are the power of cold fire
You have no will, no fear
You know not weariness nor pain
You march and slay within cold fire

Thirty times they repeated the chant. Thirty bolts of power streamed down into the bodies below. When the last of the visible energy faded, the courtyard lay in darkness.

Jovadia was pleased, judging that the transformations had gone well. She had performed this magic enough that, for her, the weariness and headache were hardly noticeable. Best of all, with these thirty, she now had nearly two hundred of the zolgars at her command.

Around her, the apprentices panted, some clutching their foreheads in pain.

No time for such weakness!

"You have done well!" she cried. "The warriors are converted; the new zolgars are born! Now you must keep focus, my students. Time to animate these creatures and march them to the dungeons below, then put them to sleep until they are needed."

Eight of the High Maestras of Montodoro stared down at Mirafra, the eyes of their bird masks gleaming.

"So you, a mere tyro, judged yourself competent to usurp the psithe of the Crested Crane!"

"Audacious." "Unlawful." "Most unorthodox." The whispers flowed from behind the masks. Mirafra could not tell which of the maestras was speaking. She had tried to explain, but the words choked her throat. She looked down at the black floor, speckled with diamond light. As the wizards' disapproval washed over her, the lights blazed brighter and brighter.

"Uhhh!" Her eyes popped open. In shadowy lamplight, she gazed at the ceiling beam of her cabin on the *Pomegranate*.

The dreams had started the first night of the voyage. Mirafra was a student in Montodoro, reprimanded in class by strict teachers. Or she was at a large practice session in a courtyard, desperately trying to match the skills of classmates. Or sitting alone on a freezing terrace as she used to do in the night when she could not sleep, staring at the towering glacier to the north, wondering if she could ever succeed as a majja.

Mirafra had always been subject to troubling dreams. But these were so unexpected. She had done nothing wrong. She had followed her maestra's orders in taking the Crane psithe. She had acted properly, even heroically.

Hadn't she?

For the first two days and nights, the *Pomegranate* had flown north, following the course of the Machtiges River. Gradually, forests and rolling farmlands gave way to plains covered in snow this time of year. Walled towns of wood and stone were replaced by villages of thatch and hides. From overhead, the travelers spotted hunting parties on horseback, trailing herds of elk or reindeer. Arwyn, along with Topiedeon, spent most of the daylight hours in the observation room on deck two or else in the wheelhouse. Arwyn was keeping a journal of their travels, and the minstrel was always looking for inspiration for songs.

On the third day, Captain Delores turned west. Ahead stood a line of dark hills, and from this altitude one could see beyond them to a range of mountains, their rugged, icy peaks fading into mist.

"There be your mountains," Dona Delores said.

Arwyn peered over the captain's shoulder at the map they had been given in Baivonne. This range, he knew, covered much of the two continents. Called the Eishaltens in Tann, they ran from the glacial ice all the way down to Khesperia in the south. The same range, with a different name, continued into western Ibor, the home of the Moldorns. Arwyn had learned all of this from his tutors back in Duneidan. Still, glimpsing the mountains for himself was stunning.

"I do hope the passes marked on this map are accurate," Dona Delores muttered. "Our dear ship was never meant for flying over such high terrain."

"Ha!" Topiedeon clapped her on the back. "But our skilled captain will see us safely through, I know."

"Ha!" She answered sourly. "Why the lady wizards had to build a separate Sanctuary, I don't know. And why they had to build it at the farthest corner of Ombernorr—that I don't know either."

"Aye, why the segregation of the sexes?" Topiedeon laughed. "Warmlanders have often wondered that. My guess is, there was too much conflict. You know how quarrelsome men and women tend to be with each other? Now imagine those endless disputes amplified by endless magic. Surely disasters would result."

"Ha!" was all that Dona Delores replied.

But Arwyn thought it an intriguing question. He decided to make a note in his journal and try to find out the answer when they reached Montodoro.

Built at the edge of the continental glacier, Montodoro spread over the slopes and summit of a long hill. The Sanctuary shone in the icy daylight, a huge, rambling structure of red, yellow, and sparkling blue stone. Turrets and spires sprouted from numerous tilting rooflines. Giant, glassy domes reflected the pale sky. But even more amazing to the eye was the rocky hill itself, which sloped down from the walls—gleaming in bands and pools that looked like precious metal.

"T'is not really gold!" Topiedeon exclaimed.

The bard watched from the front of the wheel room—along with Teron, Arwyn, Mirafra, and Clorinda—as the *Pomegranate* made its slow approach.

"Appearance only, I am sure," Teron confirmed.

"Correct," Clorinda the Ibis said. "Much that you find in Montodoro may not be what it first appears. I daresay, some mysteries may prove hard to solve—even for one as artful as the famous Mooncrow."

"I am not here to solve mysteries," Teron replied. "Only to lend my airship."

After negotiating the hazardous crags and passes of the Eishalten Mountains, the ship had sailed another day and two nights across the western reaches of Ombernorr. The territory was rolling tundra, with patches of woodland and frozen rivers and lakes. The population was sparse. Villages clustered in the shelter of hills, with some abodes dug into the ground for warmth.

Since dawn, birds had been spotted flying alongside the airship. The travelers had identified a condor, a vulture, and two hawks.

"That would be our escort," Clorinda had said. "They'll guide us to the landing place."

Just as she predicted, the raptors flew to a stretch of flat land in front of the giant Sanctuary, then rose, circling higher and higher.

"That's where they want you to land, Captain," Clorinda called.

"Yes, I understand the message from our feathered friends," Dona Delores answered.

She shouted out orders to trim the rudders and called back to the boiler rooms to vent steam. The winds were light, and the *Pomegranate* dipped easily toward the landing place. In a short while, the airship settled to the ground. Hatches dropped open, and crewmen hustled out to secure stakes and mooring lines.

At midships, Clorinda the Ibis descended the main gangway, followed by Teron, Mirafra, Arwyn, and Topiedeon. Clorinda had dressed in her wizard's finery, a white-feathered costume with cape and bird mask. Mirafra had left Duneidan with only her Tree Pipit cape. But she wore the two psithes, hung as disks on gold chains. Teron had elected to dress in a simple wool doublet and hooded cloak. He carried his psithe in its wand shape.

As they emerged from the ship, Mirafra spotted a small party of Norrlings walking toward them from the distant archway of the Sanctuary. There were four majja dressed in full Norrling regalia, moving with unhurried steps, hands folded in their capes.

As these wizards approached, four birds swooped out of the sky. The hawks, vulture, and condor settled with shrieks and flapping wings—then flashed into balls of light before landing. When the lights disappeared, the birds had resumed their human forms. Clad in feathers and masks, they stepped into line with the others, now eight wizards in all.

"I'll do the talking for us," Clorinda said over her shoulder.

"Of course," Teron answered lightly. "I am not here to talk, only to lend my airship."

His blithe attitude caused Mirafra to smile despite her nervousness.

Coming within a few paces, the eight wizards arranged themselves in a line. Clasping their hands in front, they bowed in unison. Clorinda and Mirafra returned the ritual greeting, and the rest of the party also bowed.

A majja at the center, dressed in black, spoke from behind her beaked mask.

"You are welcomed to the High Sanctuary, honored guests. We are the Congregation of Extra-Territorial Affairs. I am Lilia the Kingfisher. I present to you Prolisso the Macaw, Narcosta the Pootoo, Viola the Sky Hawk, Sengegg the Vulture, Haulli the Condor, Kalwyn the Hunter Hawk, and Surretize the Tawny Frogmouth."

Each of the majja bowed in turn, causing all of the travelers to respond in kind. Rising from her bow, Clorinda began. "I am—"

"You, Sister Maestra," the Kingfisher interrupted, "I perceive to be Clorinda the Ibis. Your communications by qorm dream have been received. Most informative. And this," she pointed a gloved finger, "I assume is the apprentice with the two psithes."

Mirafra gave a slight nod.

"And this man must be the one known as the Mooncrow."

Teron lifted his eyebrows.

"But these others I cannot identify."

Clorinda introduced them. "This is Arwyn Keltonn, the young Duke of Duneidan in Arabhedden. And this is Topiedeon, a bard and friend of Teron's."

After more bows were exchanged, Lilia said, "No need for us to stand longer in the cold. Let us proceed into the Sanctuary."

As they followed the line of majja toward the grand archway, Arwyn fell into step beside Mirafra. "I can see I'll need a lot more study of the Ombernorran language."

Mirafra had hardly noticed, but of course the whole conversation had been in Ombernorran. During the voyage, she had given Arwyn a few lessons in her native tongue. He was, of course, a quick learner, but Ombernorran and Galintaan had totally different origins.

At the front of the procession, Clorinda was speaking with the Kingfisher. Mirafra quickened her pace to listen.

"Thank you for affirming, sister," Clorinda said, "that my communications have been received. Can you say how much is now known about the concerning events in the Warmlands?"

"Specifically—?"

"Specifically the events that bring us here. Jovadia the Bittern and her misuse of psithic powers."

"We are aware there is a situation," the Kingfisher said.

"We have the information contained in your qorm dreams," Prolisso the Macaw added, "as well as other sources."

"Of course, what we interpreted from the dreams must be confirmed with you in person," Lilia added.

"What other sources?" Teron was also listening. "If I may ask?"

"Quite." Lilia glanced back at him. "Impressions gathered from birds flying into the Birdhouse, of course. That is always a source of knowledge about the Warmlands. But also intuitions received and investigated by various high maestras, some quite disturbing."

"Yes, this Jovadia must be powerful indeed," the Macaw said. "Even the high masters of Ptolloden are concerned—concerned enough to send an envoy to discuss the matter with us."

"Really?" the Mooncrow said. "That *is* surprising."

Reaching the icy entrance at last, the odd procession climbed the broad ceremonial stairs and passed through tall golden doors into Montodoro.

114

A meeting with the Congregation of Extra-Territorial Affairs was scheduled for later that day. In the meantime, Teron and his companions were led through an enormous vestibule and down a tall, sparkling corridor to an adjacent building—the so-called Pavilion of Welcome Visitors. Here they were assigned cozy apartments where the stone floors and walls were warmed by psithic magic. At Teron's request, Dona Delores and her crew were assigned adjacent quarters. The morning passed with the airship being secured and the travelers conveying their luggage to the Sanctuary.

Teron and Topiedeon were settling in to their shared room when a voice at the doorway startled them.

"Is that really my old friend Teron?"

The Mooncrow whirled to see a tall and rotund man in a dark feathered robe. It took him a moment to recognize the wizard.

"Fystus the Grackle!?"

"Ha ha!" The bearded Norrling strode into the room and clasped Teron's hand. "Advanced a rank or two since you knew me. It's Fystus the Emu now."

"Well, congratulations." Teron laughed. "It's still Teron the Mooncrow for me."

"Oh, I know! Everyone has heard of the Mooncrow!"

"Ahem!" Topiedeon cleared his throat.

"And this," Teron laughed, "is my good friend Topiedeon, also famous under the name Bandelion the Bard, composer of popular ballads."

"Which I earn a pittance for performing." Topiedeon shook the Emu's hand. "When I'm not following around the famous Mooncrow."

Teron gestured their visitor to a chair. "But what in all the ages are you doing here? Wait! Don't tell me *you* are the envoy sent from Ptolloden?"

Fystus sank into the soft chair with a sigh. "Indeed I am, and an arduous journey it was across the width of Ombernorr, let me tell you."

"No airships in Ptolloden," Topiedeon said.

"Of course not!" Fystus spread his feathered sleeves. "And being that an emu is a flightless bird, I couldn't use the quinteer and take to the skies. No! It was reindeer sled all the way for me. Took weeks—and cold weeks they were!"

"So sorry," Teron chuckled.

"Why would they send a flightless bird?" Topiedeon asked. "Was the matter not considered urgent?"

"Oh, I pleaded for the assignment," the Emu said. "A chance to visit Montodoro, to compare learning with the lady Norrlings—that does not come up often. As for the urgency, well, there are widely varied opinions, as there always are about things having to do with the Warmlands."

"But the high masters were willing to send you here," Teron noted, "so they must at least be concerned about the Bittern."

The Emu's face turned grave. "So they are, my friend, most of them. Considerable disturbances in the energy fields have been noted for some time and are growing stronger. Most agree they must be the result of unorthodox magic. There has been much discussion in Ptolloden, but no consensus on what to do about it. Sending me here to compare information was at least a first step."

"And what have you learned from the lady wizards?" Teron asked.

"Ha!" Fystus flipped his hands in the air. "They are almost as much in the dark as we. They do believe that this Jovadia the Bittern is the source of the disturbances, and that she has resurrected ancient psithic techniques. But as to what to do about her, there is no more agreement than in Ptolloden. I believe the high maestras here are hoping that you and your party will help by bringing them more knowledge."

Teron nodded. "We can give them first-hand accounts about the Bittern and her despicable magic. I just hope the maestras decide to do something."

Fystus sighed. "That remains to be seen. From what I've noticed in my time here, there are three distinct factions. I'd say the predominant group are moderates, who call themselves Adherents of Tradition. They believe the proper path is for Norrlings to live apart but to be of service to all, both Ombernorrs and Warmlanders. They mostly feel Jovadia is their responsibility and should be stopped. The second faction is called the Brood of Isolationists. Their doctrine is similar to the predominant view in Ptolloden: all wizards should be detached from the world and should not even visit the Warmlands. They say to leave the Bittern alone, that she is the Warmlanders' problem. Now the third group is one that has no parallel in Ptolloden, the Flight of Exploration. These Explorationists favor experimenting with all magical avenues, including ancient techniques. Jovadia comes from this faction, and, though they disdain her evil leanings, they would favor capturing her and learning all she has discovered. Some even argue they should first let her experiments run their course."

Teron scoffed. "If they have their way, her experiments may run their course all the way to Montodoro."

"That is indeed a worry," Fystus said. "Neither Ptolloden nor Montodoro wants to get into a war with the kingdoms of the south. But if the worst projections come to pass, that may one day happen."

Chapter 12

That afternoon, Clorinda conducted Mirafra, along with Teron and Arwyn, to the formal meeting of the Congregation of Extra-Territorial Affairs. The session took place in a council chamber with a high dome that gleamed with translucent daylight and a floor with sparkling mosaics depicting birds in various habitats. Tall podiums set on a semi-circular dais were occupied by the same eight majja who had greeted the airship on their arrival. A number of spectators occupied galleries near the entrance. Looking that way, Mirafra noticed that Teron nodded to one of them, a large and heavy man with a beard. She assumed this must be the envoy from Ptolloden, whom Teron had mentioned meeting.

Stopping at the center of the chamber, Mirafra stared up at the masked and feathered majja on the dais and tried to suppress her anxiety. As leader of the committee, Lilia the Kingfisher spoke first.

"The Congregation wishes to express thanks to our sister Clorinda the Ibis for undertaking the journey to bring us important information from the south. We shall hear first from the Ibis, then from our other visitors."

Bobbing her head up and down as she spoke, Clorinda related the political situation in southeast Tann and the growing conflict between Occitan and Llorrland. She included the tales she had heard of Jovadia the Bittern's growing powers, and described her own investigations of Jovadia using trance and qorm-dream techniques. She touched on the reported conquest of Arabhedden and the appearance of the so-called indestructible warriors, but concluded by saying she would let the others speak of these matters from their own direct experience.

Mirafra was called on next. Forcing herself to gaze directly into the bird faces, she recounted the arrival of King Alaric and the Bittern in Duneidan, and her morning encounter with Jovadia on the parapet of the castle.

"What exactly did the Bittern say regarding unorthodox magic?" Sengegg the Vulture asked.

"As best I recall, she said there were many paths, some taught long ago in Montodoro but then abandoned, others that originated in foreign lands."

"Interesting. That piece about foreign lands is new to us," Narcosta the Pootoo said.

"Irrelevant," said the Hunter Hawk. "We know that Jovadia has been appropriating psithes improperly. Therefore, we know that her powers arise from misuse of our own ancient practices."

"I'm not sure we can make that conclusion," the Pootoo answered.

"We shall discuss these details later." The Kingfisher gestured impatiently. "Let the young majja continue her testimony."

Mirafra went on to describe the attack on the castle and her discovery of Sharam the Crane as she lay dying. "She gave me her psithe and attuned it to my mind so that I could use it to escape and ..."

"Your possession of the maestra's psithe is not our concern," Lilia told her. "That matter will be dealt with by the Flock of Psithic Propriety. You will be summoned by them when they are ready to meet with you. Pray continue with your narrative."

Mirafra concluded with what she had seen of the black-armored warriors, and how she and Arwyn had escaped.

Arwyn spoke next, with Clorinda interpreting both the questions and his answers. He spoke haltingly, his face solemn as he recalled the ravaging of his home and the murder of his family. He could add little to what Mirafra had said, other than attesting to the inhuman nature of the warriors he had fought.

When Teron's turn came, he explained that he, like Clorinda, had sensed vast magical powers arising in the vicinity of Llorrland, and that he had witnessed the attack on Duneidan Castle in a psithic vision. He added further the account of the assassins' attack in Baivonne, which he and Clorinda agreed was also the work of the Bittern.

This last statement caused another round of debate among the majja at the podiums. How reliable were these new reports? How much power had Jovadia actually acquired? What, if anything, should the Congregation recommend be done?

Mirafra had always known there were different opinions in the Sanctuary as to how much interaction there should be with the Warmlands. And she had learned from Teron this morning what his friend Fystus said about the current alignment of factions. But, although the discussion from the council members was heated, she could not clearly tell which of those factions the individual members might belong to.

Finally, Lilia the Kingfisher called for silence. "Sisters, if there are no further questions for our visitors, I suggest we dismiss them and continue in private."

When no other questions were raised, she thanked the four witnesses and told them they might go. Before leaving, Teron the Mooncrow made a final remark.

"I understand events in the Warmlands seem remote here in Ombernorr. And, having been trained in Ptolloden, I know the prevailing policy there has always been rigid isolation. I can only hope that in this case, you of Montodoro will choose a wiser path."

Arwyn stood at the open door, summoning the courage to enter. On the far side of the wide chamber, Fystus sat with his feet propped before a hearth that pulsed with flameless gold fire. The Emu appeared deep in concentration, holding a psithe-disk in one hand and a large white crystal in the other. As he stared into the disk, his two hands shifted back and forth.

"You may enter, young sir," he called without looking up. "No need for shyness."

Arwyn cleared his throat and strode into the chamber. "I—thank you, majja," he said in halting Ombernorran. "I be Arwyn, Duke of Duneidan. Teron the Mooncrow ... uh, said ... to me ... to call on you."

"Indeed?" Fystus let both objects rest on his lap. "Please sit down. You may speak Galintaan. I have some schooling in the tongue."

"Thank you!" Arwyn changed to the language of southern Tann as he sank into the chair.

"What can I do for you, Duke Arwyn?"

"Oh, I have so much to learn!" Arwyn stared down at the crystal. "You are using your psithe to *read* that stone. Am I correct?"

"Yes." Fystus turned the white crystal over. "I prefer reading from written or printed books. But much of the more arcane material is only recorded on crystal."

"But how can you read that?"

"Well, you see, lines of ... uh, information are written onto the folded surfaces of the stone. Not *written* exactly, more like carved with a tiny chisel. And it's not text as you see in writing, more like sparks of light." He held up his psithe-disk, which at the moment was clear as glass. "The disk is used to draw these bits of light into my brain, where they are interpreted as words, do you see?"

Arwyn chuckled. "Not really."

Fystus set the crystal aside. "Well, the psithic arts can be hard to explain. And likely my Galintaan is inadequate to the task. What did Teron suggest you see me about?"

The young man shifted in his chair. "Well, during our voyage, the question came up as to why the Norrlings have two different Sanctuaries, one for males and one for females. Teron told me you'd be able to explain the history better than he."

"Ah, a complex history it is." Fystus propped his elbows on the arms of the chair and rose with an effort. "Would you mind if we continued our discussion outside? I'd like some air."

"No. Not at all." Standing, Arwyn followed the Emu to a glass door framed with carved wood.

They stepped onto a broad terrace that ran the length of the building. The air was frigid, and a layer of frost covered the curving pink stone of walls and balustrades.

"Hope you don't mind the cold, young sir," Fystus said over his shoulder. "I can get you a fur wrap."

Shivering, Arwyn pulled the velvet cape close to his throat. "No need. Thank you."

They stopped at the edge of the terrace, under a cloudless sky. Low hills covered in snow rolled down to a dark blue sea. From inside his robe, Fystus produced a long pipe of carved ivory. Filling it from a pouch, he explained:

"The ladies of Montodoro prefer that I refrain from smoking inside."

Arwyn stared in surprise as the majja twisted his psithe-disk into a dagger and produced a flame to light the pipe.

"Now, as to your question," Fystus said between puffs. "Where to start?"

Exhaling a stream of white smoke, he began. "After the fall of the ancient world, as you may know, there were centuries of over-heated atmosphere, resulting in melted planetary ice and a great dying-off of life forms. Then the Earth reached a tipping point and cold returned, resulting in our current age of low seas and much ice. During this transition, the Ombernorrs emerged on the tundras of this continent as a distinct racial strain—some say a human subspecies. The main difference between Ombernorrs and other humans is that some—not all—of our people have the propensity for shaping the physical world through mental effort, what we call magic. As the number of these gifted humans grew and their powers increased, a period of chaos ensued. Majja and warriors fought on the tundras and down into the Warmlands. Many people were killed, until finally a group of powerful wizards banded together to establish order. They laid down strict doctrines. Over time, these doctrines were codified into the psithic arts—the merging of a human's mental powers with the life-force of a bird. This merging both enhances our magic and helps us control it, because of the requirement to work in harmony with another life form—a sacred obligation. And, as you probably know, this is also the definition of a *Norrling*, a majja who practices the psithic arts.

"So then, at first the psithic arts were taught in houses of magic throughout Ombernorr. But, eventually, in order to preserve standards of practice, it was found necessary to maintain only two Sanctuaries. To minimize conflicts and let the majja focus on developing their powers without distraction, it was decided to segregate the sexes. So the two Sanctuaries were built in the far corners of the land, Ptolloden in the east and Montodoro in the west."

Arwyn stared out over the hills, contemplating. "Yes, all that makes sense. And from what I've heard at different times, I understand majja are only allowed to uh, engage in mating practices on certain occasions."

Fystus smiled. "That is true. In order that the Ombernorrs remain a unified people, and no elite caste of wizards should arise, it has long been the tradition that Norrlings, both male and female, mate only at certain times and only with partners who do not possess the power to a high degree."

Arwyn nodded his understanding.

"Of course," Fystus added, "those traditions are observed only here in Ombernorr. Some of the majja who emigrate to the Warmlands are known to ignore those restrictions, along with others."

"You are thinking of Teron?" Arwyn asked with a smile.

"Oh, he was among the first. But many have followed that path." Fystus pointed with his pipe. "Now let me ask you a question. Does this curiosity about our mating customs have anything to do with Mirafra the Tree Pipit? I could not help but notice how fondly you two look at each other."

Arwyn felt his cheeks flush. "I ... We were friends from the first. And after we were thrown together by danger, that friendship grew stronger. She saved my life at the risk of her own. But, whatever my feelings for her might be, I am certain she regards me as a friend and nothing more."

"I see." Fystus may not have sounded convinced.

Arwyn continued, "I ask that you do not mention this part of our conversation to her—or anyone else."

Fystus smiled kindly. "Do not worry, young lord. Emus are habitually quiet birds."

That afternoon, their second in Montodoro, Mirafra sat in front of the flameless hearth, helping Arwyn with his language lessons. Suddenly, a gray pigeon flew into the room. The bird strutted back and forth on the mantel, and produced a voice without changing to human form. This was a method sometimes employed by maestras in the Sanctuary—to temporarily use a bird as a messenger.

"You are Mirafra the Tree Pipit?" the small voice cooed.

Mirafra had risen from the couch. "Yes."

"You are summoned by the Flock of Psithic Propriety. Come at once, please."

"Where?"

"I shall lead."

The pigeon looped toward the door. Mirafra hurried after, then stopped and called, "Wait a moment, please."

She ran to her bed chamber and took the Crane psithe from the chest where it was stored. With both psithes draped over her neck, she hurried after the impatient pigeon.

In the hallway outside, she met Clorinda, accompanied by another messenger, a green sparrow.

"There you are, Mirafra. Good. It's best not to keep the Flock waiting."

They followed the birds across an icy courtyard, then through corridors and up wide flights of steps. At length, they arrived in a domed council chamber similar to the one where they had met yesterday with the Congregation of Extra-Territorial Affairs.

But here the atmosphere was far less welcoming. Eight majja sat at an ebony table. Instead of bird costumes they wore plain black robes, with white wimples tight against grim faces. No psithes or masks were visible, no hint as to the majja's names or titles, and they spoke no introductions. It all reminded Mirafra of her frightening dreams during the voyage.

"Mirafra the Tree Pipit," one of the majja said. "It is reported to us that you were involved in the improper use of an advanced psithe."

"Incorrect." Clorinda shook her head. "The Crane psithe was entrusted to Mirafra's care by her mentor, who was dying. Nothing improper occurred."

"Propriety or impropriety is what we are here to judge," another of the Flock said.

Gathering her courage, Mirafra spoke up: "I was given the psithe by Sharam the Crane. She attuned it to my mind so that I could escape with my life and, if possible, return it to Montodoro." She removed the chain from around her neck and held it up. "Which I now have done."

"That you brought back the psithe is commendable," said a majja at the end of the table.

"Still, there are questions of propriety," said another.

"Nothing improper occurred," Clorinda insisted. "The circumstances were extreme. Sharam and Mirafra both acted correctly."

"We accept that the Tree Pipit's use of the maestra's psithe was appropriate for preserving her life," another of the Flock said. "But from the testimony given yesterday before the Congregation of Extra-Territorial Affairs, we understand she has used the Crane psithe after her escape. She has, in fact, been using two psithes on an ongoing basis. This must certainly be judged improper."

"I disagree." Teron the Mooncrow strode into the chamber, inciting gasps of surprise and shock.

"What is he doing here?"

"Most improper."

"He was not invited."

Teron offered a sweeping bow. "Forgive the intrusion, honored majja. Sometimes, one must enter uninvited so that justice may be done."

"We'll decide here what is just—we, and not some renegade *male* wizard."

"Bold rascal, isn't he?"

The word "Rascal" was echoed in whispers up and down the table.

Teron ignored them. "The point is, Mirafra continued to use the Crane psithe under my direction, to build her skills in case she needed to use it again. And she did need to use it again: first to help heal an ailing queen, later to protect her life and that of others from assassins. Had she not built those skills, she might not have lived long enough to fulfill her mission and return the psithe here."

"Is what this man says true?" one of the Flock asked.

Both Mirafra and Clorinda confirmed it.

Despite their antagonism, the members of the Flock seemed swayed by Teron's words. Without asking further questions, they invoked a curtain of silence, a thick mist that descended over the table.

Now Mirafra could neither see nor hear the Flock. She glanced up at Teron and whispered, "Thank you."

The debate lasted only a few moments. Then the mist disappeared.

"Mirafra the Tree Pipit." A majja spoke from the center. "Given the extraordinary circumstances, you are absolved of all impropriety. It is the decision of this Flock that you may now surrender the Crane psithe and continue in your use of the Tree Pipit."

But Mirafra had other ideas. With courage inspired by Teron's intervention, she spoke up. "Sisters, if I may address you. I do not think I should continue with the Tree Pipit. I believe my wielding of the Crane has raised my capacity, and that limiting myself to the psithe of a tyro would risk damaging that psithe and perhaps my mind as well."

"What? Surely you don't mean you expect to keep the maestra's psithe!"

"No, that *would* be improper. I only ask that I be permitted to surrender the Tree Pipit in the Birdhouse and claim a new psithe— trusting the powers of the Sanctuary to provide one proper to my current level."

The wimpled mages looked at one another. Several nodded, and the curtain of mist descended again. The wait was longer this time, but at last the curtain lifted.

"Mirafra the Tree Pipit, it is the decision of this Flock that you surrender the Crested Crane psithe to us at this time."

The majja held out her hand. Mirafra stepped forward and placed the Crane disk on the table.

As she backed away, the woman continued, "Furthermore, after the proper period of fasting and preparation, you will be allowed to enter the Birdhouse, to release the Tree Pipit and claim a new psithe, according to our ancient tradition."

Mirafra bowed, hiding her smile.

"The Flock is now dispersed!"

Spheres of light burst at the table. The eight wizards changed into birds and flew off.

Chapter 13

Clorinda kindly offered to serve as Mirafra's mentor for her advancement. The Ibis made arrangements with the responsible high maestras. Mirafra would be admitted to the Birdhouse after the required eight days of preparation. She would be assigned a meditation cell and given the ritual texts to study.

But while the plans could be made and Mirafra could prepare herself mentally, her actual period of isolation would have to wait. Clorinda and Teron both agreed that she must be available for meeting with the Supreme Gathering. Her testimony might be crucial.

Everyone hoped the Gathering would take some action against Jovadia the Bittern, though no one was sure what that action might be.

Mirafra had another worry. If the Supreme Gathering agreed to a plan, it was likely that Clorinda would need to return to Occitan as soon as possible. Would she be able and willing to wait until Mirafra had entered the Birdhouse and claimed a new psithe?

For Mirafra, that question opened a maze of uncertainties and fears. Would Arwyn and the others be forced to leave her behind? Might she go with them carrying only the Tree Pipit psithe?

Or might it be better to stay at Montodoro in any case? Here, all was peaceful, and she was safe. She could avoid facing the terrors of the Warmlands ever again.

But that would mean abandoning her friends, abandoning Arwyn.

What was her duty? Where was her proper course?

For all she had learned since becoming a majja, she still seemed to know herself so little.

Two days after surrendering the Crane psithe, Mirafra received the summons to the Supreme Gathering. She donned her feathered cape and the Tree Pipit disk on its chain. In the corridor outside her room, she met Arwyn and Clorinda. Presently, Teron and Topiedeon joined them.

"I don't understand why I can't come along," the bard was saying. "Don't tell me it's for magicians only. Here, see Arwyn is going!"

"Sorry, you're not invited," Teron laughed. "Arwyn *was* invited, I'm sure, because they'll want to hear his testimony."

"Agh!" Topiedeon threw up a hand. "It might have made such a fine song ... 'The Birds of Montodoro, perched so high ...'"

Teron laughed. "Now remember," he said to Mirafra, Arwyn, and Clorinda, "Don't be intimidated. We must state our case forcefully. Whatever their reluctance, we must convince these maestras to take action."

"Oh! Listen to the Mooncrow in command." Topiedeon sneered. "Don't forget, Teron, you are only here to lend your airship."

"Yes, and the captain and crew of that ship are complaining to me incessantly about boredom. We must get these matters settled!"

Fystus the Emu came waddling down the hall. "Sorry if I kept you waiting. I was lost in my studies and didn't hear the messenger at first."

A sparrow flew down from the ceiling, and a voice was projected into the air: "Now that you are all here, please follow this bird."

Mirafra had nearly forgotten how far it was from the outer precincts of the Sanctuary to the central dome. After crossing the courtyard, the party marched on a circuitous route through towering corridors with crystal arches, wide stairways with marble railings, grand halls lined with murals that shimmered and moved.

At last they crossed a curved chamber, the edge of a ring supported by columns carved to resemble trees. Passing through golden doors on which birds flew among stars, they entered the central rotunda.

But though the domed space was huge, it seemed empty. As they moved toward the center, the sparrow flew off. Then lights of many colors flashed around them.

"Don't let the displays unnerve you," Clorinda said, she being the only one of them who had walked in this place before. "And let me do the talking."

A column of white light swooped down in front of the visitors. Within the column, an image appeared: a long neck and beak. "Welcome to the Hall of the Supreme Gathering. I am Eucary the Trumpeter Swan, Chair of the Gathering for this cycle."

"Greetings, Sister High Maestra." Clorinda bowed.

The others followed her example.

"This is certainly a different show than the Gathering at Ptolloden," Teron remarked under his breath.

The Swan stared coolly. "This is not Ptolloden, and your flippancy does you no credit, Teron the Mooncrow."

Teron smiled and bowed again. "My apologies, Lady. I fear I have often been called a flippant fellow."

The high maestra ignored him, eyes shifting. "These others I perceive to be Mirafra the Tree Pipit, Arwyn the Duke, and Fystus the Emu, whom we have met already."

Other pillars of light in different colors now drifted near the Trumpeter Swan. By their faces and plumage, Mirafra recognized some of the high maestra species: Flamingo, Albatross, Penguin, White Eagle.

"We have analyzed the reports of your interrogation by the Congregation of Extra-Territorial Affairs," Eucary said. "We will now ask each of you to repeat your testimony so that this Gathering can read your experiences at deep levels to gain better insight. Sister Clorinda, please begin. Tell us all you know of Jovadia the Bittern."

Calmly, the Ibis repeated her account, from the first rumors she had heard of the Bittern. While she spoke, Mirafra watched the high maestras appear and fade in their floating posts of light. Sometimes they asked questions.

"What exactly did you perceive when probing the Bittern's activities with your psithe?"

"Why are you so certain that this Count Halsark was under Jovadia's influence?"

When Clorinda had finished, the White Eagle asked, "Have you considered, Sister, that your animosity toward the Bittern might result from simple jealousy of a wizard who has surpassed your own accomplishments?"

The Ibis stretched her neck. "No, I have not. But considering it now, I find the suggestion preposterous. All I have told you is based on dispassionate assessment."

Called to testify next, Mirafra tried her best to match Clorinda's emotionless tone. Still, her voice faltered as she described the attack on the castle and the death of her mentor.

"You served your maestra well," A sympathetic bird, who identified herself as Olltalo the Penguin, spoke from an icy blue pillar. "To be precise, Sharam told you her brain had been struck by a bolt of force."

"Yes, High Maestra. She believed it must have been Jovadia."

Arwyn was called next, and he made no attempt to speak calmly or veil his emotions. As he recounted his fight with the strange warriors and the death of his family, his rage seemed to echo through the air of the magical chamber. None of the Gathering questioned him further.

Finally, it was Teron's turn. The Mooncrow provided a cool analysis of all he had perceived, from the growing sense of unnatural magic in Arabhedden, to the night of the attack on Duneidan Castle, and later his certainty in Baivonne that Count Halsark had indeed been spellbound by powerful magic. Teron also volunteered, without being asked, that Mirafra had acted properly in dealing with the psithe of her maestra, and that both she and Arwyn had demonstrated remarkable bravery.

"As one who describes himself as flippant," the Trumpeter Swan observed, "you seem to take these matters very seriously."

"Indeed," Teron answered. "Hopefully that conveys to all of you high ladies how serious these matters are. Based on my experience, I fear the high masters of Ptolloden will remain mired in indecision, doing nothing to stop this menace until perhaps it is too late." He jabbed a finger, pointing at the floating images. "I very much hope that the Supreme Gathering of Montodoro will show better wisdom."

Mirafra observed that a few of the light pillars actually fluttered at his words.

"We recognize the gravity of the situation," the Flamingo answered.

"And we will take your testimony into consideration," the Swan added.

"High Maestras, if I may?" Fystus spoke up for the first time. "Based on observing this direct testimony, have you reached any further conclusions as to the nature of the Bittern's powers?"

The air sizzled for several moments as the Gathering exchanged unspoken thoughts. Finally, the Trumpeter Swan floated near.

"The Gathering is agreed. All we have heard here supports the belief that the magical disturbances emanating from the Warmlands are the result of ancient psithic techniques, most likely methods described under the rubric *cold fire*."

"Yes, that fits." Fystus nodded. "From what I remember, those methods involved the transformation of many birds into psithes, along with techniques to coordinate their powers."

"Exactly. Practices that arose in the Age of Chaos and were eventually banned."

"So, if that is Jovadia's scheme, what will you do to stop her?" Teron demanded.

The Trumpeter Swan sighed. "Rest assured, Mooncrow, we shall decide on a course of action according to established doctrine, as is our sacred duty."

"I will communicate this new information to Ptolloden," Fystus said. "I am certain our archives contain some knowledge of the cold fire."

"We thank you, honored Emu," the Swan said. "We already have scholars studying our ancient books and maestras assigned to probe spiritual memories to discover what they can on the subject."

After another sizzling pause, she added. "The Supreme Gathering will make all efforts to learn more and will reconvene in eight days time to review our findings and determine what actions, if any, should be taken. You visitors will be invited then to attend, should you wish."

With that, the columns of light disappeared. The huge chamber lay dim in the silence.

At the close of the Gathering, Cicalia the White Eagle changed to her bird form and flew to another dome. There, she perched in a high gallery overlooking the interior and waited. She was not sure if her fellow high maestra would respond to her request to meet, but had decided it would be interesting to try.

She did not have long to wait. Presently, a gray-winged albatross swooped across the air beneath the dome and settled on the railing. The White Eagle had not changed back to human form, and neither did Salnour the Albatross.

Therefore, Cicalia spoke through audible thought projection. "Thank you for answering my invitation, honored Sister."

"Of course," Salnour replied with a guarded tone. "I assume you wish to discuss the results of the Gathering."

"Indeed. In this instance, I sense that our views, though normally opposed, might actually converge."

As a leader of the Flight of Exploration, Cicalia generally favored investigation of ancient magic, as well as expanded relations with the Warmlands. Salnour, in contrast, was known as a strict Isolationist.

"I see." Salnour's voice spoke slowly. "Because neither of us favors interfering with this Bittern?"

"Exactly. And based on this common ground, it seems we should be allies."

"That may be possible, so long as our preferences harmonize." The Albatross turned her head to stare down at the empty rotunda. "Wasn't Jovadia the Bittern at one time your pupil?"

"Indeed, an exceptionally capable majja. I was sorry when she decided to leave Montodoro, though I could appreciate how she felt suppressed here."

"Suppression that was perfectly proper, as one can see from what she has become since leaving Montodoro."

Cicalia glanced at the arcing dome. "I do not condone her present activities. I would merely point out that, under proper guidance, her talents could have flourished and been used for positive ends. In the present situation, my desire would be that we watch the Bittern's projects and learn from them. Perhaps, if she becomes a true danger to us, that we capture her and bring her back to Montodoro, where we can either reform her or, at the least, profit from all of her acquired knowledge."

"Knowledge that is forbidden, activities that have been banned long ago."

Cicalia gave an inward sigh. "There's no need to debate our differing philosophies; we both know those contrasts well enough.

The point is, in this instance, we both strongly oppose Montodoro's interfering at the present time."

Salnour considered "That much is true. So what are you asking of me?"

"Merely that you continue to express this view to our fellow high maestras, urge them toward not interfering. I shall be doing the same, of course."

The Albatross gave a nod. "I will do that much. As you say, in this cause we are allied."

"Excellent. With the two of us advocating non-interference, and the lack of recent precedent, I expect we can thwart any precipitous actions. My one reservation is these visitors, the Ibis and Emu, and the Mooncrow most of all. They may find a way to sway the Gathering. Or they might choose to attack Jovadia without official sanction. I will be keeping my eye on them, I promise you."

Chapter 14

That afternoon, Mirafra began her preparations. Because the Supreme Gathering would not meet again for eight days, she might just have time to complete her advancement in the Birdhouse and attend the council's meeting on the same day. Clorinda assured her she would not be required to attend the next Gathering, since her testimony had now been given, but Mirafra wanted to be there if she could. Above all, she wanted to make sure to secure her new psithe before Clorinda and Teron decided to return to the Warmlands.

Taking only the Tree Pipit psithe and the new feathered garments she had been given here in Montodoro, she accompanied the Ibis to a remote northern wing of the Sanctuary. Here, the maestra in charge recorded her arrival, gave her documents to study, and scheduled her entry into the Birdhouse for eight days hence. The official then conducted Mirafra to an isolation cell, a small, windowless room with only a sleeping mat and a single candle for light.

The maestra departed, shutting the door, leaving Mirafra in total darkness. With a sigh, she fumbled for her disk. It took several attempts before she managed to change it into a blade and summon a flame to light the candle.

After removing her shoes, Mirafra sat on the sleeping mat, her back against the stone wall, feet tucked at her hips. She picked up the first parchment and read in the flickering light.

It was more than two years since she last entered the Birdhouse. Still, Mirafra remembered the instructions well. They required the candidate to review her life with her present psithe. How had she developed her powers? What had she learned about herself? Most importantly, how had she been of service?

Mirafra asked herself these questions over and over, contemplation interspersed with periods of deep breathing, eyes shut in meditation. The candle would burn for twelve hours. Mirafra let it burn out, then sat in the dark for a long time before finally lying down to sleep.

Next morning, a majja knocked on her door and opened it. Without speaking, she set a tray on the floor—bread, curds, water, the candidate's one meal for the day. A new candle was also provided. Rather than lighting it, Mirafra left the door open so she could burn the candle late into the night.

After eating, she performed the required exercises with the psithe—disk, wand, cup, and blade. These wakened her muscles and helped attune her mind to what came next.

Leaving her cell, she paced in silence through the lamp-lit corridors, past other doors, both open and shut. She encountered a few majja in bird masks, but they only nodded. After climbing a narrow stairway, she pushed open a bronze-framed door.

Her cramped cell had been cold, but not nearly so cold as the terrace where she now emerged. The air hung frigid and moist, flagstones and railings coated in frost. Just beyond the terrace towered white cliffs—the edge of the polar glacier.

Two other candidates were already seated on the hard stone, facing the walls of ice. Mirafra walked past them to a spot near the balustrade. Here the aspiring majja were required to meditate each day for four hours—as marked by a bell in a tower nearby. Only the heat produced by their psithes would keep them from freezing.

Mirafra sat down on the painfully cold stone. The Tree Pipit psithe was already in its blade form. Focusing her mind, she cast in power to warm herself.

She contemplated the same questions as last night. What had she become as a Tree Pipit? How had she been of service? She recalled her time at Montodoro, all of the classes and studies. Then the surprise of being chosen by Sharam the Crane to become her apprentice, followed by the arduous journey to the Warmlands, the nervousness and excitement of discovering that whole different world with its strange and intriguing people. And her constant worries about not being worthy. Then, that terrible night it all burned down around her: the attack by the horrible warriors, the murder of Sharam and so many others.

Here in the icy cold, those memories felt all the more real and terrifying.

But here, on this second day, the ritual required her to begin asking other questions as well: What level of power did she wish to attain? For what purpose? What did she aspire to become?

Mirafra's eyes roamed over the jagged white walls, the ice that stretched all the way to the top of the world. After all she had been through, she had come back to this cold and empty place.

Now she had to find answers.

A blizzard blew in from the western ocean, the wind howling for hours.

In a large common dining room, warmed by magical stones, Teron and his entire party shared a midday meal—heated oats, cheeses, fruits, and steaming hog meat. (Fowl, of course, was never eaten at Montodoro.) Clorinda and Fystus had joined them, along with Dona Delores and all 18 of her crew, seated at three long tables.

It was the fourth day of Mirafra's isolation.

"Surely she won't go outside in this," Arwyn exclaimed, staring out the tall windows at the blizzard.

"Outdoor meditation is required each morning, regardless of the weather," Clorinda answered. "Don't worry. Her psithe will keep her warm."

"She is stronger than you think," Teron said, lifting a cup of ale.

"I know her strength, believe me." Arwyn shook his head numbly. "But I *am* worried."

"I worry about my ship," Dona Delores said from across the table. "She's never experienced weather like this, I promise you."

Till now, a few of the airmen had stayed on board the *Pomegranate* in shifts. Today, because of the storm, the stoves and boilers had been shut down and everyone brought indoors.

"We will make her airworthy again, my dear captain," Teron grinned and held up his wand. "Even if it takes some magical repairs."

"Ha!" Dona Delores clenched her lips. She had complained to the Mooncrow at least once a day that she and her crew were growing restless. When, oh when, would they be leaving?

"Perhaps a song will lighten the mood." Topiedeon stood, holding his mandolin.

"Might you be persuaded to sing for us, then?" Teron asked loud enough for all to hear.

Voices called out their encouragement.

"Well, in fact, I have a new composition, quite jaunty if I say so myself. Thank you, thank you! Since you all insist, I will sing it now!"

Topiedeon might have drunk too much. He stepped up onto the chair and almost lost his balance. Amid the hoots and laughter, he strummed and began:

I sing of my friend the magician
Whose fame you must surely know.
But is he Zeneon the Enchanter?
Or might he be Teron the Mooncrow?

Claims he's a simple a performer

On stage does clever tricks,
But also bears warnings to kings and high wizards,
Though he says he abhors politics.

I've seen him as hero and rescuer
Seen him vanquish many a foe
So is he Zeneon the Enchanter?
Or might he be Teron the Mooncrow?

Boisterous laughter and applause filled the dining room. Grinning, the minstrel played a flourish, then took his bow.

Teron changed his wand to a sword and fingered the edge. "Very witty. But you will *not* be singing that on any stage."

Topiedeon laughed at the pretended threat. "For private audiences only, I assure you."

Mirafra cast her mind into the psithe-blade, trying desperately to create more heat. With the snow blowing fiercely all around, her life depended on this tiny bit of magic. The wind stung her eyes and made her fingers numb. In all her life, she had never felt such horrible cold.

It was rare for a majja to freeze to death while meditating outdoors, but it had been known to happen. Mirafra could return inside, of course. But that would void the days she had already spent in isolation. She would have to start the preparations all over again.

That would mean admitting failure. And she feared failure most of all.

As the cold stung her face, other terrors streamed through her. Memories of fears from childhood, of the cold and dark as storms blew over the tundra. Her parents had done their best by her, but her mother had died when Mirafra was only six, and her father was often away chasing food. She and other village children were left in the care of elderly women who had too much work to do, too little strength for nurturing.

So Mirafra the child was often afraid.

The wind died down a bit. With the psithe blade blazing, she was able to regain some focus.

Concentrate on the questions: What level of power did she wish to attain? For what purpose? What did she aspire to become?

She wanted a powerful psithe, so she could go back to the Warmlands and be of service, so she could help defeat Jovadia, help King Carswell restore peace, help Arwyn reclaim his home.

It all felt impossible. She was only a small young woman, huddled against a blizzard in a dark world of wind and ice. Surely, it would be wiser to stay here in Montodoro, to spend her life in service to the Sanctuary.

Wiser and safer. Safer and less terrifying.

But also confining.

And that would be admitting failure. Wouldn't it?

If only she could be like the Mooncrow, so free and fearless, yet always willing to help, to serve the good no matter the risks.

But Mirafra was no Mooncrow, only a little person wrapped in her terrors.

What kind of psithe did she deserve? What did she aspire to be?

As the freezing wind blew, the answer rose from the core of her soul: a wizard of power, so she could return to the Warmlands and be a force for good.

If only she could find the strength.

Exactly at noon, on the eighth day after the start of her preparations, Mirafra faced the golden doors of the Birdhouse. The doors stood eight yards tall, round-arched, and cast with 640

figures—one representing each bird of the Norrling order as defined by Montodoro.

Mirafra was barefoot. She wore only a plain white robe, with the Tree Pipit disk tucked inside a pocket. Eight majja stood beside her, four on each side. They were dressed in feathered robes and beaked masks. Each carried a psithe-wand that cast a pale, quivering light in the otherwise dark vestibule.

"Sister Tree Pipit, we wish you well," said the woman next to Mirafra. And the others echoed, "We wish you well."

One at a time, each majja stepped forward and pointed her wand at the bird figure that represented her rank. One by one, the carvings rose. Each was a lever, and when all eight birds had been lifted by the levitating power of the wands, the gold doors swung inward.

After bowing to the eight majja, Mirafra straightened her shoulders and walked toward the Birdhouse. Pausing at the threshold, she reached into her pocket and clutched the psithe-disk. Then she marched forward, as steadily as she could.

The giant doors swung shut, leaving her in utter darkness.

The architecture of the Birdhouse blocked out all but a select few vibrations. This near-perfect screening of energies altered the modality of space, making the domed chamber a place of utter stillness. The few beams of vibrations that were allowed to penetrate created, by their carefully arranged intersections, the doorway Mirafra had entered and also numerous interspatial "windows" that opened out onto various spots around the world—spots chosen because they were the habitats of the 640 species of birds.

Several paces inside, Mirafra stopped, overwhelmed by a magical sense of emptiness. Opening her hand, she chanted words in the Norrling tongue, returning the Tree Pipit to its natural body. Tiny claws pressed on her palm as the bird shifted in confusion.

"I thank you, my little friend, and I am sorry that I stressed you," Mirafra said. "Fly now, and be free."

She lifted her hand, and the pipit flew off. A moment later, she glimpsed light and a flicker of wings as the bird flew back to its natural place in the world.

Mirafra heaved a deep breath. Now she only needed to wait. The forces of the Birdhouse would probe her spirit and select a matching psithe.

Presently, a faint breeze stirred, warm with the scent of flowers. Mirafra sensed a bird flying above her, circling in confusion, chirping in distress. She reached up her hand and called soothingly, imitating the bird's cries. After a few moments, the bird fluttered down and settled on her wrist.

Mirafra stroked the feathered back, feeling the life force within. Whispering ritual words, she slowed the life vibrations. A spark appeared and expanded as the bird's body faded. Mirafra glimpsed a red throat and silver feathers, bright lively eyes.

Then she was holding her new psithe, a sphere of white energy with scarlet flashes. The power felt strong, not so overwhelming as the Crested Crane, but much stronger than the Pipit.

Strong and aligned with her being—with her spirit and her purpose.

A short time later, Mirafra marched out of the Birdhouse, holding her new psithe as a gleaming red wand. The eight majja had noted which bird figure on the doors tilted up when Mirafra opened them from inside.

So they greeted her as "Sister Ruby Lark."

Chapter 15

Clorinda awaited Mirafra at the entrance to the precinct.
"You have your new psithe. Excellent! What is it?" She peered at the wand and found the answer mentally. "The Ruby Lark! Oh, very good, Mirafra. You are an adept now. Congratulations!"

"Thank you!" Mirafra knew it would take quite some time for her to absorb that fact.

"Now come, we must hurry! The Supreme Gathering is about to meet."

Mirafra was still barefoot, still dressed in the white robe of initiation. Garments to match her new rank would have to wait. She raised no objection as the Ibis grabbed her wrist and hustled her down the high corridors and stone stairways.

At length, they reached the pillared chamber that ringed the central dome of the Sanctuary. Arwyn, Teron, and Fystus stood waiting near the tall doors.

"You made it!" Arwyn cried and impulsively gave Mirafra a hug. "Are you all right?"

"Yes. I think so." She laughed, grateful to be back in the world again, back with her friends.

Clorinda leaned close to Teron and Fystus. She whispered, but loud enough for all to hear, "Ruby Lark. She's an adept!"

Teron grinned and put a hand on her shoulder. "Well done, Mirafra!"

"You'll have to tell me all about it," Arwyn said. "Well, as much as you can, anyway."

"I will," she whispered. "Later."

Her eyes roamed over the giant columns carved in the shapes of trees, the gold doors with their images of birds flying amid stars. Her exhilaration settled, giving way to fatigue—and nervousness, as she wondered what the Supreme Gathering would now decide.

The others spoke in muted voices, mostly discussing the same question, or else complaining about having to wait so long. After a time, another majja walked silently from among the columns. When she came close, Mirafra recognized Lilia the Kingfisher, leader of the Congregation of Extra-Territorial Affairs. Here to report, Mirafra surmised, on any new findings from her group. The Kingfisher stopped a short distance from the others, nodded in greeting, spoke not at all.

Finally, with a swishing sound, the doors of the central chamber slipped open. A deep, disembodied voice bid them enter.

With Clorinda leading the way, they marched into the huge chamber. Ahead of them, at the middle of the floor, the columns of light appeared, with the forms of the eight high maestras clearly visible within. Mirafra gathered that today's meeting was of a different ritual form, since the columns did not flicker and vanish but shone steadily, like solid, translucent stone. Each column even had a panel etched on the front with the name and rank of the high maestra.

Eucary the Trumpeter Swan spoke from within her column. "I now call the Gathering to order. Let it be recorded that on this 24th day of the Month of Darkest Sky, in the Norrling Year 6252, the Supreme Gathering of Montodoro met, the eight current officials all being present, by name: Alexandra the Tinamou, Tirabelle the Flamingo, Salnour the Albatross, Morgaine the Chat, Eucary the Trumpeter Swan (chairing the gathering), Olltalo the Penguin, Margaretto the Sandgrouse, Cicalia the White Eagle."

Glancing out from her column, she also noted the presence of witnesses and advisors and named each in turn. Mirafra was only mildly surprised when Eucary called her "Mirafra, the Ruby Lark." The news had traveled fast.

"We are here to discuss and vote upon a serious matter," Eucary said. "Our studies have indicated, with evidence we consider conclusive, that a renegade majja known as Jovadia the Bittern is practicing forbidden psithic magic in the Warmlands. While many wizards in these times have chosen to leave Montodoro and Ptolloden, and an unknown number of these may be pursuing unsanctioned practices, the danger of this case can no longer be ignored.

"To review what we know: Jovadia departed Montodoro six years ago, following a dispute regarding denial of her advancement to maestra. Within two years, reports were received that she had gathered a small following of renegade majja and was studying ancient techniques. Some time thereafter, she became Court Wizard to the King of Llorrland, a post she still holds. In the past year, growing disturbances have been observed, originating from the vicinity of that same Llorrland. Then, some 40 days ago, the King of Llorrland attacked the southern principality of Duneidan. Eyewitnesses to this attack have testified that Jovadia used a psithic bolt to kill one of our sisters, Sharam the Crested Crane. These same witnesses report that the attack on the castle was executed by armored warriors that seemed all but invulnerable to weapons. The night of that attack corresponded to the strongest wave of disturbances that had yet been detected.

"These matters have now been analyzed by mental probings over distance, by investigation of past-life memories, and by studying ancient texts, both here and in Ptolloden. From all of this evidence, the Gathering has concluded that Jovadia has acquired a multitude of psithes and is using an archaic technique known as the *cold fire* to focus and coordinate their powers. The cold fire can be used for multiple purposes, such as strengthening the life force and power of

Jovadia herself, and converting and animating these invulnerable warriors, which the ancient texts call *zolgars*."

Eucary paused, turning to the Kingfisher. "Sister Lilia, based on the Congregation's latest studies, do you agree with the aforementioned summary?"

"I do, High Maestra. All we have seen this week corroborates these statements."

"Do you have any new information to share?"

The Kingfisher answered solemnly, "Only that the disturbances have continued to strengthen, leading us to believe that the number of captured psithes is growing, along with the power of the cold fire."

Eucary now turned to Fystus. "Master Emu, as our ambassador from Ptolloden, do you agree with what has been spoken? And do you have any knowledge to add?"

Fystus took a step forward. "Honored High Maestras, as you know, I was dispatched from Ptolloden precisely because the high masters there are concerned about these disturbances. All that I have been able to learn from ancient records certainly aligns with your conclusions. Also, some weeks ago, Ptolloden sent a wizard to the Warmlands to attempt to infiltrate Jovadia's circle of followers. I learned this week via qorm dream that that person has disappeared without a trace. While this is dream communication and therefore not confirmable, it aligns with the understanding that the Bittern is collecting psithes by either recruiting or killing their Norrling holders."

Fystus bowed and took a step back.

The Trumpeter Swan paused to survey the birds in the other pillars. "Sisters, I believe the time has come when we must act. My own view is this: Jovadia the Bittern left her duties at this Sanctuary without permission. Since moving to the Warmlands, she has collected an unknown number of psithes in a proscribed manner. From all testimony, she has murdered fellow wizards and used their psithes to build her power. Further, she has used this power to convert men into unnatural soldiers that are her slaves. I say we must take action to stop this renegade. I open the floor for comments."

She held up her hand, staring at Teron. "Comments only from the Supreme Gathering at this time, if you please, Master Mooncrow."

Teron showed a wry smile as he bowed his acknowledgement.

Salnour the Albatross was the first to speak. "My position is well known, and I have enunciated it in conversations with many high maestras in recent days. I firmly believe defenses against this heinous renegade should be prepared, but that no actions should be taken unless and until the Bittern threatens Ombernorr. Her activities in the Warmlands should be no concern of ours."

"By the time her power threatens Ombernorr it may be much harder to stop her," Olltalo the Penguin observed. "I say we should act now!"

Sizzling and rumbling noises emerged from several pillars.

"Sisters, if I may," Cicalia the White Eagle spoke up. "While my beliefs fly far from Sister Salnour's Isolationist view, I do agree with her that we should avoid precipitous action. I strongly prefer that we observe Jovadia's projects and learn from her discoveries. Among other benefits, such knowledge would teach us the best methods to counter her if and when that becomes necessary."

Margaretto the Sandgrouse responded, "How interesting to see the Isolationist and Interventionist sisters in agreement for once. But I fear their views are equally ill-advised. As our Sister Penguin said, the longer we delay, the harder it will likely be to stop Jovadia."

After some quieter sizzling, Tirabelle the Flamingo said, "I agree we must act, and the sooner the better. The critical question is how. Do we send a force of majja against the Bittern and her king? If so, how many would be enough?"

"Would any number be enough?" Olltalo the Penguin asked. "Who knows how much power she has gathered with this cold fire?

And we would also have to contend with this Warmlander king and his army."

"Sisters, please." Eucary spread her hands. "Before we can consider what actions to take, we must first agree to *take* action. If there is no further comment, let me rephrase as a motion to put to the vote. Thus: The Supreme Gathering agrees to use whatever powers are necessary to defeat Jovadia the Bittern, to neutralize whatever heretical magic she has acquired, and to stop her from doing further harm, and that this is to be accomplished as soon as possible. Now, with this motion on the table, please simply vote Yea or Nay."

She looked to the far left of the line of columns. The Tinamou voted Yea. The Flamingo followed suit.

Salnour the Albatross simply shook her head. Beside her, Morgaine the Chat also voted Nay.

Eucary herself voted Yea. The Penguin and Sandgrouse did the same.

With five votes already against her, Cicalia the White Eagle voiced a loud and sour Nay.

Eucary nodded in satisfaction. "The motion passes by a vote of 5 to 3."

Mirafra let out a breath of relief. She glanced over and noticed that Teron, head still bowed, was smiling.

"So action must be taken, and as swiftly as possible," the Penguin said. "Now back to the question of *what* action."

"I believe we should explore all options." Eucary's fingertips pressed together before her masked face. "Capture Jovadia if we can, kill her only if we must."

"Killing her might not be enough," the Sandgrouse commented. "Remember, she has trained a number of followers. Some may have gained enough knowledge and skill to take her place."

"True," Eucary answered. "We must also discover a way, if we can, to destroy the source of her power." After a pause, she addressed the Kingfisher. "Sister Lilia, how much is written in the ancient sources about the cold fire? Are there records of measures found to be effective in neutralizing it?"

"None that I recall, High Maestra. There may be documents we haven't discovered yet."

"If I may," Fystus raised a hand. "I have not found much either, other than accounts of allowing the cold fire to eventually dissolve of its own accord. But there are some alchemical archives in your library here that may offer a solution."

"Thank you, Master Emu. I ask that you continue your efforts with all diligence." The Trumpeter Swan stretched her neck to glance at the other high maestras. "We now have a consensus of what must be done, and many routes to explore as to *how* it can be done. I direct the Congregation of Extra-Territorial Affairs to explore any and all alternatives: ways to capture Jovadia and to nullify her power."

"Difficult and unprecedented problems," the Flamingo observed. "And, as I mentioned earlier, it may mean raising a force of majja to fly to the Warmlands and do battle. And how large a force will we need?"

"Those ideas must be considered," Eucary agreed. "Sister Kingfisher, please ensure such options are included in your investigations. Recruit help from other assemblies in Montodoro as needed."

A solemn quiet settled over the assembly.

"If there is no further discussion ..." The Trumpeter Swan surveyed the shining columns and the witnesses. "Then I propose we reconvene in eight days to hear the report of the Congregation of Extra-Territorial Affairs, and make every effort then to decide on a course of action. I now declare the Gathering closed."

Chapter 16

"Another eight days!" Dona Delores threw up her hands in dismay. "Really, Senor Teron, this is too much!"

Teron and Topiedeon had come to the captain's apartment to give her the latest news. Several of the crew were relaxing in the comfortable antechamber, including Emilio and Ricardo, Dona Delores' two cousins. All had stood up when the wizard and bard entered.

"I agree, Captain, far too much." Teron showed a grimace of disdain. "The dawdling of these lady high wizards is maddening—endless committees and postponements! I'm starting to think they are even less effective at taking action than the masters of Ptolloden!" His shoulders heaved in a sigh of frustration. "Still, in their defense, I must admit they are dealing with unprecedented and dangerous affairs."

"I understand the dangers," Dona Delores complained. "But we have been anchored for 11 days in this icy wasteland, with nothing to do but sit around eating and drinking. My crew is restless, and who knows what all this freezing weather is doing to the *Pomegranate*?"

"Senora Captain." Young Emilio spoke up. "Perhaps you should ask Senor Teron about our proposal."

"Agh! Well, why not?" She turned back to the Mooncrow. "Emilio and some of the others were thinking, if we were delayed longer, that we might take the ship and explore the coast. They have been pestering me with this idea, and now that we must wait another eight days ..."

"You know that the coast north of here is all glacier," Teron said.

"Yes, but south of here! There must be villages, and eventually cities. Sea vessels of Ibor are known to sail this coast, some even as far as Ombernorr. Remember, we are keeping logs and providing maps to be of interest to the Airship Guild. These will be worth much more if we survey the western coast!"

Emilio and Ricardo were grinning with excitement.

"I can see the added value," Teron admitted. "But I am wary of the risk. We need the ship here when we are ready to leave."

"We can be back before eight days," Dona Delores promised.

"I like the idea," Topiedeon said. "In fact, I'll go along. Sailing the coast might give me inspiration. And there's not much for me here since I am barred from attending your wizard gatherings."

Teron started to object, then shook his head. "I can see I am outvoted. You have my permission, Captain, but only three days out, then three days back. That will leave two days margin. The ship *must* be back here and ready to sail when the next Gathering meets."

The captain smiled her agreement. The crew members cheered.

"Don't worry, Mooncrow," Topiedeon laughed. "You can trust me to keep the captain in line."

"Oh, I doubt that," Teron said. "But then, I don't need to." He stared at Dona Delores. "Our captain is much too wise to cause a Norrling wizard any trouble."

Cicalia leaned her elbows on the onyx rail of a high terrace overlooking the tundra. The late night was clear and cold, lit only by stars and the warming gleam of her psithe-sword.

Footsteps drew near. The White Eagle turned her head with a smooth movement. "Greetings, Sister Salnour. Thank you for accepting my late invitation."

"I do not mind," the Albatross replied, stopping to rest one hand on the rail. "Though I must wonder what there is left for us to discuss, since our position on not interfering with the Bittern was outvoted."

"Yes." The White Eagle stood erect. "The vote was unfortunate. But I prefer to view it as a setback rather than a defeat."

"Meaning what, precisely?"

"Well, bear in mind: any plans of action that our sisters may design are bound to be problematic, their chances of success uncertain at best."

"So what do you propose?" Salnour asked.

"That we stay the course, continue to point out the risks and to urge delay."

The Albatross paused, touched a finger to her lips, then nodded. "Yes, I think we can do that, possibly delay any decision to act for several more meetings at least."

"Good. We are agreed."

"There is that other problem, though," Salnour added. "The Emu and Mooncrow, as you have mentioned. If they come up with a plan against Jovadia, they might decide to act without the Supreme Gathering's approval."

Cicalia's mouth twisted. "Indeed. I will continue to watch them. If necessary, I am certain I can find ways to thwart any actions they may devise."

The throne room of Castle Tonnsburg was illumined by skylights in three domes and by tall casement windows above the side arcades. Ranks of sentries stood among the pillars, and numerous servants and attendants clustered near the dais.

A blare of trumpets sounded, and a herald at the rear of the hall announced Duke Baglan of Duneidan. At long last, Baglan's wait was over.

For six days he had ridden with a detachment of troops—over the hills and valleys of the Arm of Arabhedden, then the broad, well-kept roads of Llorrland. Arriving at last in Tonnsburg, he had been kept waiting another two days before finally being admitted to the presence of the King—the King who had summoned *him* here and claimed he would brook no delay.

Wearing a breastplate, leather breeks, and boots, with a steel helmet tucked in his arm, the Duke strode the length of the red and gold carpet. Approaching the dais, he locked eyes with King Alaric, who watched him with a smile. Flanking the king were his closest officers and ministers, who Baglan remembered from Duneidan, and also one other, who Baglan could never forget.

Yet Jovadia the Bittern, tall and resplendent in her feathered robe and wimple, looked different to him—somehow younger, more feminine. Baglan wondered at the rumors he had heard, that the Norrling wizard had replaced the King's other mistresses, that even Alaric's Queen had left court, retiring to the country. Some even claimed that Jovadia would soon be crowned the new Queen.

Scant evidence for that, Baglan thought, as she gave him a charming smile. For the King to dispose of his Queen, replace her with a Norrling wizard: that would be outrageous indeed.

Of course, stranger things had happened—especially in these strange times.

Baglan stopped at the bottom of the steps and gave a deep bow.

"Ah, Duke Baglan." Alaric spoke as if he had noticed the visitor for the first time. "Good of you to come. Ehh, what is your report, if you please?"

"Your Majesty, as you ordered, your allies in Arabhedden are marshalling their forces. Some lords in the southern highlands are prevaricating, but their numbers are small. Elsewhere, the troops are prepared to march at your command. Of course, this includes the soldiers of Duneidan, consisting of 35 knights and squires and 250 bowmen and foot soldiers."

Jovadia leaned over and whispered in the King's ear. Alaric nodded. "On your return, send riders to these hesitant southern lords. Inform them again that delay will not be tolerated, that if I must, I will send my airships to burn their castles to the ground."

Baglan clenched his lips and bowed.

The King's voice softened. "Thank you, Duke Baglan. You are a loyal vassal. So I will tell you the reason for urgency. I do not plan to wait for spring, but will launch a surprise attack on Occitan as soon as one month from now—that is, as soon as the armies can be ready. This invasion will advance on three fronts. The lords of Arabhedden and southern Llorrland will cross the lowlands in the south. Other troops will attack on the northern flank, with the main forces driving from the center. Occitan's armies will be overwhelmed by the surprise attack and by our superior troops. King Carswell's capital will fall within days, weeks at the most. That is our plan."

Later that afternoon, Baglan was summoned to witness King Alaric's superior troops on display. The forward barbican of the castle overlooked a broad city square, with the gables and roofs of Tonnsburg spread beyond.

Baglan accompanied the King, high-ranking courtiers, and a number of visiting lords. They mounted steps inside the barbican and positioned themselves on the high parapet. Far below, the square stood nearly empty, guarded at the edges by sentries, with a small number of townspeople gathered behind them to watch the parade.

"Now you will see," the King asserted, "a sample of the invincible soldiers who will soon conquer Occitan, and later bring order and peace to all the lands of Tann and Ibor, for that, gentlemen and ladies, is our glorious cause."

Below, trumpets sounded and the march began. First came cavalry, knights by the hundreds riding fine steeds and followed by their squires. As they passed the parapet, they silently raised their lances in salute to the King. Next came ground troops, rank upon rank of spearmen and archers marching in step to loud drums.

Lastly came the zolgars, the deathless warriors in their black armor, striding in perfect cadence. Each carried two longswords, held with arms crossed over their chests. Duke Baglan watched in amazement tinged with horror. The night they took Castle Duneidan there had been thirty. Now he counted over 400.

Below, the drumming ceased. The zolgars turned and faced the high parapet. Raising their swords in salute, they shouted in unison.

"Long live the King. Long live his glorious cause."

An involuntary shiver ran through the Duke's body. Then, he heard a whisper at his ear.

"What do you think, my lord?" Jovadia the Bittern asked.

Collecting himself, he answered sternly. "Most formidable."

"Do I sense disquiet? Remember, there is no room in our alliance for hesitancy or qualms."

"I have none." His voice sounded taut.

"Then show me," the Bittern said.

Baglan stared into her face. Suddenly, he dropped to one knee, raised a hand in salute, and shouted.

"Long live our King! Long live his glorious cause!"

"How is the research going, Master Emu? Any progress?"

Arwyn and Fystus looked up as Clorinda the Ibis approached their table. They sat in a huge circular library under a diamond-white dome. The chamber, hundreds of feet across, was crowded with bookcases, lecterns, couches, and stone tables. It contained more books than Arwyn had ever imagined existing in one place. Fystus had said this was only one of four libraries in Montodoro. Arwyn had answered that he might happily spend the rest of his life in this one room—if he could only master reading the language.

The young Duke had accompanied the Emu here each afternoon. He assisted by fetching volumes from the shelves, helping Fystus find certain pages he had read before, and listening and asking questions while Fystus sorted through his thoughts and theories.

Only four days remained till the Supreme Gathering met again. Clorinda seemed anxious to hear if the Emu had found any solutions.

Fystus stood respectfully, then gestured for the Ibis to take a seat. The vast chamber was empty except for a few lady wizards and birds. They could therefore converse in private.

"We are making some progress, I think," Fystus said. He had taken out his pipe and held it near his mouth, though he did not light it. "One line of inquiry in particular seems promising. We've found several accounts of the use of cold fire as a weapon during a wizards' rebellion in the 31st Century. These accounts are more detailed as to formulas and methods than anything I've read before."

"Will these accounts help us find a way to defeat Jovadia?" Clorinda asked.

"Too early to tell, I'm afraid."

"Well, was a way found during this rebellion to neutralize the cold fire?"

Fystus frowned. "There are conflicting stories. A few accounts mention draining away the power of the cold fire by a spell devised for this purpose, called the *sun fire*. But I've found no record of how this was done. There is also one tale that claims a ring of simple wood fires was able to generate enough heat to negate a small cauldron of cold fire. The common thread is that a conflagration with sufficient heat is tapped to drain away the cold energy."

"I see." Clorinda nodded. "So in theory, we would need to first create a suitable heat source, and then find a way to plunge that heat into Jovadia's cold fire."

"Yes. The second is an interesting problem. In the sun fire accounts, a certain distance between the two energies was deemed an advantage, so that the heat of the sun fire was not itself neutralized. Instead, a conduit was created, forming a one-way connection to draw the cold energy away from the cauldron and into the heat."

"Would neutralizing the cold fire also overcome Jovadia's unnatural warriors?"

"I believe so," Fystus answered. "That is mentioned in the one account I've found that describes the zolgars. And it makes sense, according to the laws of magic. Since their unnatural power is drawn from the cold fire, when the cold fire vanishes, they would become what they were before, mortal men."

"Very good," said the Ibis. "I suppose we would need to find the location of Jovadia's cauldron in order to insert this conduit device."

"That's another problem, to be sure. But first we must find a way to produce sufficient heat. I'm thinking up some experiments to ascertain if that's even possible."

Most of each day, Mirafra practiced with her new psithe: sometimes in an outdoor courtyard, sometimes in a domed chamber reserved for such exercise.

The power of the Ruby Lark amazed her. Her rank of adept was two levels above that of tyro. An advancement that skipped an entire level of the hierarchy was not unprecedented, but it was unusual.

With this rank, Mirafra had no assigned mentor. But both Clorinda and Teron offered coaching.

The psithe-blade could now become either a knife or a sword at her command. She practiced fighting techniques with Arwyn, while Teron watched and offered tips. With the cup, Mirafra could now easily distill water from the air. She studied formulas for creating medicines and tinctures. Concentrating on the wand, she could lift heavy objects with no difficulty. But most thrilling of all was the disk, the qorm attribute. She could now cast complex illusions, could walk the halls past other majja without being noticed. Again, she spent many hours in the library, memorizing chants and spells for advanced uses of the disk.

Three days after the Supreme Gathering, two days after the departure of the *Pomegranate* for its tour of the coast, Mirafra was working in an empty hall near her quarters. Using the wand, she had lifted herself 30 feet into the air and was testing how long she could keep afloat.

"Very good!"

Startled, she looked down to see Teron leaning on a pillar, watching.

"Your endurance is improving, I see."

Careful not to lose concentration, Mirafra lowered herself to the floor.

"Have you attempted the quinteer yet?" Teron asked.

Quinteer, the fifth, quintessential power, the merging of the wizard with the psithe, her body actually becoming the bird. The quinteer was reserved for adepts and maestras, for only they had sufficient control to ensure their minds would remain intact.

Mirafra shook her head. "I haven't been brave enough."

"Well, you are an adept now," Teron said. "So, of course, you must decide these questions for yourself. If you want me to talk you through it, let me know."

Mirafra watched him walk off down the hall. When she was alone again, she gazed down at her wand. Intent on resuming practice, she focused on levitation and rose into the air.

But now she felt challenged.

Teron was right. As an adept, she must not be afraid to test her powers.

She sank down till her feet rested on the shiny floor.

Of course, she already knew the method of the quinteer. Ambitious to try it one day, she had studied and memorized the incantation long ago.

At her will, the psithe resumed its pure-energy form. A sphere of white light rested on her palm, pulsing with faint sparks of scarlet and gold. She stared into the radiance, imagining her body transformed into a ruby lark.

"I invoke the quinteer," she whispered. "I become the bird."

The psithe quivered. She repeated the words in the ancient magical tongue: *"Nyr solelleum quinteer, nie te porm."*

The sphere of light pulsed with her heartbeat. Eyes wide, Mirafra repeated the incantation again and again, focusing her will, calling her power.

The glimmers of color in the psithe became sparks. The sphere burst into a globe of multicolored light. Mirafra's sense of the world dissolved.

The burst of light shrank and vanished—leaving a lark flapping its wings in the dim hallway.

With a cry of delight, she fluttered her wings and flew off.

She was the bird. She was the Ruby Lark.

She looped through the air, soared to the arches of the ceiling, circled high, then dove toward the floor. She recalled that, since early childhood, she had fantasized about this moment, this wild exhilaration.

Soon enough, human thoughts reasserted themselves. She would have to change back. What if she failed?

Reluctantly, she slowed her flight, carefully circled down to settle herself on the floor. In her mind, she recited the words to reverse the spell: I dissolve the quinteer. I am the majja.

Nyr pollocette quinteer, nie te majja.

Her nerves sizzled as the energies separated. Light flashed for a blinding instant.

Then Mirafra was standing alone in the hall, the sphere of the psithe floating before her eyes. With a laugh of delight, she reached out and caressed it.

She *was* the Ruby Lark.

Chapter 17

Arwyn was struggling to understand. "You are going to use the psithe-disk to create two fires, one of them the so-called cold fire?"

"Not exactly," Fystus replied. "Remember, the magic of the disk does not work on the physical plane but on the mental plane. The fires will be mental constructs. According to our teachings, the physical plane that we know is simply a lower expression of the mental plane. So, if our experiment discovers a process that works on the mental plane, that process must also work in the physical world—assuming, of course, we get all the factors right."

They sat in the Emu's apartment. Outside the tall windows, night had fallen. But the comfortable chamber was warm and bright with lanterns.

"But the factors," Arwyn said, "are simply the amounts of energy in the two fires, correct?"

"Yes. But to estimate that, we need both the burning temperature and the quantity of fuel. That is, for the hot fire."

"What about the cold fire?"

"That's actually simpler. The cold fire comes from the conversion of psithes. We don't know how many birds Jovadia may have acquired, so we'll estimate a range of numbers. Say 10 psithes at the low end, perhaps 100 at the high. Of course, more powerful birds yield more energy, but basing our calculations on a mid-range average should suffice."

Fystus straightened in his chair, holding the psithe-disk in both hands. "Now, I'll begin by casting the two fires. Then I will attempt to

163

neutralize the cold fire with the hot. As I make each attempt, I will adjust and call out the projected energy levels. You write those down and the results."

Pen and paper in hand, Arwyn nodded eagerly. He watched as Fystus gazed into the psithe-disk. Soon the disk took on a hovering white glow. The glow rose from the disk and then split into two spheres, which floated in the air in front of the wizard. As Fystus projected more energy, one of the globes turned yellow, burning with flame as in a fireplace. The other shimmered and began to sparkle, white like fallen snow.

"First attempt," the Emu murmured. "Energy of 10 psithes in the cold fire. The hot fire to contain the heat of a cordlet of wood, burning at an average of 110 degrees on the Vexium scale."

Arwyn scribbled the notes. He watched as a tendril of energy flowed from the cold fire to the hot. It penetrated but seemed to have no effect. After a few moments, the tendril disappeared.

"No result from this minimal heat," Fystus confirmed. "As we might have expected."

Again and again, the Emu repeated the experiment—first adding wood to the hot fire, then increasing the estimated energy of the cold.

When the wood fire simulated a tall oak burning, Fystus reported that the cold fire had begun to lose power. But this effect vanished as soon as he increased the projected number of psithes from 10 to 20.

Next, the Emu tried simulating hot fires that burned different grades and amounts of coal. These fuels produced higher temperatures and showed better results. Arwyn recorded the progress made with each adjustment.

After many attempts, Fystus discovered that a hot fire burning a wagonload of hard coal actually neutralized the smallest cold fires. Expanding the amount to ten wagonloads made it possible to drain cold fires formed by up to 30 psithes.

But that seemed to be the upper limit.

Fystus took a rest, massaging his eyelids. "I'm afraid it's no good. We have to assume Jovadia might have as many as 100 psithes captured in her cauldron. For this plan to have a chance, we'd need considerably more energy in the hot fire."

"What about Moldorn fire?" Arwyn asked. "That's the fuel they use in airship bombs."

Fystus lifted his eyebrows. "Yes, I've heard of it. But we'd have to know how hot it burns."

"1400 degrees Vexium," Arwyn said. "That's in the initial explosion, which lasts several seconds, until the fuel is gone."

Fystus gaped. "How do you know that?"

Arwyn shrugged. "I was curious, and the alchemists at King Carswell's court were kind enough to answer my questions."

"I wonder if we could acquire sufficient quantities?"

"Well, each bomb stores about a quart of fuel, and I imagine the King is stocking up a large supply as he prepares for war."

The Emu frowned, flicking his fingers in the air as he calculated the numbers. Finally, he picked up the disk. "Let's try a few more."

Soon the two glowing spheres emerged from the psithe-disk and took on the images of heat and cold. Arwyn watched with pen and paper ready.

"The hot fire contains the fuel of five Moldorn fire bombs, burning at 1400 degrees," Fystus said. "The cold fire stores the energy of 50 psithes."

Presently, a stream of light flowed from the cold sphere to the hot. The cold fire flickered and disappeared.

Fystus turned to Arwyn with a grin. "I think we're on to something!"

They experimented late into the night, adjusting for greater and lesser quantities of Moldorn fire, adding psithes to the cauldron. Fystus also folded in other calculations, such as the possible loss of energy in the transmission through the conduit, and if the Moldorn fire did not burn at optimum temperatures.

In the morning, they repeated the most successful trials, verifying the results. Arwyn carefully checked his notes, then went over them with Fystus.

"Good. Very good," the Emu said. "I think it's time to show the others. But before I can cast any more demonstrations, I'll need some breakfast, and a nap, and a smoke."

"I have summoned you here for an important casting," Cicalia the White Eagle told her three apprentices. "It involves an historical technique we have not used before, a form of weather magic."

She stood on a wool rug woven with magical glyphs. The circular room was part of her private apartment, perched high in a tower on a south-facing wall of the Sanctuary.

Cicalia's trusted apprentices faced her with alert expressions: Jenvi the Starling, Vonna the Mockingbird, Tula the Pintail. All three were adepts and stalwart members of the Flight of Exploration—the faction of which Cicalia was an unofficial leader.

"Psithes in wand form, if you please," Cicalia told them. "You three will use your wands to summon a wind of extreme strength and focus. Using my disk, I will then cast that wind to a distant location."

"What is the purpose of this, High Maestra?" the ever-curious Mockingbird asked.

Cicalia did not mind explaining. "As we've discussed, I am intent on delaying any interference with the activities of Jovadia the Bittern. I firmly believe that her projects are recovering lost knowledge from which we of Montodoro can eventually benefit. At the moment, my most pressing concern is a plan being developed by our visiting male majja—the Emu and Mooncrow. In seeking a way to counter their efforts, a simple solution occurred to me. As you may have heard, the Mooncrow's airship departed some days ago, but is expected back before the next meeting of the Supreme Gathering. By summoning this wind, we will drive the ship far off course, perhaps far enough that its return to Montodoro will become impossible, but at least far enough to delay that return for some days."

"But how will delaying the airship solve the problem?" the Mockingbird asked.

In fact, this was only one of the measures the White Eagle had in mind. She considered divulging her other plan, but decided against it. That magic she could accomplish alone, and the fewer who knew about it, the better.

She answered, "Without their ship, it will take months for our visitors to return to the Warmlands. That should leave more than enough time for Jovadia's current projects to bear fruit—and for us to prepare other measures to capture Jovadia and reap her knowledge, which is our proper goal."

"But if our magic wind only delays the ship for a number of days?" the Mockingbird said.

"I shall monitor its position. If necessary, we will repeat this casting again and again." Cicalia lifted her disk high. "Now, stare into my psithe, and heed my words."

Focusing her mind, she sent a steady pulsing light into the disk. "Raise your wands high, my majja! Circle the tips overhead. By your power, draw wind from north and south, east and west. Circle that wind above this tower, stronger and stronger, higher and higher!"

Moving her disk through the air, Cicalia chanted in the ancient tongue. *Nosca elorbum. Nosca vobalum.* She watched the wands circulate, saw in her mind the winds gathering and spinning above the tower, their force growing and growing.

When the winds had built to the highest level her mind could contain, she lowered the disk and stared into its depths. On the mental plane, she called forth the image of the airship. She found its location many leagues to the south.

Focusing on that image, she drew down the power of the winds, collected the power in her psithe, then thrust it violently away.

"*Tabulatum!*" she cried. "Release!"

Enormous power flowed from the disk, the energy throwing her off balance. But in her mind she glimpsed the devastating effect, the airship swaying from its course, flowing far out over the ocean.

"Are you all right, High Maestra?" the Starling asked anxiously.

"What? Yes!" Cicalia blinked, her vision coming back to the tower. "Yes. Well done, my majja. Well done!"

That afternoon, Teron and Mirafra interrupted their practice session and followed Arwyn down the hall to the Emu's apartment. A messenger had also been sent to Clorinda, and she joined the group a short time later.

Fystus sat in a wooden chair, his back to the wide hearth. The others faced him, seated on a fur-covered couch and soft chairs with footstools.

"I take it you have good news for us," Teron observed.

The Emu lifted up his disk. "I believe I do. Thanks in no small part to this Warmlander lad. I never would have thought of Moldorn fire."

With the notebook in his lap, Arwyn dipped his head and smiled.

"What are you talking about?" Clorinda asked. "Does this have to do with your experiments?"

"Yes. Yes, it does. Let me demonstrate."

Holding the disk in his lap, the Emu stared down with eyes wide. The disk shimmered and shortly produced two spheres of light that floated into the air. Fystus cast more power, and the spheres took on the appearances of flame and ice.

Fystus explained, "One represents Jovadia's cold fire, the other a hot fire that we will produce."

The Emu demonstrated seven of the Moldorn fire simulations, with Arwyn reading from his notes to specify the parameters for each. Mirafra only dimly understood the calculations, but she noted that both Teron and Clorinda seemed surprised and excited.

"To summarize," Fystus said after letting the balls of light fade. "Given sufficient quantities of the Moldorn fire fuel, I believe we can neutralize Jovadia's cold fire. I estimate that if her cauldron has the power of 50 psithes, our probability of success is 95%. If she has acquired as many as 100 psithes, I still see an 85% chance."

Mirafra smiled and squeezed Arwyn's wrist.

The Mooncrow grinned. "Excellent work, Fystus, and Arwyn too."

"Very good news, I agree." Clorinda stood and began pacing. "Now, for this scheme to work, our other problem is how to locate Jovadia's cauldron and seed it with the conduit device."

The mood in the chamber turned thoughtful. Mirafra glanced around to see Fystus gazing glumly at his psithe, Teron pondering.

"Can your High Maestras not discover the cauldron's location by magical means?" Arwyn asked.

Still pacing, the Ibis shook her head. "Not with enough precision. We know the source of the disturbance is the city of Tonnsburg, but pinpointing the cauldron is another matter. Jovadia's concealments are strong."

Teron straightened in his seat. "Well, it seems obvious then that we need someone to infiltrate Jovadia's circle, gain her confidence if possible, or otherwise get close enough to find the cauldron."

Fystus and Clorinda nodded, but neither spoke.

Teron shrugged with a laugh. "Sounds like a task for the Mooncrow."

"Oh, I don't think so," Fystus said. "You certainly have the skills, my friend. But you are too well-known. Jovadia would see through you at once."

"Yes," Mirafra said. "Remember, Jovadia sent assassins to kill you, so she already knows you're involved."

"True," Teron stroked his chin. "But my being known to her might be something I could twist to my advantage—if I can come up with the right story."

"Perhaps a double maneuver." The Ibis touched her lips. "We send Teron to distract her attention, and another majja who pretends she wants to join Jovadia's circle."

Mirafra's heart pounded in her chest. The answer to that seemed obvious, and despite her fear, she spoke it: "That sounds like a task for the Ruby Lark."

Everyone stared at her, Fystus and Clorinda shocked, Teron surprised but perhaps calculating, Arwyn simply aghast.

"I wasn't thinking of you," Clorinda explained, resuming her seat. "Rather, a more experienced adept that we send from Montodoro. Someone Jovadia does not know."

"Yes, she knows me," Mirafra said. "In fact, she told me I have talent and hinted that I might become her apprentice. That gives me a perfect reason to approach her."

"No!" Arwyn grasped her hand. "I won't let you do this. You know what Jovadia is. You could be throwing your life away! And for what? A plan that might have little chance of success."

She turned to Teron, who reluctantly shook his head. "No, I must agree, Mirafra. You are gifted, but also young and inexperienced. Intrigue and deception are whole sets of skills that you have not learned. I'm afraid you'd be no match for Jovadia."

This brought a surge of anger. Irrational though they might be, she let her emotions speak: "Please don't underestimate my abilities. I do that too much myself!"

When this brought no answer, she added, more reasonably. "At least consider it. If no better plan can be found, my idea will be an option."

"Fair enough," Teron answered. "But you think it over also. Before you commit yourself, make sure you believe this is your true course."

He rose to his feet. "Let's all keep studying our options. We still have three days till the Gathering meets."

A moon sharp like a sickle floated over the frozen marsh. Wind shifted and brushed the browned grasses and reeds. Mirafra was a tiny thing, a tree pipit with a broken wing. Unable to fly, she hopped over the ice and snow, fleeing for her life.

A giant bird stalked her. She heard it crashing through the rushes. Jovadia the Bittern.

"I'm coming for you, little pipit," the harsh voice cried. "It won't be long now."

Mirafra reached the edge of a frozen pond. Frantically she scanned both directions, searching for cover.

Nowhere to run. Then the Bittern was upon her, crushing her down with one clawed foot.

"You should never have left Montodoro," she mocked. "Now you're just one more piece for my collection."

The Bittern's beak dropped and snapped up the pipit's body. Mirafra experienced a moment of squeezing pain, then pure terror as she was thrown into the air. She sailed out over the frozen pond. Her body turned to ice as she died.

She woke from the nightmare, sat up in bed.

She had not left Montodoro. She was still here.

Still safe.

Variations of the same dream had haunted her now for two nights. Once again, she wondered at herself. Why had she spoken up so recklessly, volunteering to infiltrate Jovadia's lair? Was it courage or merely stupid pride? Could that really be her true course?

So much more sensible to stay here in Montodoro, resume her studies. She still had so much to learn. Here everything was peaceful and well-ordered.

And safe.

But that would be letting her friends down. Arwyn, Teron, even Clorinda and Fystus—all of them mattered to her.

But if she went on this mission and tried to deceive the Bittern, would she really have a chance? And when she failed, wouldn't that be letting her friends down in a worse way?

Mirafra needed answers. She got out of bed, pulled on a fur robe, and took up the psithe-disk. Like most of the apartments in the visitors' sector, this one adjoined a long terrace. Mirafra opened the glass doors and stepped outside.

The night was icy cold. The moon hung like a sickle—just like in her dream. She set a cushion on the stones and sat down to meditate. She shaped the psithe into a sword and cast in energy for warmth.

As time passed, Mirafra moved deeper and deeper into the core of her soul. In Norrling teaching, the soul opened into infinity, so there was no end to that journey. Deep peace suffused her mind and emotions. She asked to be shown her true course.

First, she saw herself moving through the halls and grand chambers of Montodoro. As she walked, her spirit grew bigger and brighter, accumulating more knowledge and power. But that journey seemed to have no end, and soon the halls and even the giant domes felt small and cramped.

Then she visualized herself in the Warmlands, the beautiful city of Baivonne, the green hills of Duneidan. She walked the battlements of the castle, recalled her meeting with Jovadia.

Returning to the Warmlands—what would come of that choice, she could not tell. Instead, her visions kept returning to memories of the attack, the rampage of the horrible warriors, Arwyn's parents and brothers murdered, Sharam the Crane dying in her arms.

I must go back and try to set things right, she thought. Otherwise, I will never know peace.

Mirafra opened her eyes. It was morning, the light almost blinding. Turning her head, she saw Teron watching her through the door of his room. She glanced down at the sword on her lap.

Standing, she walked over toward the Mooncrow, carrying the sword. Teron opened the door when she came near.

"I believe I know my true course," she said. "If the Gathering agrees, I will sail with you and infiltrate the Bittern's circle. That is what I must do."

Chapter 18

The day before the Supreme Gathering was to meet, the *Pomegranate* had still not returned. Teron stalked back and forth along the terrace, lifting his head to scan the open sky.

"They should have been back yesterday or the day before," he told Mirafra. "I knew this would be trouble."

"Is there anything we can do?"

The Mooncrow held up his psithe, a formless light. "That's why I called you here. I'm going to invoke the quinteer and search for them. You inform Fystus and Clorinda so they know. If I don't return by tomorrow, they might need to ... adjust their plans. The Gathering might agree to send more birds to search for us."

"I can go with you now," Mirafra said. "I mean, if it would help, and after informing Fystus and Clorinda, of course."

Teron considered, then smiled. "Well, since you've volunteered. Two birds searching would be better than one. Are you sure you're up to it?"

"I've been practicing the quinteer the last three days. I'll be careful."

"All right. You fly directly south. I'll go southwest and follow the coast. If you spot the airship, get on board. Tell Dona Delores that the Mooncrow said to get the ship back here as fast as possible."

Teron tossed the psithe into the air and mouthed the incantation. Dazzling light burst, and in a moment a black crow with a yellow bill and crest flapped its wings over the terrace. With a loud caw, he flew off above Mirafra's shoulder.

The Ruby Lark hurried inside. She found Fystus in his sitting room, leaning over a table piled with books and crystals, an unlit pipe in his mouth. She informed him of Teron's plan to search for the airship.

"Yes, I have been wondering about the ship," he said, distracted.

Mirafra met Arwyn in the corridor. She told him Teron had gone to search for the *Pomegranate*, and that she would be busy all day and would not likely see him till tomorrow. Not wanting to worry him, she didn't mention that she too was taking to the air.

In the depths of her psithe-disk, Cicalia watched the Mooncrow flying along the coast. On that course, she realized, he would likely find the airship later in the day. This actually played into her plans. Once the wizard was onboard the ship, she would gather her apprentices and cast another powerful wind, blowing the craft and the Mooncrow even farther away, preventing any return until long after the Supreme Gathering met.

Meantime, Cicalia had other work in mind. As a high maestra, she had developed the skill of remote vision to a powerful degree. Of course, it was especially effective within the confines of Montodoro. This was how she had learned of Fystus the Emu's experiments and his plan to destroy the Bittern's cold fire. Cicalia thought the scheme brilliant, especially in its blending of ancient magic and Warmlander alchemy. She also believed it had an excellent chance of success.

Which was why she was determined to stop it.

Finding the best method to accomplish this had taken considerable thought. But in the end, all her reasoning circled back to one simple fact: creating and working the conduit device to drain the cold fire required skillful magic. That work would be done by the Emu, using his master-level psithe.

Cicalia had studied several techniques for draining the power from another majja's psithe. Such methods were common in the Age of Chaos, when wizards of different tribes fought across Ombernorr. Today, of course, such practices were forbidden, deemed heinous.

But the White Eagle would not let that stop her. Sabotaging the male wizard's psithe would do him no harm. And Cicalia strongly believed that adherence to rigid doctrines should never prevail against a greater good.

Sitting cross-legged on the rug in her tower, Cicalia gazed into her psithe-disk. She called to mind the Emu in his apartment in the visitors' pavilion. Soon, his image appeared—a bearded, overweight fellow in a feathered robe, reading in a stuffed chair, a pipe clenched in his frowning mouth. His disk with its chain rested on his chest.

Peering hard, Cicalia poured her thought into the Emu's disk, matching the vibrations of her brain to its rhythms. Slowly, the attunement became a stream of power. Cicalia began to chant— ancient words in the magical tongue that translated as:

The psithe is empty

The bird has flown

The Emu frowned over his book, shifted a shoulder, but otherwise showed no reaction.

Eyes wide with excitement, Cicalia sensed the spell beginning to work, the energy of the Emu psithe flowing into her disk.

So intent was she on working the magic that she did not hear the fluttering of wings, birds circling her tower, gathering outside the windows. Only when sizzling lights exploded within the chamber did she look up.

Eight high maestras stood in a circle around her.

Cicalia jumped to her feet. "What—What is the meaning of this?"

"Stop what you are doing," Eucary the Trumpeter Swan commanded. "And surrender your psithe."

"I will not." Cicalia clutched the disk to her heart. "Why do you invade my privacy?"

"Surely you know why," Salnour the Albatross answered. "Your concealments around this tower are potent, but not enough to hide your activities from eight high maestras."

Glancing at the others, Cicalia saw that seven were members of the Supreme Gathering. The one other high maestra, it seemed, might be taking her place.

Eucary held out her hand. "Your psithe, Sister."

The White Eagle forced a smile. "I realize my activities are unsanctioned, but surely not so unlawful as to—"

"Your actions are not only unsanctioned but pernicious," Salnour replied. "By placing the airship of a welcomed guest in danger, you violated our rules of hospitality. But now, attempting to damage the psithe of another majja, you have broken the sacred doctrine of fellowship."

Cicalia's shoulders sagged. "What do you intend to do with me?"

Eucary answered. "First, you will surrender your psithe. After that, your penalties will be decided by the Flock of Psithic Propriety."

The most rigid-minded majja in Montodoro, Cicalia reflected grimly. She could expect no sympathy from them.

Reluctantly, but with no other choice, she held out the White Eagle disk. Bitterness made her speak: "You can punish me, strip me of power, exile me to some freezing outpost on the tundra. But my spirit will not be crushed. And the Flight of Exploration will continue. Montodoro will not live forever in the past, despite what you close-minded maestras may wish."

South of the Sanctuary, the western coast of Ombernorr stretched in hilly tundra and frosted black rocks that tumbled down to the blue ocean. After flying for half a day, Teron spied patches of forest, tall conifers covering the slopes. He was able to pause and rest in the branches.

Late in the afternoon, he spotted the airship, a tiny dot out over the sea. The wind was against him, and it took all the power Teron could cast into the crow's body for him to finally reach the ship. Exhausted, he perched on a window frame in the prow and cawed loudly. Soon one of the crew noticed him and summoned Dona Delores. The captain was unsure what to do until Topiedeon appeared and burst out laughing.

"It's Teron, dear Captain. Let him in!"

The window was slid open, and the Mooncrow hopped to the floor. He parted the quinteer and emerged in his human body.

"Senor Teron! What are you doing here?" Dona Delores cried.

"Looking for you, of course!" Teron panted, slumped on the floor against the wall. "You were supposed to be back two days ago."

"Oh, Senor, I know. I must apologize. We were just turning back—after flying three days as you ordered—when a strong wind came up and blew us out to sea. Senor Topiedeon will confirm what I tell you."

Teron glanced at the bard, who nodded, amused.

"And this wind!" the captain cried. "She was terribly strong. And she appeared out of nowhere. No storm clouds about, no turbulence in the seas below. The wind seemed pointed directly at our ship!"

"Really?" Teron touched a finger to his chin. "That is unusual."

"Sorcery, do you think?" Topiedeon said.

"Have you made enemies of those lady wizards?" Dona Dolores asked suspiciously.

"Some, perhaps." Teron climbed to his feet. "But for now you must get us back to Montodoro with all speed."

"Of course. Of course. We are flying as fast as we can!" After a moment, Dona Delores added, "The voyage itself was worthwhile, though. We saw not only villages, but a good-sized town."

"You didn't try to land?" Teron said.

"No! This crazy bard wanted us to land, so he could sing to the people and learn their stories. But I knew it might be dangerous and would certainly delay us. Ah, but the villages! They have not only fields and fisheries, but also mines. There must be metals, perhaps silver or gold—excellent opportunities for trading! This will make the Airship Guild even more interested in our logs and maps!"

"That's fine." Teron said. "Just get us back to Montodoro now."

Guided by the fading stars, the Ruby Lark soared high over the tundra. She had flown all day yesterday without finding the airship. At sunset, she reluctantly turned back, and flew all night so as not to miss the Supreme Gathering.

As the sun appeared over the distant hills, Mirafra worried that she might have miscalculated and lost her way. But at last she spotted Montodoro, the domes and spires gleaming on the gold-splashed hill. Flying closer, she was relieved to spot the *Pomegranate* moored on the field in front of the Sanctuary.

Swooping low, she glided over the roof of the entryway, then settled into a courtyard near the visitors' pavilion. After dissolving the quinteer, she sank to her knees in exhaustion. She had taken frequent rests during the night, but had not wanted to stay too long on the icy ground. Instead, she had forced the tired bird body back into the air.

Panting, she reminded herself that this was still no time to rest. It was already mid-morning. No telling at what hour the high maestras would meet.

Struggling to her feet, she hurried inside to get ready. In the corridor outside her room, she met Arwyn, pacing up and down.

"There you are!" He ran to her, grabbed her shoulders, peered hard into her eyes. "Are you all right?"

Still breathless, she nodded. "I'm fine."

"Then why did you deceive me?"

"I'm sorry." Mirafra moved past him. "I didn't want you to worry."

"Oh! So I wake up this morning, and no one knows where you are. And then Teron tells me you flew off as a bird to look for the airship. But the airship is back, and you're not. If you didn't want me to worry, that was not the best plan."

She opened her door and leaned on the handle. "I'm sorry. You're right, it was not a good plan. But Teron found the airship, and it's all right?"

"So they tell me, ready to fly."

"And the Supreme Gathering?"

"Nothing yet. We're waiting on the summons."

"I'd best get ready."

As Mirafra started into her room, Arwyn grabbed her wrist. "Yes. But please, in the future, when you decide to take on some mad, dangerous task, at least share your decision with me."

Mirafra smiled. Abruptly she gave him a hug. "I will. I promise."

Chapter 19

The Supreme Gathering was in session. Mirafra and her friends had been waiting for some time under the circular colonnade. Mirafra and Clorinda were arrayed in their wizard garb, feathered costumes with bird masks set over their heads. Fystus wore a feathered robe, while Teron and Arwyn were dressed in simple Warmlander garb.

They were not the only ones waiting. Other majja came and went, summoned through the gold doors to speak with the Gathering, then leaving again. Clorinda explained that these were representatives of different councils and committees. The entire Sanctuary, it seemed, had been put to work on the matter of the crisis in the Warmlands.

"You might also notice a slight difference in the membership of the Gathering," Clorinda added. "Cicalia the White Eagle has been replaced, owing to, uh, certain infractions."

"What sort of infractions?" Teron asked.

"That information the high maestras have not disclosed to me."

"Hmm. I wonder if they might have something to do with conjuring unnatural winds to blow a certain airship off course?"

Clorinda frowned and lifted a shoulder.

Fystus spoke up. "Well, I don't suppose they might have anything to do with attempting to drain energy from another majja's psithe?" On the long walk to the central dome, he had mentioned noticing an unusual flickering out of his psithe's power. Fortunately it had only lasted a short time, and the Emu psithe now seemed perfectly normal.

"I really could not say," Clorinda answered.

"The White Eagle was one of those opposed to interfering with Jovadia," Mirafra remarked. "With her vote gone, that might help us get the Gathering's approval."

"Here's another question," Arwyn said. "Do we even need their approval? We have our plan, dangerous though it may be." Here he glanced at Mirafra and Teron. "And the fuel will come from King Carswell. It seems to me we could go ahead whether the Gathering agrees or not."

This had not even occurred to Mirafra. She looked over at Clorinda.

"I cannot speak for Mirafra," the Ibis said, "but I could not take on such a task without the Gathering's approval. Of course, my part is small. No doubt, Fystus would be able to manage the hot fire component without my help."

The Emu pressed his lips, considering.

At that moment, the gold doors swung open. A tall majja emerged, dressed in blue and green feathers. As she passed, a disembodied voice called from within.

"Would our visitors from the Warmlands please enter?"

With Clorinda leading the way, they marched over the threshold and across the enormous, silent chamber. They stopped near the center, before the shimmering columns of light in which floated the images of the eight high maestras.

"We thank you for attending, esteemed visitors," Eucary the Trumpeter Swan said. "You will note that one of our members, Cicalia the White Eagle, is no longer in the Gathering, owing to matters that need not concern you. Seated in her place is Augaton, the Crested Owl." She gestured to a column at her left, where the Owl gave a solemn nod.

"As you are aware," Eucary continued, "we have been meeting this morning to review the matter of Jovadia the Bittern. And we understand that your group may have found a means of neutralizing her power."

"We would like to hear your proposal," Tirabelle the Flamingo said.

Clorinda deferred to Fystus for explanations. The Emu summarized what he had read in the archives about the cold fire and possible means of negating it.

"It seems that a heat source is needed to drain the power of the cold fire, sufficiently strong so the heat itself is not neutralized. The only promising accounts I found involved a formulation known as *sun fire*. But I could find no records of how that was created."

"We are aware of the sun fire stories," Ollato the Penguin interrupted. "The technique was suppressed because it was deemed too dangerous."

Fystus nodded. "I surmised as much."

He went on to explain how, with Arwyn's help, he had discovered a new source of heat energy, the Moldorn fire, which could be used to destroy Jovadia's cold fire. Briefly, he reviewed his experiments and the calculations behind them, and concluded that, with sufficient fuel for the hot fire and a conduit placed into Jovadia's cauldron, he was confident of success.

"All this sounds plausible," Margaretto the Sandgrouse said. "But how do you propose to place this conduit device into the cold fire?"

Fystus tilted his head toward Teron. "I will let the Mooncrow answer, as that is his part of the plot."

Teron smiled and bowed. "The plan is this: two of us, Mirafra the Ruby Lark and myself, will infiltrate Jovadia's circle. Arriving at different times, we will present ourselves as majja seeking to join her cause and learn from her. We know she is recruiting Norrlings, so the chances for one or both of us to be admitted seem good."

"Infiltrating the Bittern's circle has been tried before, with unlucky results," Olltalo the Penguin said. "Surely Jovadia will be on her guard against such tactics."

"Indeed," Teron agreed. "That is why, in my experience, such deceptions must be improvised, played as the situation demands. Planning in much detail is useless."

"Your reputation for deception is well known, Master Mooncrow," Alexandra the Tinamou observed. "But what about you, Sister Ruby Lark? You know the peril you'll face. Are you equally confident in your skills for deception?"

Mirafra cringed inside. This was a question she had vigorously avoided asking herself. She replied in a hesitant voice, "I am confident that, between Teron and myself, one or both of us will find the cauldron and destroy the cold fire."

After she spoke, Mirafra sensed the minds of the high maestras probing her, reading her brain and spirit. She fought to keep her body from trembling.

"Sister Clorinda," the Trumpeter Swan said. "What is your assessment of the viability of this plan?"

The Ibis took a deep breath. "I confess that the esteemed Emu's calculations are beyond me, but I have confidence in his intellect. And I have great confidence in the abilities of both Teron and Mirafra." After a pause, she added. "May I ask if the Gathering has found a more promising plan for neutralizing the Bittern's power?"

"None at all," said Olltalo the Penguin.

"From all we have deduced," Eucary answered. "No remote attack, other than the one you propose, would have much chance of success. And that leaves no alternative except to send a force of majja against Jovadia's circle. But that course is most perilous. It would certainly result in bloodshed and could easily end in failure."

"Then it sounds like you need to approve our plan," Teron stated bluntly.

"We will withdraw and consider," the Trumpeter Swan announced.

Within the columns, the images of the high maestras faded away, replaced by colored clouds. Mirafra and her companions waited, shifting on their feet, glancing at one another.

Finally, after several minutes, the high maestras reappeared.

"The Supreme Gathering has decided, on a vote of 6 to 2," Eucary declared, "that your mission to disarm the cauldron of Jovadia the Bittern is approved. We commend your intelligence and courage and ask that you proceed with all haste."

Across the hall, the gold doors swung open, letting in more daylight. Mirafra and the others bowed and started to leave.

"Sister Clorinda," Eucary said. "We direct you to stay behind for further discussions."

Mirafra opened her eyes and sat up in bed. A faint disk of light hovered in the room.

At first, she thought she must be dreaming—yet another nightmare. The airship was leaving in the morning, and Mirafra's sleep had been fitful.

But no. A woman stood beside her bed—Clorinda the Ibis.

"Maestra. What are you doing here?"

Clorinda leaned over, holding the disk. "I am sorry to have to do this, Mirafra."

The psithe-disk glinted and sparkled, circling with spirals that Mirafra could not resist watching. Energy throbbed in her skull ... And then she was falling.

She had been the Ruby Lark, sailing through the sky. But now suddenly her wings were gone. She plummeted through endless night, pieces of herself flying away.

Then she was back in her body, in her bed in the dark room, staring at the Ibis and her disk.

She was Mirafra again. But parts of herself seemed lost. "What did you do to me?" she cried. "What did you do?!"

Part 4
The War of Cold Fire

Deception is a constant danger. An initiate must always analyze their feelings and motivations. But even with relentless self-reflection, a wizard may be deceived—either by another's magic or, worse yet, by their own failure of self-awareness.

— *Master Aswell's Book of Rules and Meditations*
(The Golden Book).
Norrling Year 4263.

Chapter 20

Dressed in her Norrling regalia, Mirafra walked across the broad city square of Tonnsburg. A small young woman clad in gray and red feathers, she attracted only a few curious glances. But then, the folk of this city were accustomed to strange sights.

Mirafra ignored them, her jaw set, her eyes fixed on the castle walls that towered over the square. In the cold of the late winter morning, she approached the massive barbican and its main gates.

Six sentries in steel helmets and chain mail stood before the gates, armed with swords and pikes. They stared at her sternly. When she walked close, one of the guards called out.

"Halt and state your business!"

"I am a Norrling from the Sanctuary of Montodoro. I am here to see Jovadia the Bittern."

The captain who had spoken exchanged an anxious glance with another man. "Wait here," he said, then tilted his head, gesturing the other man inside. The subordinate nodded and hurried through the gates.

Mirafra held her place, breathing slowly, staring straight ahead.

Sometime later, the guard returned, said something to the captain, then resumed his post. The captain pointed his pike at Mirafra.

"Someone will come. Step aside now, if you please, so you are not blocking the way."

Mirafra gave a nod and moved two steps to the left.

Later, a young man appeared, dressed in brown wools and a yellow-feathered cloak. After consulting with the guards, he approached Mirafra.

"I am Lando the Golden Sparrow, one of Jovadia's apprentices. Kindly tell me your business."

"I speak only with Jovadia."

The young wizard was taken aback. "That will be difficult. She is very busy. You must tell me what you want with her."

"You may tell her I bring word of Montodoro."

Lando stared at her face for a long moment, then shrugged and walked back inside.

Late in the afternoon, another majja walked from inside the castle: a broad-shouldered woman in a brown-feathered cape, with a bird mask worn on the top of her head. She walked close and peered sharply at Mirafra.

"I am Andelica the Tawny Swift, Jovadia's second. What is your business with her?"

"I speak only with Jovadia."

"Whatever you have to say, you can say to me!"

Mirafra stared straight ahead.

Andelica growled. "Would you prefer to speak to me or be arrested and thrown in the dungeon?"

Mirafra looked the woman over, her face expressionless. "If you take me to the dungeon, I will wait there. If you have the guards kill me, I will die. But then Jovadia will not hear my warning."

Andelica's sharp eyes widened, then narrowed. "You're going to get cold standing out here all night."

Mirafra said nothing.

With a grunt of frustration, the Tawny Swift whirled and stalked back into the castle.

At twilight, the guards changed, and lanterns were lit along the gatehouse walls. Mirafra sat down on the stones, her back to the low wall of the walkway. When the cold became severe, she made her psithe into a sword and cast enough heat to keep herself warm.

Sunrise found her standing at the same spot.

At mid-morning, Andelica came out of the gate. She approached Mirafra but did not speak. After waiting expectedly for less than a minute, the Tawny Swift snarled in frustration and marched back into the castle.

A short time later, Jovadia appeared. The sentries stood at sharp attention as she passed. Dressed in a fur robe and wide, plumed hat, she strode easily up to Mirafra.

"Yes, I remember you," she said with a smile. "The Tree Pipit, I think. Only now you have a new and better psithe, if I am not mistaken."

Mirafra nodded, concealing a surge of fear.

"I understand you have a message for me," Jovadia said. "But there's no need for us to stand in the cold. Come inside."

They walked side-by-side through the barbican and across a wide inner courtyard. Though weak from hunger and thirst, Mirafra determinedly matched the Bittern's smooth stride. Her fear had vanished, leaving her numb. Vaguely, she wondered what she was going to say.

Inside the palace, they entered a richly-appointed reception hall. Jovadia led her to a couch in front of a burning fire.

"You must be hungry as well as cold," Jovadia said kindly. "Can I offer you some breakfast?"

"Some water, please?"

"Of course."

The Bittern waved to the servants who stood at a distant doorway and called for water. She relaxed on the couch, waiting till the water had been brought and poured. When the servant had moved back to his place, well out of earshot, she leaned forward.

"I wondered if I would see you again," she remarked. "You escaped from Duneidan after stealing your maestra's psithe. Am I wrong?"

"I did not steal it. She gave it to me."

"Of course. But then you used it to escape? Quite an accomplishment for one of your rank. And you also rescued the Duke's young son."

Mirafra set down the cup. The water seemed to have revived her.

"Yes, I helped him escape from you and King Alaric. We went to Baivonne. Later, I travelled to Montodoro and returned my maestra's psithe. And there I acquired my new psithe." She gestured with her fingers at the cape and the mask perched on her head. "Now I am Mirafra the Ruby Lark."

Jovadia's eyes gleamed. "Most impressive."

Mirafra stared back. "You told me once that I had potential."

"Indeed. I was not wrong. But why are you here now, Mirafra the Ruby Lark?"

"Because they betrayed me—the Supreme Gathering, I mean. I wished only to remain in Montodoro, to pursue my studies. But they insisted I come back to the Warmlands to help fight you. They said that because I had contact with you in the past, I might be of use. I tried to refuse, but they forced me."

"How did they force you?"

"An enchantment. They submerged parts of my soul. But I was not so weak as they thought. They planned for me to come to you, but not to tell you the truth." She stared with hollow eyes into the fire. "They betrayed me, so I decided to betray them."

Jovadia watched her, assessing. "So they planned to insert you here as their agent, to spy on me?"

"More than that." Mirafra reached into the pocket of her robe and took out a small spiral carved of wood. "I was to discover the furnace or cauldron that gives you power and to throw this into it."

Mirafra dropped the spiral into the Bittern's open hand. Mouth open, Jovadia examined it.

"And this tiny thing was meant to damage my power?"

"I only know what they told me to do."

Jovadia placed the wooden thing in her robe, then set a hand on Mirafra's knee.

"You have done well to tell me the truth, Ruby Lark. And I understand your motives. I too was betrayed by those self-important maestras of the Sanctuary. I am glad you have seen the truth of them." She stood up. "Come with me."

Mirafra followed her out of the chamber. They walked through a high-arched corridor and up a grand stairway. More hallways and stairs brought them to a remote upper story of the castle. Stopping before carved wooden doors, Jovadia used her wand to twist locks and slide a bolt. Once the doors swung open, they stepped into a grand chamber decorated with colorful rugs and tapestries.

"This is where I and my apprentices live and do our work." Jovadia explained.

At an open space in the center, three Norrlings were practicing with their psithes—the Tawny Swift, the Golden Sparrow, and one other. They paused and watched silently as Jovadia and Mirafra passed.

Down another corridor, they entered a small bedchamber. A narrow window near the ceiling let in daylight.

"This will be your room for now," the Bittern said. "You will be kept here until I determine what is to be done with you."

Mirafra eyed her, fearful again.

"There is much hidden in you. But I will discover it." Jovadia held out her hand. "Give me your psithe."

Mirafra stiffened. But she could see no other choice. She took the disk and chain from over her head and handed them to the Bittern.

"I ... only wish to learn from you."

"We shall see."

White clouds floated through a deep blue sky, the air cool and clear. From this high parapet of Carswell's castle, Arwyn could see past the city to the river, across stretches of wetlands, all the way to the sea.

Deep in thought, he was startled by a footstep and three notes of string music. He turned sharply as Topiedeon walked up beside him.

"A beautiful morning." The bard breathed deeply. "The air is sweet with a hint of spring, I think."

"I had not noticed." Arwyn's gaze turned to the distance, to the west.

"Thinking about your lady Mirafra, I suppose," Topiedeon said.

When Arwyn made no answer, Topiedeon plucked four notes. "A most intriguing character, that one. One day, perhaps I'll write a song about her."

"About her death, I fear."

"Oh, my lord! Don't be so gloomy. She has a good chance."

Arwyn shook his head. "I don't understand any of it. I knew she was taking on this mission. But on the voyage back from Ombernorr, she hardly spoke with me. And when I talked with her, she seemed changed, not herself at all."

"Yes, I noticed that too," Topiedeon admitted.

"I asked Teron and Clorinda about it. They would say nothing. Did they not notice the change, or only pretend not to notice? And then, after we landed here, Mirafra left without even telling me goodbye."

The bard strummed a low chord. "I know how you feel, my lord. I lost the only lady I ever loved, years ago."

The young Duke eyed him with surprise. "I did not know."

"Mirabelle was her name. A lovelier soul I've never met. She was killed when the cursed Moldorns bombed their own city."

The minstrel was quiet for a moment and then started playing again, a doleful tune. Arwyn let his gaze wander down to the airfield. There, three of the king's ships were moored for refueling before flying off again to patrol the borders. That was also where Fystus the Emu was stationed, supervising preparations for the hot fire that was supposed to help destroy Jovadia's power.

The mood of the music lifted. "But there is hope for your Mirafra. Teron will be following her to Tonnsburg soon. Between the two of them, they might well topple King Alaric and the Bittern both ... Oh, what a fine song that will make!"

"How can you think of making songs with all that is happening?"

Topiedeon plucked more notes. "My young friend, with all the sorrows of this world, making songs is all that keeps me alive."

Day and night, Mirafra sat in the locked chamber of Jovadia's tower. Without her psithe, she could not practice, could not even seem to meditate. Her mind was broken, consciousness flowing in a crooked stream that sank away and rose again with no sense of time having passed. She could not tell when she had slept, dreams and imaginings equally unreal.

She struggled to regain her memory. Something had been done to her, changed her into this confused, angry creature. But was this really her, or was it some part she was forced to play? Had she been enchanted by the high maestras in Montodoro? Or perhaps by Jovadia herself?

Twice a day, one of the Bittern's apprentices would unlock the door and deliver food and drink. In the evening, they would also light a candle. The fireplace held ashes, but they would charge it with their psithes, casting in enough heat to last through the night.

The apprentices mostly remained silent, except to give her their names: Zaria the Snowhawk, Maarit the Curlew, Lando the Golden Sparrow, whom Mirafra had met outside the gates. Of them all, he seemed the gentlest. But all of them appeared grim, perhaps frightened.

How long would she be kept here? They could not or would not say.

Then, on the third day, Andelica the Tawny Swift came into the room. Mirafra stood, instinctively frightened as the tall woman moved through the daylight streaming in from the high window. Andelica carried her psithe-sword.

"You've had enough time to reflect. Are you ready now to tell us the truth?"

Mirafra backed away. "I told Jovadia the truth."

"You're lying!"

She sprang forward, holding the sword parallel to the floor. Mirafra threw up her arms, but without a psithe she was helpless to defend herself. Andelica pressed her against the wall and held the shining blade to her throat.

"Now," she said softly and slowly, "tell me the real reason you are here."

Mirafra's voice trembled. "I told Jovadia all I know. I gave her the spiral device. She has my psithe. What more do you want from me?"

"The truth!" Andelica's fierce eyes stared, burning into her brain, probing her soul.

Mirafra sobbed. "I don't know. I don't know!"

At last, Andelica backed away. Mirafra collapsed to the floor, weeping.

"You are a pathetic thing, Ruby Lark," Andelica said. "And you have no idea of the danger you are in."

With that, she turned and stalked from the room, bolting the door behind her.

Later that day, another apprentice, Varma the Bunting, came and conducted Mirafra from the locked room. Mirafra was allowed to bathe and dress in fresh clothes. Then she was led to a round chamber on an upper floor of a tower. Jovadia and all five of the apprentices sat in a circle on high-backed chairs like thrones. Mirafra stood in the center, on a thick carpet woven in a panoply of scenes— hills, roads, towns, and castles. The air smelled sweet, yet with a hint of dust.

"Welcome, Ruby Lark," Jovadia said with a smile. "You may stand at ease. We have all probed your spirit and concluded that there is no falsehood in your story."

Mirafra bowed her head, not sure if she could trust the sense of relief creeping over her.

"And yet," Jovadia said, "I remain perplexed, because I sense there is yet a great deal hidden in you."

The other majja watched Mirafra impassively, except for Andelica, who glared.

"But perhaps," Jovadia continued, "this is because there are things you are hiding from yourself. I have seen this before in other majja. They repress elements of who they really are in order to adhere to the strict Norrling teachings."

"That might be it," Mirafra answered. "I confess, I am confused."

"But you still believe the high maestras betrayed you?"

"Yes ... Something they did changed me. I lost parts of myself." She looked up at Jovadia. "You told me they betrayed you as well. What did you mean?"

"Ah, yes," the Bittern reflected. "They stifled me in Montodoro, denied me advancement because they did not approve of my more esoteric studies. When I defied them, they placed me on probation and threatened to take away my psithe. That was when I left Montodoro—a decision I have never regretted."

Her eyes locked with Mirafra's. "Now you also have left their order behind. But what is it you want, Ruby Lark?"

Mirafra considered. "What I have always wanted, to cultivate my powers, to grow them to the highest degree."

"Even if that means leaving behind the rules and strictures of Montodoro?"

"I have already left them behind."

The Bittern smiled. "Indeed. I like your answers. And you have done me a service by revealing the Sanctuary's plot against me and surrendering the spiral device." She lifted up the chain with Mirafra's disk. "In recompense, I give you back your psithe. You will also be given texts to study and permitted to observe the workings of our circle. In time, if you prove worthy, you may be allowed to join us."

She extended the chain, holding it in both hands, smiling but with fire in her eyes. Mirafra stepped toward her, then dropped to both knees and let Jovadia place the chain over her head.

The Bittern disk stirred with trails of emerald light and quivering black clouds. Jovadia's eyebrows arched high as she stared into the depths, contemplating all that she had set in motion—and all that she had yet to accomplish.

She blinked and looked up as two of her followers approached. The anteroom was bitter cold, the balcony doors deliberately left open to the night.

Andelica and Zaria bowed.

"Forgive the intrusion, maestra," the Tawny Swift said. "But there is a dispatch from King Alaric."

She handed over a rolled-up paper. Alaric had left the capital with the main body of his army three days ago. They were expected to reach the Occitan border in another day. Jovadia broke the seal and scanned the message.

"Very good." She glanced at the apprentices. "The army is proceeding on schedule. The zolgars are performing in perfect order. The King sends us gracious compliments."

She handed back the paper with an attitude of dismissal.

But the two subordinates lingered.

"Something else?" Jovadia asked.

"Eh, yes." Andelica spoke hesitantly. "Zaria and I have been talking, maestra. We are ... concerned about this Ruby Lark. We don't think she should be trusted."

"Of course she should not be trusted!"

"But to let her observe our workings—"

"Will do no harm. If she is concealing some other plot against us, this is the best way to draw it out. If not, and she is as she appears to be, she might become a valuable addition to our circle."

The Tawny Swan and Snow Hawk exchanged uneasy glances.

"The risk is small." Jovadia changed her disk into a sword. "So long as we stay on guard and are ready to destroy her in an instant."

Chapter 21

"My lords and ladies, I have summoned you here to discuss the latest airship reports, which bring us dire, though not unexpected, news. An army of King Alaric's, estimated to be at least 5,000 strong, is advancing toward the center of our border with Llorrland. We believe the invasion is imminent."

King Carswell stood at the table on the high dais in his grand council chamber, flanked by his Queen, his son Prince Darien, Clorinda the Ibis, and other courtiers. Tables spread below were occupied by perhaps another fifty soldiers, lords, and advisors. Arwyn sat at one of these, along with Teron, Topiedeon, and Fystus the Emu.

"No new buildup of troops has been reported at the southern and northern positions," Carswell continued. "However, 2 to 3 thousand men are still encamped in both locations. So we must expect the invasion to come on all three fronts, with the main thrust at the center."

So the waiting was nearly over, Arwyn thought. Ten days since they arrived back in Baivonne. Ten days since Mirafra disappeared. A twinge of fear surfaced in the midst of his grim resolve. He glanced at the faces of his three friends and saw, he believed, similar emotions.

"Tomorrow morning," the King said, "I will march with those troops currently encamped outside Baivonne to reinforce our center position. I ask those lords who still have men in reserve on your lands to send riders at once to alert them. They are to proceed to whichever of the three positions was previously ordered. Finally, our airship corps will continue to patrol the border and the coast. At the first attack, they will be ready to counter against Alaric's airships and his ground forces."

"But why should we wait?" one of the ministers at the high table asked. "Why not use firebombs to weaken Alaric's army now?"

Arwyn had wondered that as well. He had studied enough about warfare to know that bombing worked best on stationary targets such as towns and castles. The dropping of firebombs had limited accuracy, and mobile armies could simply scatter and avoid much harm. Still, he was surprised by Carswell's answer.

"I will not be the first to take aggressive action and thereby justify Alaric's invasion. No, my lords and ladies, I am determined that we not be the ones who start this war, but that we shall be the ones to finish it."

A murmur of agreement moved over the assembly. Arwyn had to admit the King was honorable. Sadly, that by itself would not save his kingdom.

"In my absence, a token force of city and castle guards will remain in Baivonne," Carswell said. "And, I am grateful to say, that my dear Lady Esmeralda has recovered her health to the point where she can take charge of the city in my absence."

The Queen stood with a grim smile, clasped the King's hand and held it up. Across the chamber, many stood and bowed, while others called out their appreciation of the lady. Arwyn noticed a satisfied smile on the face of Clorinda.

"Now, lords and ladies," the King called out. "We open the floor to further discussion."

After a few moments of silence, an officer stood at the table next to Arwyn's. "Are there any further reports on the position and number of those black-armored foot soldiers, the so-called deathless warriors?"

The King's expression darkened. "Indeed. The airships spotted columns of men in black armor on the central front. They estimated close to 1500."

Uneasy whispering greeted these words. The King held up a hand.

"We cannot be sure these are the same magically empowered creatures that ravaged portions of Arabhedden. Some may simply be men in similar costume. Still, we must assume our army will have to face a large number of these zolgars, as they are properly called."

"If they are truly impervious to wounds and weapons, what can be done against them?" a lord in armor asked.

"If they invade our land," Carswell replied, "our first defense will be bombing their columns from the air. We do not know how well they may resist the Moldorn fire. Secondly, there is a plan being worked on by our Court Wizard, Clorinda the Ibis, along with our esteemed allies from the Sanctuary of Ptolloden. I will not disclose details here, but I am hopeful that their work will counteract the sorcery that gives the zolgars power. When that happens, to whatever degree Alaric's army has relied on these unnatural creatures, our enemy will be disarmed."

Arwyn noted the reactions around the hall—hopeful, worried, skeptical, determined. For himself, he would do his best to cling to the hopeful.

Arwyn stared at his reflection in the looking glass—a slender young man, long of limb, dressed in chainmail, a plumed helmet in one hand, a knight's longsword in the other. More like a squire than a knight, he thought. But the tabard worn over the armor held the crest of House Duneidan, and he would wear it with pride.

All of the apparel and gear were gifts from King Carswell. The gracious ruler had even offered to furnish him a horse, but Arwyn had almost no training in mounted combat. Instead, he had chosen to fight on foot, joining with the King's forces at the southern border. There, he knew, were marshaled the warriors of Arabhedden who now served King Alaric. If he was lucky, Arwyn might even encounter the new Duke Baglan who had betrayed Duneidan.

"Your pardon, my lord." A steward had appeared at the door. "The Lady Lorraine wishes a word with you."

Setting down the helm and sword, Arwyn followed the man to the antechamber. Lorraine stood waiting, tall and somber in a velvet gown. She smiled fondly when she saw him.

"Oh, you look fine in your armor!"

"Thank you. King Carswell is most generous."

"You have earned it. You and all your friends have done much for Occitan." She hesitated. "I was afraid I might not see you in the morning, and I wanted to bid you goodbye and wish you well."

"Thank you, dear cousin."

They embraced, rather stiffly because of the chainmail. Lorraine held his shoulders and looked down at the tabard.

"Your father and mother would be so proud."

His throat tightened. "I will do my best to uphold our family's honor."

"I know you will, Arwyn." She sighed. "I am no warrior, but I will do my best here at court, serving the Queen in whatever she needs of me. I am so thankful that her health is restored. Please, express my gratitude again to Teron—and also to Mirafra, when you see her."

Arwyn wasn't sure how much Lorraine understood of the danger Mirafra faced. Perhaps she knew and was trying to inspire him with hope.

He simply nodded and said, "I will."

Teron the Mooncrow descended the gangway of the *Pomegranate*, Topiedeon the bard a step behind. Around them, the airfield basked in the bright morning, the air warming as the world turned toward spring.

"I must say," Topiedeon remarked, "Dona Delores seems much more content to wait and do nothing than she did last time we were in Baivonne."

"So she should," Teron chuckled. "She doesn't want to go flying into an airship battle, and as things are developing, that might occur wherever she took the ship."

"I suppose. But how long will she wait?"

"Till the war's over, if she's smart." They strode from under the shadow of the balloon. "Oh, and there might be another reason she is content to wait. If I do not return from this little adventure, I have arranged that the ship will pass to her."

"What?" Taken aback for a moment, Topiedeon chose to make light of it. "Let me guess: After you put out Jovadia's cold fire in Tonnsburg, you're planning to fly to Ptolloden and resume your detachment from the world? Or perhaps you will journey back to Montodoro and plead to be admitted as their first male wizard?"

Teron laughed. "That might not be a bad idea. Now, let's go and say goodbye to Fystus."

At the edge of the airfield, away from all the buildings and moored vessels, lay a circular pit thirty yards wide. In the days since Teron's party arrived back at Baivonne, the pit had been dug by steam shovel and now lay filled with canisters of fuel for the Moldorn fire.

Some distance away, a metal shack stood beside the fence that bordered the airfield. Fystus the Emu sat on a bench in front of the shack, smoking his pipe.

"Still smoking, I see," Topiedeon smirked as they drew near.

"Yes," Fystus gestured with the pipe. "I fear I'm developing a taste for these Warmlander weeds. Most pleasurable."

"We came to check on you before we leave," Teron told him.

"I believe all is ready." Fystus lifted his chin toward the fire pit. "The King provided even more fuel than we requested, and the containers have been placed three layers deep. Should make quite a fire when the time comes."

Teron smiled. "Just don't fall asleep and miss the signal."

"Don't worry about that. Either Clorinda or I will be on watch here at all times. But what about you, Teron? You have all the devices with you?"

"Yes." Teron pulled a wooden spiral from the pocket of his cape. "The false device for Jovadia to confiscate and the two little beads hidden inside my belt." If Mirafra failed to reach the cold fire with her two magical devices, Teron's would provide a second chance.

"Just remember," Fystus said. "Timing is crucial. Drop in one bead, count to thirty, then the other."

"A question," Topiedeon said. "I understand how the beads work. The first signals you to light the hot fire, and the second opens the channel to drain the cold fire into the heat. But surely so much fuel will make a grand explosion. How are you going to light it, Fystus, without blowing yourself to bits?"

"Hah! Simple." The Emu lifted up his disk. "I receive the mental message through the disk, then immediately change the disk to a sword. I cast a ball of fire from the sword and drop it into the pit, touching off the explosion. Easily done from this distance—uh, that is, with the psithe of a master. Clorinda and I have both practiced it with no problem."

"Quite an orchestration," Topiedeon observed with admiration. "I'm sorry I can't be here to watch."

"Why don't you stay?" the Emu asked. "I could use the company ... Oh, you're not planning to go to Tonnsburg with Teron, are you?"

"Not permitted," the bard answered. "No, I'm going to follow our other young hero, Duke Arwyn. He's taking an airship to join the King's forces in the south. I think he's hoping to meet up with some of his former neighbors—now turned enemies."

"I see." Fystus reflected. "He's a smart and noble young man. Do your best to protect him, won't you?"

"Sure, and I will," Topiedeon chuckled. "But, might I ask, who is going to protect me?"

Under a starlit sky, a ring of psithe-disks sparkled in different colors. The circle of majja stood on the parapet of Jovadia's tower, with the Bittern herself at the center. Mirafra stood with the others on the edge—an observer, not yet an apprentice.

Still, she had been instructed to focus her mind and follow as best she could. This was her third time practicing this work called the *Animation of the Zolgars.*

"Cast your thoughts into the psithe," Jovadia chanted, holding her own disk high. "Let them follow my direction."

Mirafra stared into her disk, held in cupped hands. Diamond and ruby lights flashed, like the stars but nearer and brighter. Then the sparks seemed to circle and flow down, a whirlpool receding into distance. The whirlpool drained into an utterly black sphere.

Then the blackness burst into dazzling white.

"Now you see the cold fire! Draw from your psithe all energy and cast it in!"

Mirafra obeyed, sending all her power into the cold fire, watching in wonder as it pulsed and gleamed. She had not been told the location of the actual cauldron, but she sensed it was somewhere far below her feet, somewhere under the castle.

Texts she had read described this ritual. Written in Old Norrling, translated from crystals by Jovadia herself and appended with her comments, they described all that was remembered of the cold fire from the remote past. While several techniques had been developed to combine the energies of many psithes, the cold fire had proven the most effective—capable of drawing vast power from the mental realms. Over time, the records showed, Norrling reformers had banned all of these "joined-psithe" techniques, calling them abominations because they usually resulted in the destruction of the bird life-forms. Usually, but not always. There were accounts that claimed that when the cold fire was extinguished, the psithes returned to their natural state, became birds again.

Mirafra watched the light changing as she slipped into a vision. She saw the cold energy rising from the castle, arcing into the night sky like a rainbow. Traveling on that arc, she followed the energy over hills and valleys to the west, to descend at last on the encampment of King Alaric's army. There, while soldiers and horses were bedded down, rank upon rank of zolgars stood, silent and still under the stars.

Then Mirafra saw another vision—more like a dream or imagined future. She watched the zolgars fighting in daylight, in a rampaging battle of knights and foot soldiers, trumpets blaring, arrows flying. Through it all, the zolgars raged, invulnerable to weapons and wounds, invincible.

Mirafra shuddered, the energy of the cold fire that filled the zolgars also filling her. More magical power than she had ever known, ever imagined. The horror of the battle no longer mattered. All she felt was the thrill of that overwhelming power.

Later in the day, Mirafra sat cross-legged on her narrow bed, studying. She had finished the historical accounts and was now reading Jovadia's notes of her own experiments. At first, the Bittern had worked only with her own psithe, imbuing individual warriors with power to make them resistant to pain. In fact, it had been the ancient accounts of the zolgars that had led her to the idea of using cold fire. The early experiments proved successful but extremely draining for the Bittern. Jovadia had to control the zolgars directly, sending them commands moment by moment. Gradually, through trial and error, she succeeded in giving the zolgars limited sentience. The hundreds who now marched with King Alaric's army had brains attuned to their human commanders and obeyed simple commands—attack, retreat, rest.

Mirafra recalled her vision from the ritual last night. Wincing, she set down the page as if it burned her fingers. The irresistible power of the zolgars as they killed men and horses with their swords—the memory filled her with horror. And yet, at the time, the power had excited and thrilled her.

What was she becoming?

If only she could remember better what she had been ...

A knock at the door startled her. Varma the Bunting called that it was time for afternoon practice.

Dutifully, Mirafra pulled on her boots and cape. Taking her psithe, she followed the other apprentices to a lower level of the castle. At the base of the tower lay an open courtyard. Twice a day, by Jovadia's orders, the apprentices practiced here, maintaining their traditional Norrling skills.

Each attribute of the psithe was invoked and exercised. First, they formed the cup and drew water from the air. With their wands, they levitated themselves and each other. Holding disks, they cast concealments and simple illusions. Lastly, with their swords, they invoked heat and also practiced their fighting skills.

In the days she had been here, Mirafra had regained some of her composure and presence of mind. She enjoyed the practice sessions and felt mostly satisfied with how she performed.

She was dueling Maarit the Curlew, easily parrying and dancing away from the blade, when she became aware of another majja watching them. Mirafra halted the contest with a salute and bow. She turned to find Andelica and Daria standing near.

"Our Ruby Lark is quite the swordswoman." The Tawny Swift showed a mocking smile. "Some of your moves I've not seen before. Learned from Warmlanders, I gather."

Her casual cruelty sparked rage in Mirafra. She bowed to hide her face, then saluted with her blade.

"Oh, are you offering me a lesson?" Andelica asked.

"If the lead apprentice wishes."

"Well, how can I refuse?"

Andelica shrugged off her cape and handed it to Zaria. The others were drawing near to watch. The Tawny Swift took a sideways stance and pointed her blade. The courtyard had grown quiet.

Mirafra leveled her point but stepped to the side, forcing Andelica to turn. In the midst of the turn, Mirafra thrust, forcing the Swift to parry and almost lose her balance.

Mirafra danced away, exhilarated. She clearly remembered how Andelica had taunted her, holding the blade at her throat. Then another memory flashed in her mind—the vision of the zolgars fighting on the plain, the energy of their killing rage.

That same energy moved Mirafra now as she circled. Andelica had regained her balance. Her point hovered, ready to feint or thrust. Mirafra waited.

Andelica made a double-bluff and then lunged. Mirafra did not try to parry. Instead she launched her body dangerously close to the other sword and stabbed hard at Andelica's shoulder. The Tawny Swift gasped and stumbled back, dropping her sword, falling to the ground.

Mirafra leaped forward, setting her foot on the discarded sword. She raised her blade, poised for a killing stroke. Then she regained her self-control and stepped back.

Two apprentices rushed in to support Andelica. The others stared at Mirafra with shocked faces.

"She's bleeding," one of the majja said.

Mirafra let the sword sink in her hand. "Forgive me," she said to Andelica. "I seem to have wounded you, by accident."

"It's nothing." Adelica's eyes flashed with hate. "I've had blood drawn before." With the help of the two majja, she climbed to her feet. "My cup will heal me in no time. After that, I am sure, we'll have another match."

Chapter 22

The War of Cold Fire started on the 17th day of the second month after Midwinter. As King Carswell expected, invasions were launched on three fronts along the Occitan border. Only the day before, the King had arrived with the main body of his army at the central front, near the town of Ellysee.

Also as Carswell predicted, the conflict began in the air. The King was wakened at dawn by news that three Llorrland airships were crossing the border. By the time the King was armored and mounted, his own ships were flying to intercept.

The King sat on his palomino charger at the crest of a long hill south of the town. Next to him was his son Darien, eighteen years old and just recently knighted. On the King's other hand sat his commander-in-chief, General Mendosa. On the plain below, the knights and foot soldiers of Occitan were assembling to march.

But the King and his aides had their gazes fixed on the sky. Carswell had been wise to concentrate his air forces here at the central border. From north and south, four of his airships now approached the flight paths of the Llorrland ships. Before the enemy vessels could reach his army to drop bombs, they were forced to swerve aside.

"My lords, we are witnessing history," the King murmured. "Though I wish it were not so."

Indeed, this would be the first battle where multiple airships fought each other in the skies. When the Moldorns first developed lighter-than-air vessels, they were the only nation that had them. Their warships were used strictly for bombing and as transports.

Since the retreat of the Moldorn Empire, only a few instances of ship-to-ship combat had been recorded. Each of those involved only two ships—a Moldorn patrol vessel against a rebel or pirate craft. More recently, here in Tann, King Alaric had used airships on occasion to firebomb castles and towns. But those ships had flown unopposed.

"Now we shall see how well our training has served," Mendosa said.

"Training and engineering both," the King answered.

Alaric's ships were known to be armed with ballistas—giant crossbows capable of launching fire bolts. After learning of this, Carswell had equipped his own ships with the weapons, two ballistas on each side and one in the prow.

But launching a bolt from a moving ship in the air to accurately strike a moving target? That had proven extremely difficult—unless the two ships flew very close. And flying so close exposed your ship to the enemy's bolts.

The royal engineers had come up with a solution. First, they designed more powerful ballistas, ones that swiveled on bearings, both side-to-side and up-and-down. The exact angle of launch could be set according to horizontal and vertical scales engraved on the weapons. After judging the speed and flight path of the two ships, the archers consulted calculations provided by the engineers and used them to adjust the barrel just before launch.

Months of practice and refinements had gone into this new weapon. Now the King, staring through a spyglass, observed the results. After forcing the Llorrland ships to change course, his own vessels retreated, drawing the enemy away from his army.

A short time later, the Occitan ships turned again, coordinating angles of attack according to their training. Bolts from the ballistas arced across the sky. At first they fell short or missed their targets, the bolts falling to the fields below, where impact fuses caused them to burst into flame.

But then, as one of the Llorrland ships was beginning a turn, fire exploded on its envelope near the tail. Trailing black smoke, the vessel began to lose altitude—inside the envelope, one of the air-filled ballonets had been pierced. As the ship turned back toward the border, a cheer went up from Carswell's army on the plain below.

The other two Llorrland ships maneuvered to continue the attack. They launched bolts of their own, but these all fell short of the Occitan ships. When flame appeared on the lower hull of a second Llorrland vessel, it too turned to retreat. Soon after, the third ship gave up the fight and headed back to the border.

Carswell shifted his spyglass to the distant ground, where Alaric's army was spread in loose formations along a front a mile long. Most prominently, in the center stood rank upon rank of soldiers in black armor. Carswell grimaced as he estimated their number at well over a thousand.

Even as their airships withdrew, the army of Llorrland began to advance.

"Now we shall see how invulnerable those creatures really are," the King said.

Even as he spoke, his airships flew to the attack. As previously arranged, they would concentrate their bombing on the zolgar lines. With the enemy ships routed, the Occitan ships could swoop low and drop firebombs with accuracy.

Each airship carried at least a dozen bombs. Soon the ground where the zolgars marched exploded into orange flames and spouts of black smoke. Carswell watched, hopeful of the effect.

But it soon became clear that bombing alone would not defeat the supernatural creatures. As the smoke dispersed, here and there a few zolgars lay on the ground, crumpled and unmoving amid the fires. But the majority continued their relentless march—even those whose black armor glowed with heat or flamed with the clinging gel of the Moldorn fire.

And now, on both flanks, Alaric's cavalry was advancing.

"We must ride." The King lifted his lance and shouted to his knights. "May Fortune be with you, my lords. For Occitan!"

As he led the horsemen down the hill, the King's thoughts were of his son, who rode with him this day, and of his Queen and young daughter, far away in the beautiful city. Carswell had not wanted this war. But there had never been a question in his heart that if the invasion came, he must fight with all his power—for his people and their freedom, for his family most of all.

As he reached the front ranks, rows of crossbowmen were already firing, their arrows streaking toward the enemy lines. The King dispatched Mendosa to lead the right flank and ordered Darien to ride with him. He commanded another duke to lead the charge on the left. Carswell himself would take the center, advancing against the zolgars. As King, he viewed this most perilous post as his duty.

At his command, trumpets sounded and the army moved forward—first lines of knights with lances and shields, next armored foot soldiers with pikes and swords, then crossbowmen in the rear, pausing at intervals to load and fire.

Soon arrows flew in from the Llorrland side as well, forcing the King and his knights to lift shields and duck their heads. Still, a few fell wounded.

Glancing to the right and left, Carswell could see the other flanks also advancing. Directly in front of him, the lines of zolgars marched out of the smoke and fire, drawing ever nearer.

The King shouted for his men to charge. Lowering his lance, he spurred the palomino to a gallop. The horses beside him kept pace, their hooves thumping over the field. Ahead, the zolgars loomed, raising long swords in their two armored fists.

The forces met with tremendous crashes, collisions breaking apart the zolgar lines. Carswell's lance drove through the chest of one enemy, the king himself nearly unhorsed by the impact. Regaining balance, he drew his sword.

A melee surrounded him, zolgars charging from right and left, swinging and stabbing at men and horses alike. The King yanked the reins to turn his steed, but too late. Long swords stabbed the palomino in the flank and chest, penetrating its armor. The animal screamed in pain and collapsed, the King falling with it and crashing to the ground.

Far away, on the parapet of Tonnsburg Castle, Mirafra worked with the other apprentices, casting power into the cold fire. She had performed this exercise twice a day since being admitted to Jovadia's circle.

But today was different. Today, Jovadia had told them, the zolgars marched into battle.

All of them could feel the difference—more urgency and intensity. Today, it seemed, the energy flowed away as quickly as it was given.

As at other times, Mirafra's mind flowed with the power. But the vision she saw today seemed more immediate. She knew it was real and happening now. She watched and felt the zolgars swinging their long swords, hacking and lunging. She watched and felt men and horses falling, saw blood flying, heard screams of agony and death.

This time Mirafra felt no thrill, only torment. She could not escape the truth that the men and animals bleeding and dying were real, living beings like herself.

She could not bear it. Could not *contribute* to it. With a gasp, she drew her mental focus away from the cold fire, back into the psithe. She wrapped the power around herself for protection.

She did not dare to look at the other majjas, fearing they might have noticed her withdrawal. She kept her gaze lowered.

Only after a long while, when Jovadia finally declared an end to the session, did Mirafra dare to look up.

The Bittern was staring at her. Her failure had been noticed. Terrified, Mirafra cast her eyes again at the stone floor.

King Alaric savored red wine from a jeweled goblet. The vintage from the region of Ellysee was justly famous, he thought. But tonight the wine tasted especially sweet.

The King was in a jolly mood, having enjoyed a good dinner. He sat at table in his pavilion, which had been moved and reassembled following today's victory. Sitting with him, generals and high-ranking nobles listened to reports from the battlefield.

Overall, it had gone exceedingly well. True, his airships had been routed by superior weapons and, perhaps, better airmanship. And, while the Occitan forces on the left and right flanks had fought his own troops nearly to a standstill, those formations were simply distractions. The main thrust, of course, had been the middle, where the 1500 zolgars had devastated the enemy troops. It was even reported that Carswell had been wounded after foolishly leading the center attack himself. Unfortunately, the King of Occitan had escaped capture.

Still, Carswell's army was in full retreat. Moreover, only a few dozen zolgars had been lost to the aerial bombing. The rest stood outside in the field, safely at rest and ready to march again at dawn.

In summary, Alaric felt there was much to celebrate. The King was puzzled therefore that some of the nobles seemed less enthusiastic. Still, after his third cup of wine, he decided to ignore the matter.

That was until he had dismissed the gathering. Four of the lords, led by Duke Strasser, the Prime Minister, begged a word with him in private.

The King poured himself more wine. "What is it? We won a great victory today. Why do you all look so sour?"

"Forgive us, Majesty," Strasser said. "The victory is great indeed. Still, today's events raise concerns that we ought to discuss."

"Go on."

"First, our airships were defeated rather handily by—"

"By superior ballistas and better flyers. But our pilots will learn from today. And once we conquer Occitan and confiscate their airships, those weapons will be ours. What is your second concern?"

Strasser paused, looking glumly at the other lords, then continued. "Our land forces only won today because of the zolgars. But they are unnatural creatures and might not always be ours to control."

The King leaned back, letting out a sigh. He saw the problem now, one that had been festering for some time. "You worry about our Court Wizard and her powers. And now that we are away from the capital, far from Jovadia, you finally have the courage to voice your concerns."

Lips clamped, the Duke gave the slightest of nods.

The King laughed, setting down his cup. "I know. You wonder who holds the real power now. Are we as much Jovadia's puppets as the zolgars? Well, perhaps we are. But if that is a role I must play to expand my empire—yes, I said *empire*—then so be it!"

The noblemen looked at each other, appalled.

"Fools! Don't you see it? The Bittern is not using me. It is I who am using her. Yes, I have become intimate with her, deposed the Queen and replaced all my other paramours with Jovadia alone. But this intimacy also gives me easy access to her person. If and when she becomes a threat, a knife delivered without warning ends the threat at once. You see, my lords, even great wizards can die."

Weary and disconsolate, King Carswell rode in a supply cart on the trail west of Ellysee. Over the fields and through the woods all around him, the army marched in retreat through the twilight.

The King's knee was swollen, the leg injured when the palomino fell on him. Fortunately, the physician believed that no bones had been broken. Carswell had been lucky indeed that one of his knights had rushed to his aid in time to lift the King onto his own horse.

Seeing the slaughter all around, Carswell had immediately ordered retreat. Bowmen and foot soldiers covered the withdrawal, and the Llorrland forces soon gave up pursuit. Though virtually invulnerable to attack, the zolgars were not swift in the field. That much, at least, was in Occitan's favor.

"Your Majesty, are you badly hurt?" A horseman had galloped up beside the cart—General Mendosa.

"No. I'll be all right. My son—?"

"Darien is well and fought bravely, my lord. He is helping to supervise the care of the wounded. Our company withdrew only when we heard the retreat sounded, and we took only moderate losses."

"That is good news, Mendosa. Thank you for your noble work."

"What are your orders now, my King?"

Carswell stared into the gathering dark. "We retreat to the riverside across from Baivonne. There we must make our stand. I've already sent riders to the airfield with instructions. Our ships will continue to harry the enemy. Although I hate to set fire to parts of our own land, this will at least slow the zolgars."

"Yes," the general said. "There seems to be nothing else to do."

"Agreed ..." Carswell voice was tight. "Those cursed creatures ... unbelievably strong. I fear no human army will stop them."

That left only one hope: Clorinda and her allies. If their wizardry could not stop the zolgars, all would be lost.

Chapter 23

Many thoughts moved through Jovadia's mind. Under the night sky, she leaned on the parapet of her tower, the castle and the city quiet beneath her. She needed these times of solitude to balance her energies, to contemplate all the forces she had set in motion.

And to settle unanswered questions.

In the past day, the powers she commanded had risen to new heights. On that far battlefield near Ellysee, the zolgars had performed majestically. In her mind, Jovadia had seen King Carswell's army routed, Alaric's forces sweeping the field—their first great victory of the war. It seemed inevitable now that Occitan would fall, and soon.

The power driving that victory had come from this castle, from the cauldron of cold fire underground, and from the psithes that directed it. The circle of apprentices had performed well, and yet ... That had raised one of those unanswered questions.

Mirafra the Ruby Lark. She had drawn back her will from the cauldron, used the energy to shield herself. Mirafra remained a mystery. Was she as painfully confused as she seemed? Or was that all a skillful masquerade?

It might be best to dispose of the Ruby Lark and be done with it.

But Jovadia hated unsolved mysteries. And killing the girl might set other, unknown forces into motion.

A sudden rustling caused the Bittern to whirl, facing the center of the parapet. Faint in the starlight, a large crow swooped in and settled.

Jovadia knew at once this was no ordinary bird. With a flick of her wrist, she made her psithe a sword. She leveled the point as white light burst in the air, enveloping the crow.

A man stepped from the light, clad in black feathers. Seeing Jovadia with her sword drawn, the man tilted back, holding up his hands.

"Forgive my abrupt entrance. I mean you no harm."

She said nothing, only waited.

The man continued, "Perhaps you can help me. I seek a great majja, Jovadia the Bittern ... Could that by chance be you, my lady?"

"What is your name?"

He offered a bow. "I am Teron the Mooncrow."

Rising from his bow, Teron eyed the Bittern's sword. Having flown for two nights and a day in the bird form, he felt tired, in no condition for a fight. He had hoped to land unnoticed and spy out the castle before presenting himself. Circling over the tower, he had failed to pick out the still and silent figure leaning at the wall.

Careless of him. But no help for it now.

"I assure you, Lady, I mean no harm. Are you indeed Jovadia?"

She smiled, the expression eerie in the psithe-light. "I am. What is your business with me, Mooncrow?"

Teron spread his hands. "Well, I hoped we might become partners. I've just come from King Carswell's army, you see. I know something of his troop deployments and quite a bit about his airships."

"Interesting. But why come to me with such information? Why not King Alaric? If you come from the location of the battle, he was much closer to you."

"Yes. But I feared the King might act stupidly and have me killed without hearing me out. I trusted a wizard of your reputation to act with better wisdom."

Her smile widened. "You are a clever fellow. I expected we might meet one day, ever since I heard that you were at Carswell's court. I learned from my agent there that you had helped the Duke of Duneidan's son escape when his father's castle fell. In fact, I assigned that same agent to have you and the young duke killed."

"Fortunately, he failed," Teron laughed.

"So, at least up till that time, you were Carswell's ally. What made you decide to change sides?"

"Ah. I was riding in an airship that patrolled the border when I spotted your black-armored creatures below. I remembered how formidable they had shown themselves at Duneidan, and I saw well over a thousand of them on the march. I realized then that I was on the wrong side of this war. So, at the first opportunity, I invoked the quinteer and flew away."

"Sounds reasonable." The Bittern lowered her sword. "You've flown quite a distance then, and it's rather chilly up here. Why don't we continue our talk indoors?"

Teron grinned. "I'd be delighted, and most grateful."

Still holding the blade, Jovadia directed him through a doorway and down a curling stair. She was careful to make the Mooncrow walk ahead as they emerged in a lamp-lit corridor. At this late hour, no guards or servants were about. This part of the castle, Teron surmised, belonged to Jovadia alone.

She showed him to a sitting room, to a chair before a stone hearth. No fire burned, but Jovadia used her sword to send heat into the ashes.

"May I offer you food or drink?" she asked, gesturing at a pitcher and cups that rested on the mantel.

"Don't bother, please." Teron held up his psithe-cup. "I'll just fix myself a little water."

The Bittern smiled with amusement. She took the chair beside his and changed her psithe from sword to disk.

"Even if you don't need me to defeat Occitan," Teron said, "I might still prove a useful partner. I've visited many lands and studied obscure magics. And, should your military ambitions eventually reach to Ibor, I know all about the Moldorns and their neighbors."

"As I said," Jovadia replied, leaning back in her chair, "you are a clever fellow. Still, you claim to have betrayed King Carswell and come to me with information. I find this somewhat hard to believe, since it is exactly the same story I heard from the Ruby Lark."

"Oh, yes ... Mirafra, wasn't it?" Teron frowned as though trying to remember. "I believe Montodoro's plan was for her to come here and somehow sabotage your power. No one would tell me the details. I assume she has been captured and killed?"

"No. She still lives." Jovadia lifted the disk, pulsing with power. "How long the same may be said for you is another question."

Irresistibly, Teron's eyes were drawn to the gold and silvery sparkling around her hands. He felt Jovadia probing his mind and responded by blanking his thoughts.

He smiled at her.

"Your will is strong," Jovadia observed.

Jovadia lowered the disk, then suddenly held it high. Blinding power flashed in Teron's brain, and he lost all awareness.

"Awake, Mooncrow."

Rough, damp fabric pressed against his face. The air held a moldy smell. Teron blinked, grimaced at the pain throbbing in his skull. He was lying on a cot.

Nearby stood Jovadia, holding her disk, and another majja whose sword lit the narrow cell. Teron sat up and heard the clinking of metal. His hands touched his neck: he wore a steel collar chained to the wall.

His fingertips pressed his forehead. "Why did you put me here?"

"To learn the truth, of course."

"But I've already told you ..."

"Don't bother to lie." Jovadia held up the small wooden spiral. "I've already found this, just like the one I took from the Ruby Lark. I know it's meant to somehow disrupt the cold fire, though I don't yet understand the process."

Teron hung his head, a show of defeat.

"So I can only surmise," Jovadia went on, "the high maestras sent the Ruby Lark here to destroy my cauldron. Either she betrayed them, as she claims, or simply failed. So, next they sent you on the same mission. But is that really all, or are there other twists to the plot that I am missing?"

The Bittern lifted the psithe over her head and spoke in a commanding voice. "Tell me why you are really here."

Teron stared into the psithe, his head swimming. But deep within, he clung to his determination and suppressed all coherent thought.

After several moments, Jovadia lowered the disk. "I congratulate you, Teron the Mooncrow. Your resistance is indeed formidable. But we'll see how strong it is after two or three days without food and water."

"Maestra," the apprentice said. "Wouldn't it be safer to kill him now?"

"No, Andelica. Not until we know for sure why he came here." She started to turn away, then paused and stared at Teron. "Without a psithe, he is no danger at all. Oh, yes, Mooncrow. I have taken your psithe and already added it to the cauldron."

With that, Jovadia and her apprentice left. The door clanged shut, leaving Teron in darkness.

Teron sat on the cot, folded his legs, and took deep breaths to calm his body. Gradually, the headache faded.

The Bittern was right, of course: there was more to the plan. In fact, after the high maestras decided to cast their enchantment on Mirafra, Teron and his friends had constructed three plans—one wrapped inside the next.

Plan One called for Mirafra to break through the enchantment on her own and regain her memory. By then, she might know the location of the cauldron or be able to find and defuse it on her own. Teron had never placed much hope in Plan One.

In Plan Two, Teron would come to Tonnsburg and either conceal himself or inveigle the confidence of Jovadia long enough to discover the cauldron. That was why he carried copies of the wood spiral and the two beads. The spiral decoy had been taken, but not his belt, so he still had the beads, the actual conduit devices. But escaping from this cell without a psithe seemed impossible.

Well, Teron had always believed that the third plan offered the best chance. Time now to put it into motion.

Teron relaxed, letting his spirit settle to deeper and deeper levels. After a long time, he reached out with his mind, out and up through the walls and floors of stone, searching. Visions passed through him: the roofs and towers of the castle, gray in the twilight of morning, the inner halls and long corridors, faint in lamplight. In his thoughts, he called gently, over and over.

Mirafra.

Mirafra stirred, rolling over in bed. She had not slept peacefully since arriving in Tonnsburg, tormented by frightening dreams, by the confusion in her mind, the blank strands of memory.

Now someone seemed to be calling her, whispering her name— one more symptom of the madness that plagued her in this castle. She sat up, wrapped the blanket over her shoulders, hugging herself, straining to shut out the intrusive whispers.

Yes, she had guarded herself like this since yesterday, since drawing back from the cold fire, from the gruesome realization. Before, in the practice sessions, she had found the visions of the zolgars fearful but also exciting—the weird thrill of their power. But yesterday, watching the actual killing had struck Mirafra with horror. She saw clearly then that the zolgars were evil, that Jovadia and her circle were evil. That was why she had withdrawn her energy, wrapped herself in protection.

But what next? Perhaps she could escape from Jovadia, invoke the quinteer and fly away from Tonnsburg. But to where? Where could she go? Not back to Montodoro. The high maestras had betrayed her and sent her here. She recalled Duneidan, being happy there, with Sharam the Crane as her mentor. And with Arwyn. But Sharam was dead and Duneidan conquered. And Arwyn? Fighting in the war, no doubt, possibly dead already.

Mirafra desperately needed to clear her thoughts, to find some other path. She must keep herself shielded until she could piece together what had really been done to her, how she had ended up here—and what to do next.

Mirafra ... Mirafra.

That voice again. She summoned more energy to block it out.

Eventually, Teron gave in to exhaustion and slept.

When he woke, after what seemed only a little time, he was still in total darkness. The cell had no windows, only the barred opening in the door that he had noticed before. No light came through there, even though it must be day by now. Doubtless, the cell was in a dungeon underground.

He sat up and focused on contacting Mirafra. He had not expected this part to be so difficult. On the airship traveling back from Montodoro, under Clorinda's direction, Teron had attuned his mind to the Ruby Lark psithe—and so to Mirafra herself. This attunement should have allowed his voice to reach her across the mental planes, to speak the words that would lift the enchantment and restore her memory.

That was the essence of Plan Three.

Teron had to keep trying. Without food or water, he didn't know how long his strength would last, how long he could resist Jovadia's penetrating his mind and discovering the truth.

And there was no Plan Four.

Chapter 24

Peering through a spyglass, Arwyn scanned the distant lines of the enemy army.

Late morning, and for the second day in a row the Llorrland side showed no signs of attacking.

So far, there had been only one battle on the southern front—on the day Arwyn and Topiedeon landed, set down by the airship with a few dozen other reinforcements from Baivonne. Alaric's forces marched over the border, archers and foot soldiers led by a small number of cavalry. Arwyn donned his armor in time to join the counterattack. But, stationed in reserve in the rear, he did no actual fighting. Soon after the initial assault, the Llorrland side withdrew. The Occitan forces chased them to the border, but no farther.

Arwyn suspected he knew one reason the enemy might be reluctant to engage. The banners he recognized above the tents and campgrounds belonged mostly to nobles of Arabhedden, the southern peninsula Alaric had conquered. The flag of Llorrland flew only before the cluster of pavilions at the center.

Many of the conscripted troops from the south were probably not enthusiastic about fighting Alaric's war. This idea had been discussed last night at a council of commanders that Arwyn attended. Another theory was that the placing of forces at the southern front was simply a diversion. Some of the commanders argued that they should stop waiting and attack. But King Carswell had ordered that his army not cross the border, only defend it. Some suggested they should withdraw at least some of their men to go and reinforce the King's army in the north—where, they had heard, Carswell had suffered heavy losses and was in retreat. In the end, the lords had voted to obey their standing orders for now and wait.

That was when Arwyn came up with a plan of his own.

He had mentioned it to no one except the bard Topiedeon, who had seen him walking this way, armed for battle. They stood together now at the edge of the Occitan camp.

Across the empty fields, Arwyn spotted what he was searching for—the coat of arms of Baglan, the usurper. Under that banner would be stationed the men from Duneidan. Arwyn folded up the spyglass and turned to Topiedeon.

"Time to march."

The young Duke discarded his helmet, bent over, and struggled to pull off the chainmail hauberk.

Shaking his head, Topiedeon assisted. "I will say again, young lord. I think you are mad to try this."

"Perhaps." Arwyn straightened. He now wore a wool surcoat and a wide belt with his scabbard and sword. He picked up a spear. On its point he'd hung his tabard, with the coat-of-arms of House Duneidan.

"But *you* are *certainly* mad to come with me."

"Oh. I agree." Topiedeon had slipped the mandolin from over his shoulder and now strummed a chord. "But I cannot deny myself the chance to witness such bold madness! Besides, they're less likely to harm a poor minstrel."

Arwyn laughed. "I wouldn't count on that."

Lifting the spear high, he marched down into the field.

Walking beside him, Topiedeon plucked a tune. "Maybe a bit of music will charm the fellows."

Arwyn smiled grimly. He had debated with himself through a sleepless night whether to actually do this. He thought it highly probable that he was marching to his death.

But with all that he had lost, what was left for him in life? This deed at least seemed a righteous way to honor his family. And if

Mirafra and Teron, who had far less to gain from this war than he, could risk their lives on wild gambles, how could Arwyn do less? Added to that was the small chance that he might succeed. If the men of Arabhedden were as disaffected with the war as Arwyn suspected, he might just convince them to change sides.

Ahead, crowds of men gathered to watch their approach. The music and the sight of two lone figures crossing the field alone would certainly rouse curiosity. Arwyn waved his tabard like a flag. He spotted a few bowmen, kneeling and pointing their weapons. But none fired.

When they reached within thirty yards of the massed soldiers, a knight in plate armor ordered them to halt. Arwyn planted his spear into the ground and raised his sword.

"Greetings, clans of Arabhedden," he shouted. "I am Arwyn, last son of Rhys Keltonn and the rightful Duke of Duneidan. I seek Baglan, the usurper, that I may kill him in fair combat."

An uproar spread over the gathered crowd—muttering, arguing, even some laughter. Topiedeon picked a dramatic tune, though Arwyn thought the playing a bit nervous.

Finally, the knight who had spoken before waved his hands for quiet. "Duke Baglan is in camp," he shouted. "Your challenge will be conveyed to him."

Arwyn stood his ground and waited. More and more soldiers were arriving, hurrying in from all over the camp. They formed a wide circle, with Arwyn and the bard at the center. Some of the soldiers Arwyn recognized by their tabards as neighbors from the highlands near Duneidan. Others wore the armor and tunics of Peltaine or Llorrland.

A man broke from the circle and approached, a broad-shouldered warrior with wild red hair and beard. As he drew near, Arwyn recognized him—one of his father's trusted vassals.

Staring hard, the redbeard exclaimed, "By the hills in moonlight, it really is you, young Arwyn!"

"Not so young anymore, Sir Crowley."

"Lad, I am happy to see you alive. But not so glad to find us on opposite sides."

Arwyn nodded. "I follow the path of honor, as I must, Sir Knight. And I bear no ill will to you or any of my father's allies who have been forced to fight under Llorrland's flag." Setting a hand on the old knight's arm, he lowered his voice. "But I ask you to consider this: Should I win my challenge, I will call on all loyal men of Duneidan, and all free men of Arabhedden, to rebel and join me in fighting the tyrant Alaric."

Crowley leaned back, lips parted. "But lad ... It is a noble dream, but you are still a youngster. I fear you have no chance against Baglan."

Arwyn hefted the sword in his hand. "We shall see. Think over what I've said."

Crowley bowed and walked back to the lines. Arwyn watched him exchanging words with other clansmen, some of whom the young duke recognized. Then that section of the circle parted, and a new group of knights emerged, dressed in mail coats and helmets, carrying pikes. Arwyn's eyes narrowed as he recognized Baglan.

When the usurper saw Arwyn, his teeth flashed in a grimace. He ordered his men to stay behind, drew his sword and strode across the open ground. Arwyn glared at the man but kept his own sword lowered. Topiedeon stopped playing and stepped back.

Baglan halted a few yards away and said in a low, scornful voice, "Go back to your books, boy. Leave the fighting to men."

Arwyn pointed his sword and shouted for all to hear. "Count Baglan, before this assembly, I, Arwyn Keltonn, son of the rightful Duke, name you traitor to Duneidan. I charge you with conniving in the murder of my family, by means of foul sorcery. And I demand satisfaction under the code of arms."

"This is absurd!" Baglan spread his arms, facing the lines. "I'm not even sure this boy is who he claims!"

Voices murmured through the crowd. "He is Arwyn!" Sir Crowley bellowed. "We know him!" Others from the ranks of Duneidan shouted their agreement.

"But how can I fight him under the code?" Baglan scoffed. "Besides that he is not full-grown to manhood, he wears no armor!"

"I fight as I am!" Arwyn yelled. "As the challenged party, Baglan has the right to choose weapons and armor. But only for himself! This sword of Duneidan is enough for me to vanquish a traitor."

Groans of surprise and hoots of approval sounded along the lines. Arwyn smiled to himself, for now he had the Count cornered. Challenged and insulted before the whole army, Baglan could hardly refuse the duel. And, after proclaiming Arwyn less than a man, it would be deemed a disgrace to fight him with superior weaponry.

"Conniving puppy!" Baglan glared from under his helmet. "I will make you pay for this." He turned and shouted aloud. "Honor leaves me no choice but to fight this misguided boy as he stands, with only a sword and no armor. I shall try to make his death quick and merciful."

He marched back to the lines, where vassals assisted him in removing his chainmail.

"Well, this is turning out better than I expected," Topiedeon remarked through the side of his mouth. "Conniving puppy, indeed."

Arwyn gave a wild grin as he warmed up, swiping his blade through the air. Dressed as a knight, with shield and armor, he would have stood little chance against the stronger, more experienced Baglan. But this way, relying on quickness and the swordsmanship he had learned from the Mooncrow, he might just win the duel.

His reverie was shattered by gasps and groans. Without warning, Baglan was charging, sword raised high. Arwyn just had a moment to gather himself and spring to the side, avoiding a vicious downstroke. He leaped again and parried as the Count stabbed upward.

As he landed, Arwyn's foot slipped on the soft ground. Seeing him off balance, Baglan stepped in, lifting his blade overhead. Arwyn launched himself left and rolled onto the ground. The Count's violent slash met empty air, and this time threw him off balance. Arwyn scrambled to his feet, darted in, and thrust. Baglan parried the stroke with ease.

"You should have died in Duneidan with the rest of your family," the Count hissed. "But I will mend that oversight now."

Hate surged in Arwyn, inciting a reckless courage. He stepped in, too close for safety, inviting the Count to thrust. Arwyn shifted. He took the point under his shoulder blade and, at the same instant, lunged hard. That drove the steel deeper into his shoulder, but his own point stabbed Baglan's throat.

The Count staggered, gasping, clutching at his neck. He fell sideways, rolling onto his back. Arwyn leaned down and thrust again, driving the sword up under the jaw so that blood spurted out.

Only when the death spasms stopped did Arwyn pull his blade free. He glanced down at his shoulder and clutched the wound, which was bleeding badly. All around him the soldiers were staring in shocked quiet.

Snarling, Arwyn faced them, shaking his sword in the air. "Men of Duneidan, with this traitor's death, my debt of honor to my family is satisfied. But you, all of you clansmen of Arabhedden, you have been forced to march under the flag of a tyrant. Bear it no longer! I, the rightful Duke of Duneidan, call on you to join me. Throw off the yoke of Alaric. Join the forces of King Carswell and take back your freedom!"

Along the lines, the silence returned, but only for a moment.

"Long live Arwyn, Duke of Duneidan!" someone shouted.

More voices took up the call, and then other men roared. Arwyn saw arguments and disputes rising through the throng, skirmishes breaking out. Men from Duneidan rushed in to surround him. One lifted the spear with his tabard; others hoisted him on their shoulders. From the new vantage point, Arwyn could see altercations spreading across the camp—men gesturing as they argued, others shoving each other or drawing steel.

Cries reached his ears: "Long live Arwyn! Long live Duneidan!" "Death to the tyrant Alaric!"

Dizzy, Arwyn gazed down at the blood seeping from between the fingers where he held the wound. His chin drooped forward as he blacked out.

Chapter 25

Mirafra strained to calm her thoughts as she practiced her midday meditation. Since yesterday morning, she had been mostly successful at shielding herself from disturbances.

But now, for some reason, she could not stop thinking about Arwyn.

In all her struggles to reconstruct the past, she had never believed that Arwyn betrayed her. No, for him she felt only friendship and deep affection.

Perhaps he was in danger, and her feelings for him had been activated by that? Perhaps, indeed, he had died on some battlefield ... *No!* She could not bear to think of it. If Arwyn was gone, who in all the world was left for her?

Only one person came to mind: Teron the Mooncrow. He was a strange and distant man, but he seemed to care for her and Arwyn, had taught them both new skills, indeed, had gone out of his way to help them, at cost to himself.

Where was Teron now? She couldn't even guess.

Mirafra. Mirafra.

That voice again. She had blocked it for so many hours. Over time, it had all but vanished. Now, suddenly, it had a different tone.

Mirafra. Hear me.

"Teron?" she whispered

Yes, lady! I have reached you at last.

"I-I don't understand."

Listen closely. You were enchanted by the high maestras in Montodoro. Parts of your memory were hidden.

235

"Yes, I know."

Know also this: The enchantment was cast without my knowledge or agreement. The Supreme Gathering decided that your only chance to make the Bittern believe that you had been betrayed was for you to believe it yourself. Once the enchantment was done, I saw no choice but to play along.

"Where are you?"

Nearby. I came here to lift the enchantment. Listen to these words and repeat them. Cosma deciduloas, megurum nee sellee.

As she whispered the words from the magical tongue, her mind translated them to the more familiar, modern Norrling: "Confusion is lifted. I am my true self."

And when she repeated the chant a second time, the meaning flowed into truth. Fragments of her mind and memory, broken and scattered, fell back into place.

She remembered Clorinda the Ibis waking her on that last night in Montodoro, saying she was sorry to do this as light from her disk blazed into Mirafra's eyes. And Mirafra recalled what came before: how she had agreed to take on this mission, to travel to Tonnsburg alone and try to locate Jovadia's cauldron—to destroy the cold fire.

Mirafra, Teron's voice called in her mind. *Have your memories returned?*

"Yes. Yes! But I failed, Teron. I gave Jovadia the wooden spiral."

That was a ruse. The real devices are two glass jewels, the eyes of your Ruby Lark mask. Do you still have your mask and psithe?

"Yes." Mirafra stared at the bird mask, set on a chair beside the bed.

Have you found the cauldron? Teron asked.

"No. Jovadia keeps its location secret. But I know it's under the castle. I think I can find it by following the energy trails."

That will have to do. Best start at once.

"Yes." She stood, picked up the psithe-disk. "But where are you, Teron?"

In a dungeon below the castle, I think. Don't worry about me. First, the cauldron. Throw one of the eye jewels into the cold fire, then count to thirty, then throw in the other one. Do you understand?

"Yes, Teron, I understand."

Hurry! Time may be short.

Mirafra pulled on her boots, donned the cape, set the bird mask on her head. The apprentices would be gathering soon to cast power into the cauldron. Usually, they did this on the parapet, but sometimes in a circular chamber below. Either way, Mirafra would likely be seen if she tried to leave the tower. She would need to weave a concealment. The disk on its chain hung close to her heart. She set both hands over it, feeling its power.

Feeling *her* power.

At last, she felt whole again. She *was* the Ruby Lark.

Focusing her mind, she chanted to invoke the concealment, draping the energy over her body, feeling its power grow.

After sealing the enchantment, she went to the chamber door. Cautiously, she pushed it open, looked in both directions, then stepped into the corridor.

As she moved toward the stairs, she heard footsteps coming behind her. She pressed herself against the wall as two majja approached—Maarit the Curlew and Varma the Bunting. They chatted excitedly. The zolgars were on the march. There might be a battle today. Mirafra held her breath and sent more power into the psithe.

The apprentices walked past without seeing her. Mirafra waited until they reached the steps and started up. Then she hurried after them and went down.

"Teron," she whispered. "Are you still with me?"

Yes, Mirafra.

The connection in her mind felt fragile. "Are you hurt? Did they torture you?"

Just weak ... lack of water. Please, focus on the cauldron.

"All right. But after that, I will find you, I promise."

The days of practice had attuned Mirafra's psithe to the cold fire, and now she could use the disk to follow the powerful emanations. At the bottom of the tower, she entered a broad corridor with high arches and polished floors. She passed sentries guarding certain doorways and servants going about their business. Because of the concealment, no one noticed her.

Near the center of the castle, she came to an iron gate with stairs leading down. The gate stood open, the way guarded by two zolgars in their black plate armor, silent and unmoving. Mirafra reinforced her concealment, then walked past them, her heart pounding.

After descending three flights of steps, she entered a cramped hallway. No lamps burned here, but she did not need light. The faint trail of the cold fire guided her through the darkness. The underground of Castle Tonnsburg was a maze, she realized. Somewhere in the maze, Teron was held prisoner. And somewhere, near the bottom of this labyrinth, like a drain where water flowed out, Jovadia had established her cauldron.

The Ruby Lark psithe did not fail her. Seven levels below ground, at the end of a short tunnel, silver light shimmered through the bars of a dungeon door. Confident she had found the cauldron, Mirafra ran to the door. She used her psithe-wand to slide the inner bolt. The door shuddered on its hinges as she pulled it open.

Inside, at the center of the chamber, the cold fire blazed—frosty flames leaping and shuddering from a pit several yards across.

In front of the pit stood Jovadia, holding her sword. "Come in, Ruby Lark. I've been waiting for you."

For just a moment, Mirafra froze in terror. Then, gathering her nerve, she forced herself to walk calmly, to show no sign of panic. She called in her mind to Teron but sensed no response. Looking down, she saw that, without thinking of it, she had changed her psithe to a sword.

Mirafra stopped a few steps from the Bittern, their eyes locked.

"Yes," Jovadia explained. "I felt you communicating with the Mooncrow, and of course I knew the reason. I sensed all along that there were plots within plots involving the two of you."

She pointed her sword. "But now the plots are ending, I think. Will you walk into the cold fire, or must I force you?"

Mirafra stepped back, crouched in a fighting stance. The Bittern smiled and matched the posture.

Jovadia attacked, thrusting, her blade flashing white. Mirafra parried and retreated.

The icy flames of the cauldron rippled and hissed. Jovadia was drawing on its power. Realizing this, Mirafra opened her own mind to the cold fire, as she had practiced doing these past days. Even as she circled, tensing and feinting, she could feel the wild energy pulsing in her limbs.

Mirafra swung the sword, knocking the Bittern's blade aside. She thrust low, then high, stabbing close to Jovadia's neck.

The Bittern leaped back, laughing. "Oh, you have done well, Ruby Lark. A pity you were against me from the start. You would have made a fine apprentice—might even have replaced Andelica one day."

She was speaking to distract. Just after her last words came a fierce lunge, the blade dazzling. Mirafra was just able to jump back. But she lost her balance and tumbled to the floor.

Rolling over quickly, she scrambled to her feet just in time to parry.

"Nice." Jovadia stepped sideways. "But that was a close thing. You won't last much longer."

Even as the Bittern's sword flashed with renewed light, Mirafra knew her words were true. Desperately, Mirafra called in her mind to Teron, hoping he might lend her power.

No answer came.

But, as Mirafra circled, forced closer and closer to the cauldron, another thought ran through her mind: *What would the Mooncrow do?*

A daring answer came: one last, mad ploy.

Close to the cauldron's edge, the Bittern lunged. Mirafra cross-stepped and fell on her back. She rolled over, careful to place the sword beneath her body.

"No!" She cried, lying face down, covering her head with both hands. "Please spare me! You are right. I betrayed you. But I was betrayed! I was forced into it!"

Without looking up, she felt the Bittern standing over her. Hidden under her body, the sword became a disk.

"Please! Please!" She sobbed. "The high maestras' enchantment is lifted now. I could become your apprentice in truth. I would serve you well!"

Jovadia waited—either considering Mirafra's words or simply enjoying her suffering.

Into the Ruby Lark psithe, Mirafra cast an illusion: the very image of herself lying there, pleading for mercy.

An instant after sealing the illusion, Mirafra rolled over, changed the disk to a wand, leapt to her feet.

Jovadia blinked and looked up as the illusion vanished. She had been fooled for only a moment, but that was enough. Mirafra threw herself on the Bittern. She shoved hard, with all the power of the wand and all the strength of her body.

Shock on her face, Jovadia reeled back. She lifted her arms too late as she fell into the cold fire.

Mirafra gasped, jumping back. Jovadia's body was lifted by the flames. Her arms flailed like wings, then stiffened. A faint scream sounded from her throat. Her body sparkled as it changed into ice. Even as the ice rippled into being, it shattered into fragments that tumbled down into the pit.

Panting, Mirafra clutched her forehead, gathered her wits ... The Ruby Lark mask, the two jeweled eyes!

She pulled the beaked mask off her head, squeezed one of the eyes. Her fingers couldn't loosen it. She picked up the psithe, formed it into a knife, used the point to pry the jewel free. It popped out and tumbled to the floor. Mirafra picked it up, stepped forward, and tossed it into the cauldron.

Chapter 26

Many leagues away, at the edge of the airfield in Baivonne, Fystus the Emu was snoozing in the shade. His chair leaned against the wall of the shack where he slept—where either he or Clorinda the Ibis stayed constantly on watch, ready to light the hot fire.

Suddenly he woke, startled. The psithe-disk that rested in his lap was screeching, like the cries of innumerable birds.

Fystus shook himself. "At last! At last!" he muttered.

Grunting, he pulled himself to his feet. As he hurried across the open field, he changed the disk into a sword. Stopping at what he considered a safe distance, he summoned power into the sword. As the intensity of heat and light grew, he uttered an incantation.

Suddenly, he pulled the sword back over his shoulder and swung it forward. A fireball sprang from the point, flung in the direction of the fuel pit. The ball rose high and arced down—falling twenty yards short of its target.

"Oh, dear me," the Emu grumbled.

He waddled closer to the pit and summoned another fireball. As soon as it landed at the center of the pit, he turned and hurried away.

Behind him, brief explosions sounded. Then the entire pit erupted into roaring flame and gouts of black smoke.

Mirafra finished counting to thirty and tossed in the second bead.

For a long moment, nothing happened.

Then, suddenly, the cold flames shot higher, writhing and flapping against the stone ceiling. The floor beneath her feet shook. Mirafra retreated to the open doorway.

Glancing back, amid the rushing of wind and rumbling of stones, she heard shrieking and chattering. To her astonishment, birds were flying out of the cauldron—dozens of birds, changed back from the psithes that had been thrown into the cold fire. Of many colors and types, they darted and wheeled about the chamber. Some found their way to the door and flew past her. Mirafra ducked her head amid the rushing of wings. When she looked up, she saw that the flames had subsided again, sinking back into the pit.

Then the chamber rumbled and shook. Stones fell from the ceiling, the arches cracking as more and more energy rushed down into the cauldron. Mirafra turned and fled into the corridor as the chamber caved in behind her.

The whole castle might collapse, she thought.

She had to find Teron.

The Mooncrow felt the dungeon cell shaking around him. The thought occurred that Mirafra must have succeeded. But, as the rumbling increased, another thought tempered his elation. The whirlpool of energy caused by the draining cold fire might bury him alive—not a particularly glorious end to Topiedeon's ballad cycle about the Mooncrow.

Standing, he tried once again to pry the metal collar from his neck, then to yank the chain from the wall. Hopeless, of course, and even if he succeeded, he had no way to open the cell door.

Teron. Can you hear me?

Mirafra. Yes! You cast in the eyes? Well done!

I am trying to find you.

Don't worry about me. The whole castle may collapse. Please, save yourself.

No!

A cawing from the dungeon door interrupted his thoughts. Then he heard a fluttering of wings as a bird flew in through the bars.

Could it be? Fystus had theorized that if the cold fire was drained, the psithes imprisoned in the cauldron might change back to their bird forms. Teron had hoped that his mooncrow might be freed. But he had hardly expected that the bird might come and find him.

Well, they had been together for a long time.

The crow screeched. Teron reached out his hand in the dark.

"Come, my friend. Time for both of us to leave this place."

As the bird settled on his arm, Teron caressed the head and uttered the words Fystus had taught him. *Cossomos teeala mactor lann.* It was a trick taught to masters in Ptolloden, changing a bird that had once been through the Birdhouse into a psithe, or the psithe back to the bird.

Teron was no master. But he had never been strict about adhering to the rules.

A sparkle of light appeared in the dark. Next moment, Teron held his psithe.

The floor beneath him shuddered yet again.

Teron? Are you all right? I felt something.

I'm all right, Mirafra. I have my psithe back. Find your way out, and I'll do the same.

Really?

Trust me, Mirafra! Go!

Mounted on horseback, King Carswell peered through his spyglass at the enemy lines. Their advance had paused, and a keen hope lifted the King's heart.

His own army stood mustered around him, ready to march. After retreating for two days, they had made a stand on the banks of the Machtiges River, across the wide channel from Baivonne. Carswell counted on the marshy ground to help slow the enemy. His airships had also harried their advance with bombing attacks. Still, with the black-armored zolgars in the vanguard, Alaric's army had pressed on relentlessly.

Until now.

A short while ago, Carswell had heard an explosion. Turning his telescope back toward the city, he had watched the promised hot fire bloom over the airfield. The plot of the wizards, he thought, might save his kingdom after all.

At first, he had seen no effect on the Llorrland army. But after a short time, the black-armored creatures seemed to slow. Carswell watched in growing elation as their ranks broke, some of the zolgars stopping motionless in their march, others crumpling to lie on the ground. Their human commanders ran among them, shouting and waving swords, but to no avail.

All of the Llorrland army had now stopped. Carswell folded up the spyglass.

"Sound the advance," he ordered, drawing his sword. "Fortune is with us. Alaric's creatures are vanquished. Now, we drive the invaders from our land!

The force of Teron's thoughts had convinced Mirafra. She stopped trying to locate him and instead concentrated on finding her own way out of the underground. With the sword gleaming in her hand, she did her best to retrace the path she had taken down.

The rumbling and shaking came in waves, rising and subsiding, but growing stronger each time. At last, Mirafra came to an upper passageway. At its end, she saw daylight shining on the wide stairs where she had descended.

As she ran up the corridor, the worst quake yet shuddered through the walls. The stairway broke and collapsed, part of the upper floor sagging with them. Mirafra changed the sword to a wand. She dashed forward and jumped, levitating herself up and over the fallen steps.

Landing on the floor above, she found the two zolgars that she had passed before, now lying collapsed in their black armor.

All around was chaos, guards and servants shouting as they fled from doorways and down steps, crossing the hall toward the castle gates.

Then Mirafra saw a group rushing toward her—Andelica and the rest of the apprentices.

"She's come from the cauldron!" the Tawny Swift shouted, raising her sword. "Where is Jovadia? What have you done?"

Panting, Mirafra changed the wand back to sword. "She is dead. It is over."

The castle trembled around them.

"We had better leave!" Lando the Golden Sparrow, started away. Two of the others moved to follow him.

"We'll leave." Andelica pointed her sword. "But first, this one dies."

Lando and the two others looked at her, at each other, and then ran toward the gates. Zara the Snowhawk drew her sword and stepped beside Andelica. Above them, the beams of the tall chamber groaned.

Mirafra crouched, moving her point back and forth as the two majja separated, readying to attack her from two sides.

246

Then a loud cawing sounded, and a black crow flew overhead. It circled and settled behind the apprentices. In a flash of light, Teron appeared, holding his sword.

"Can I lend you a hand with these two?" he asked.

Mirafra laughed and stepped forward.

Zara glanced at the two points approaching her from opposite sides. She threw down her blade and ran.

The floor shuddered.

Andelica gave a cry of despair and fell to her knees. "Please, don't kill me!"

Mirafra pressed her point close to the majja's chest. "Drop your sword."

Andelica obeyed, and Mirafra picked up the psithe-sword. Teron had already retrieved the one dropped by the Snowhawk. He looked up at the ceiling, where cracks were spreading through the beams.

"I suggest we all go outside now."

Followed by the Tawny Swift, Mirafra and Teron ran to the main gates. As they crossed the footbridge, the ground shook and the outer walls of the barbican sagged inward. The loudest crashing yet was heard as part of the roof collapsed.

Panting, Andelica stared at the castle, then at the Mooncrow and the Ruby Lark. After a moment, she turned and fled across the square. Teron uttered some words over her sword, and it changed to its bird form.

"I didn't know you could do that!" Mirafra marveled as he released the swift.

"A little trick they teach in Ptolloden," Teron said.

He repeated the incantation for the other captured psithe. The snowhawk cawed and lifted off. Following it with her eyes, Mirafra stared in wonder. Dozens of birds of different species circled over the castle.

Teron smiled at her. "If you're able to invoke the quinteer, I suggest we join them."

Mirafra nodded. "A fine idea."

Moments later, the Ruby Lark and the Mooncrow wheeled in the sky over Tonnsburg Castle, before setting off to the west.

In the time that followed, historians would record how the War of the Cold Fire ended less than a month after it began.

Without the support of the supernatural zolgars, the army of Llorrland was routed in the "Battle by Baivonne." Forced to retreat, King Alaric's forces were cut off two days later near the border. Rebels from the southern front, led by clansmen of Arabhedden, had changed allegiance and intercepted the King. Compelled to surrender, Alaric was marched back to his capital as a prisoner. There, the armies found Tonnsburg Castle in ruins—and no sign of Jovadia the Bittern or her apprentices.

After grueling negotiations that involved the nobles of both Llorrland and Occitan, Alaric agreed to abdicate. At first, it was suggested King Carswell might take advantage of the victory and crown himself King of Llorrland. But Carswell claimed no such ambitions. Instead, it was decided that Alaric's displaced Queen, Lady Summerton, would take the throne. Alaric himself would spend the rest of his life in exile and under guard—ironically, at the same northern estate where his Queen had recently been confined.

Epilogue
A Feast in Duneidan

For no bond, natural or mind-engendered, is stronger than that of a perfect empathy between two sentient beings.

—*The Humble Book of Exquisite Wisdom*
(The Emerald Book).
Norrling year 1640.

Candlelight danced across the great hall of Castle Duneidan, shining on the banners, weapons, and shields that adorned the walls. Rows of tables buzzed with happy conversations as nobles, townspeople, and servants enjoyed a rich dinner with plenty of wine and ale.

Mirafra sat at the high table, staring across the chamber in a weary, dreamy mood. So much had happened in the few months since she fled from this castle—so much terror and loss, but also affection and friendship, accomplishment, and thrilling magic. She had left here a Tree Pipit and returned a Ruby Lark.

And yet, she still felt unsure of herself, and of what her rightful course should be now.

"Enjoying yourself, Mirafra?" Arwyn leaned close, his shoulder touching hers, his voice a bit slurred from drinking.

"Of course." She smiled at him, her beloved friend—Or was he even more than that?

With them at the high table sat Teron, Fystus, and Topiedeon the bard, along with Sir Crowley and other nobles of Duneidan.

The feast was in celebration of Arwyn's official crowning as Duke. He wore velvet robes and a silver amulet signifying his title. He had insisted on removing the sling from his arm, which he had worn since being wounded. That wound might have cost his life had the loyal clansmen not come to his aid. Still, despite the bandages and weakness from loss of blood, Arwyn had ridden with the rebel forces as they moved north to intercept King Alaric. Now, after weeks of healing treatments by Clorinda the Ibis and Mirafra herself, his shoulder was mostly recovered.

The chamber grew quiet as a herald marched to the center of the floor. After stamping his pike, he made an announcement. In honor of the duke's coronation, the visiting bard Topiedeon would now sing a ballad composed for this great occasion and performed here for the first time.

Amid the applause, Topiedeon rose from his seat. Picking up his mandolin, he stepped down to the floor in front of the duke's chair.

Teron leaned over and whispered to Arwyn and Mirafra. "I've heard him working on this. I think our minstrel has outdone himself."

Topiedeon bowed theatrically to the high table, then to the rest of the hall. After strumming three chords, he sang in his deep, melodious voice. The ballad opened with young Lord Arwyn marching alone across the field to face the army of Llorrland. It told how he carried the banner of House Duneidan on a spear and, before all the warriors of the highlands, challenged the usurper Baglan to a duel. The song noted that the young lord carried no shield and fought in his surcoat.

The bold Duke wore no chainmail,
Only armor of highland wool.

Topiedeon sang those lines as a chorus with each of the final verses, which described the swordfight and how Arwyn, though bleeding badly, rallied the men of Arabhedden to his cause.

When the song ended, everyone leaped to their feet, roaring and applauding. Mirafra smiled at Arwyn and held his wrist. Topiedeon took many bows before returning to the table.

"Well done, my friend. Well done. I will treasure your song always." Arwyn removed a jeweled ring from his finger. "Please accept this as a token of our friendship."

Topiedeon bowed yet again as he accepted the ring. "I thank you, my lord. It is my honor to sing for one so brave."

As he slipped the ring onto his finger, he glanced at Mirafra. "I do have another ballad in the works, though it's taking me longer to compose. It's about a brave young wizard, the Ruby Lark, and how she vanquished the evil Bittern."

"Ah, it's a shame you could not sing that tonight," Arwyn said. "And that you must leave tomorrow. You must certainly return someday, when that song is finished, and sing it in this hall!"

Everyone was looking at Mirafra, who cast down her eyes, embarrassed. Arwyn laughed and touched her hand.

"Dear Mirafra, you must learn to expect such honors, now that you are a hero!"

As the banquet drew toward its close, Arwyn persuaded Mirafra to walk with him out to the terrace. A crescent moon glowed in the west, and the sky was full of stars. They strolled along the parapet.

"I may have drunk too much, but I don't care," Arwyn said abruptly. "I will ask you one more time, Mirafra. Must you really go?"

She had expected this. Sadly, she gazed down at the meadow, where two airships were moored. One was Teron's, leaving in the morning to convey Fystus the Emu back to Ptolloden. The other ship belonged to King Carswell. It was finishing a tour of Arabhedden, carrying the King's envoys to visit and solidify alliances with the local lords and princes. Mirafra would travel on that ship back to Baivonne, and from there journey on to Montodoro to resume her studies.

That was her plan.

"It hurts my heart to leave you, Arwyn. But I truly feel I have to. If I am to become the best majja I can, I must go back. I still have so much to learn."

"There is much you could learn here." Arwyn stared at the moonlit hills. "About these beautiful highlands and their people. And about helping me deal with being Duke. There is much I have to learn about that."

He had offered to make her Court Wizard. As she was now an adept, and with what she had accomplished in the Warmlands, there was little doubt Montodoro would approve such an appointment.

"I just don't feel ready. I'm sorry. Maybe, in a few years, when I've advanced as much as I can ..."

Arwyn nodded, lips clenched. "I understand."

They stood in awkward silence for a moment, and then both turned at the sound of footsteps. Teron and Fystus walked toward them.

"Sorry, we did not mean to interrupt," Teron said. "We're about to retire."

"That's all right." Arwyn stirred himself. "I'd best go and bid my other guests goodnight. I will be sure to see you all off in the morning."

He nodded to Mirafra, bowed to Teron and Fystus, and headed back inside.

When he was gone, Teron leaned his elbows on the parapet. "Our duke seems melancholy."

"Yes." Mirafra changed the subject. "You, on the other hand, seem content, Teron. Have you decided what you will do? I mean, after you return the esteemed Emu to the Sanctuary?"

In recognition of his services, Teron had been offered a post at King Carswell's court, or at the castle of any of several of the King's vassals. The Mooncrow had demurred, saying such official appointments were not for him.

"Actually," he answered now, "one of Carswell's ideas has aroused my interest. He wants to send a delegation to the Afrique lands, to establish relations and negotiate trade agreements. He asked if I might be willing to convey his envoys in the *Pomegranate*. And I've just about decided to say yes."

"Really?" the Ruby Lark asked. "Have you discussed this with Dona Delores?"

"Oh, yes. She's rather excited about the idea. The King will pay us well. Besides, her journey to Ombernorr seems to have widened the captain's views. She's become enthusiastic about being an explorer as well as getting rich."

"And Topiedeon will go, of course?" Mirafra said.

"Oh, yes. He'd not miss a chance to cross the ocean."

Mirafra laughed. "It sounds like a suitable venture for all of you then."

"It does indeed sound intriguing," Fystus remarked wistfully. "I'm almost tempted to tag along."

"Well, you better decide by morning," Teron laughed. "Dona Delores will not be pleased to fly you all the way to Ptolloden for no reason."

"I see your point." Fystus chuckled. "No. Tempting as it sounds, I really must return to the library and finish my *Histories*. I still have at least ten volumes to write—and now there is so much more to include for this century!" He glanced at them both and gave a bow. "Now, I shall tactfully withdraw and let you say your farewells."

Mirafra gave the Emu her hand and thanked him for all of his help. When he had gone, she turned to the Mooncrow, her expression earnest.

"I wish you good fortune, Teron, in all your travels. And, since we may not meet again, I want to thank you for being such a good mentor."

He appeared surprised. "No. I have hardly been your mentor."

"Oh, but you have. You taught me so much, by example—to be courageous, to use my psithe in unexpected ways, above all, to follow my own conviction as to my rightful course."

He nodded thoughtfully. "Well, you know, Mirafra, you have also taught me things—by example."

"Really? What things?"

"To care again. To have hope."

Mirafra smiled, bowed her head.

"But tell me, Ruby Lark," Teron said. "What is your conviction now about your rightful course?"

Turning her head, she gazed solemnly down at the meadow. "As to that … Well, sometimes it is hard to be sure."

Early the next day, Arwyn and a group of his courtiers stood in the meadow and watched the airships lift off into a gray and windy sky. First, Teron's ship, captained by Dona Delores, set off for the north. A few minutes later, the Kings' ship, with Mirafra on board, rose from the field and turned northwest.

Arwyn, beset by a crushing sadness, hastened back to the castle. Dismissing his attendants, he ascended alone to the roof of the high tower. There he stood with his spyglass extended and watched the King's ship sail away into the distance.

But then a speck of motion caught his eye. Staring intently, he watched as a bird flew rapidly from the direction of the ship, beating its wings hard as it drew nearer. Arwyn lowered the telescope, staring round-eyed, wild emotion stirring in him.

As the bird swooped toward the tower, he spotted scarlet feathers at the throat and wings. She settled on the roof and flashed into a ball of light.

"Mirafra! You decided to come back?"

She ran and embraced him. "Yes, my dear. I could not leave you."

Arwyn hugged her tight. "I am so pleased."

"So am I," Mirafra said. "I am sure this is my rightful course. This way, we can continue to watch out for each other."

Author's Note

A sequel to my novel *Mooncrow*, *Ruby Lark* is Book 2 of the series, *Tales of the Norrling Wizards*. A third title is in the works and, if the Muses agree, will be published in the not-too-distant future.

My thanks to cover artist Masa Radanic of bgsauthors.com and to Laurence O'Bryan of BGS for publishing advice.

And thank you for reading! If you enjoyed the story, please consider leaving a rating and review on Amazon, as well as other sites. The algorithms of the publishing business make this extremely important to a book's success.

I love hearing from readers! You can connect with me at triskelionbooks.com, as well as at:

Substack: speclectic.substack.com

Facebook: www.facebook.com/AuthorJackMassa

X/Twitter: @JackMassa2